TEST
PATTERN

TEST PATTERN

MARJORIE KLEIN

WILLIAM MORROW AND COMPANY, INC. NEW YORK

Grateful acknowledgment is made to reprint the following:

Dialogue excerpt from *The Outer Limits*. Reprinted by permission. © 1963 Daystar-Villa DiStefano-Metro-Goldwyn-Mayer Studios Inc. All Rights Reserved.

Lyrics of "There's No Business Like Show Business," by Irving Berlin. © Copyright 1946 by Irving Berlin. © Copyright Renewed. International Copyright Secured. All Rights Reserved. Reprinted by Permission.

"Chattanooga Choo Choo," by Harry Warren and Mack Gordon. © 1941 (Renewed) Twentieth Century Music Corporation. All Rights administered and controlled by EMI Feist Catalog Inc. All Rights Reserved. Used by Permission. WARNER BROS. PUBLICATIONS U.S. INC., Miami, FL 33014.

"Hey There," by Richard Adler and Jerry Ross. © 1954 Frank Music. © Renewed 1982 Lakshmi Puja Music Ltd. and J & J Ross Co. All Rights administered by Songwriters Guild of America. All Rights Reserved. Used by Permission. WARNER BROS. PUBLICATIONS U.S. INC., Miami, FL 33014.

It is the policy of William Morrow and Company, Inc., and its imprints and affiliates, recognizing the importance of preserving what has been written, to print the books we publish on acid-free paper, and we exert our best efforts to that end.

Library of Congress Cataloging-in-Publication Data
Klein, Marjorie.
Test pattern / Marjorie Klein. — 1st. ed.
p. cm.
ISBN 0-688-17284-9
I. Title.
PS3561.L3486T47 2000
813'.54—dc21
99-16423
CIP

Printed in the United States of America

First Edition

1 2 3 4 5 6 7 8 9 10

BOOK DESIGN BY JO ANNE METSCH

www.williammorrow.com

For Joshua and Bennett.
The future is yours to see.

ACKNOWLEDGMENTS

I am grateful to many people for their help and support:

Lynne Barrett and John DuFresne, for their inspiration and guidance.

Aaron Priest, my agent and champion, for his belief in me.

Betty Kelly, my editor, for her enthusiasm and wisdom.

Frances Jalet-Miller, for her editorial insight.

Lucy Childs, for her perception.

Also, Norma Watkins and Meri-Jane Rochelson, for their reading of the early drafts and their encouragement.

Melissa Simpson, library manager of the Newport News *Daily Press*.

Barry Massin, the Wizard of Welding.

Maddy Blais, for her good counsel.

And of course, to Donny, Allison, and Ken.

There is nothing wrong with your television set. Do not attempt to adjust the picture. We are controlling transmission. We will control the horizontal. We will control the vertical. For the next hour, sit quietly and we will control all you see and hear. You are about to experience the awe and mystery that lead you from the inner mind to . . . *the outer limits.*

The Outer Limits,
ABC television,
September 1963–January 1965

C A S S I E

1 9 5 4

MOM IS DANCING the tango in front of our new TV. Her silhouette dips and glides, slides flat as a shadow across the silvery screen. She's one step behind Arthur Murray, who is demonstrating the Magic Steps That Open the Door to Popularity.

"Come on, dance with me," she says to Dad. She grabs his hand, tries to pull him off the couch. He scrunches down, crosses his arms, shakes his head. Dad doesn't believe in dancing.

Maybe he's tired. He started moving the furniture as soon as he got home and saw the TV was here. Mom directed, pointing here, no here, no maybe it'd be better over there, until finally everything was lined up, TV on one wall, couch on the other, Naugahyde chairs parked so they'd face the TV, too. Now our living room looks like the Paramount Theater.

Dad's still in his work clothes, his Dickies shirt smeared with dirt and stuff from the shipyard, hair all sticking out and sweaty. Mom couldn't wait for him to change, just rushed us through dinner so she wouldn't miss *The Arthur Murray Party*. She's so bossy about it, you'd think it was her very own TV.

It came this afternoon when we kids were playing kickball. "Yay!" we cheered as we spotted the delivery guy balancing the big box on his cart, then we jitterbugged behind him in a wacky parade up the sidewalk to our house. Mom waved him through the doorway, her hands all white from making biscuits. I wanted to die. She was wearing her ratty gray robe and those dead-squirrel slippers. Her hair was knotted in pincurls stuck to her head like snails.

The guy grabbed one corner of the box with a hairy fist and ripped off the side of the carton. There it was, our new TV, wobbling on pointy little feet like a dog that's been bumped by a car. "Magnavox," Mom whispered, reading the gold letters beneath a screen that shone silver as a nickel. The guy plunked the rabbit-ears antenna on top like a beanie, fiddled around with some wires and stuff, then plugged it in.

"Not much on right now," he mumbled, flipping channels, wiggling and stretching the rabbit ears in every direction. Circles and lines appeared on the screen, faint and fuzzy at first, then clearer until he stood back, squinted, and said, "Pretty good picture."

The test pattern stared back: a giant's eye, round and square at the same time. "That's all, folks," the guy said before he snapped it off.

After he left, the kids stayed outside, quiet. Then Margaret asked, "Can we watch?"

"Go on home," Mom said, shooing them off with her flour-stiff fingers. "Nothing's on."

"Come back later, okay?" I yelled as they straggled away. "Come back when it's Howdy Doody time."

"Never you mind," Mom said so they couldn't hear. "And keep it off till Dad gets home." Sometimes she acts like I don't count, like what I think doesn't matter.

Soon as she went into the kitchen, I clicked on the TV. I couldn't get much, just a bunch of snow, but the test pattern came in clear. Black-and-white. Bull's-eye. Spider's web. Round and spoked as a wheel. I stared. It seemed to breathe. I couldn't get away. And then it spoke to me: *Hmmmm*, it said. *Hmmm hmmm*, grabbing my ears like the pattern grabbed my eyes.

I heard Mom talking. Far far away.

"Cassie, Cassie—*Cassandra*. What is the matter with you?"

I stared into the eye of the test pattern. Saw me looking out at myself, looking in at myself. I couldn't get away from me.

"Cassie!" Mom's hands, big and warm as cats on my shoulders, turned me around to look at her. Her mouth moved around my name. I blinked like I just woke up.

"That's enough," she said with a frowny face, and switched the test pattern off. She didn't turn the TV on again until after dinner when it was time to tango with Arthur Murray.

I CAN'T SLEEP. The house is still. Bony branches of the chinaberry tree clack witch fingers against my windowpane. Nights like this I'd stay warm in bed, but this night things have changed. There's a TV in our living room, and I hear it calling to me.

I tiptoe barefoot down the stairs, creep into the darkened room. In the gloom, the couch seems alive. It cradles its cushions in its arms like fat babies. Deep shadows from the porch light shift and hide like small quick animals.

I change my mind, turn to go back upstairs. The TV stops me with its silvery face. I get that same loopy feeling I get on the Tilt-A-Whirl, like I just ate a handful of jumping beans. I touch the knob of the TV. My hand seems to belong to someone else. My fingers and toes prickle like they've fallen asleep, and my whole body freckles with electricity.

I hear its hum before I see it, the circle with spokes like a wheel. The blacks get blacker, the whites get whiter and then I see it clearly: the test pattern. It starts to spin, then whirs like a pinwheel and sucks me into its eye. I'm inside a space that's inside of me.

I hear voices. Music, weird music. Flash of red, flicker of green. Somebody—just my reflection, just me? Or . . . ?

"What the bejesus do you think you're doing?"

Yikes. It's Dad.

And here comes Mom in that ruffly cap she wears over her pincurls at night, eyes all pooched with sleep. But her mouth is wide-awake. "Get your bee-hind upstairs. Are you out of your mind, watching the test pattern?"

"There's nothing else on," I mumble.

"Get to bed," Dad says, and snaps off the TV.

Even when I'm back in bed, the test pattern is still with me. Sharp and clear and real as a dream, it presses against my closed eyes.

2

L O R E N A

ORENA'S IN THE kitchen pounding dough. *Bam, bam,* she punches away at the soft fleshy mound, flattens it with the rolling pin into a quivering blanket spread over the wooden board, blizzards it with flour. She wields the biscuit cutter like a circular sword, smashes its sharp edge repeatedly into the pale dough, deals the limp rounds into neat rows on the baking pan. She has done this every day since she married at twenty. She figures she will do it till she dies.

The screen door opens in a metallic whine, slaps shut. Here comes Cassie. "Mom!" she calls.

"What?" Lorena blots her sweating forehead with a dish towel, balls it up, throws it into the sink.

"Can we watch TV?"

"Not now." Lorena can hear the crowd of kids jostling each other outside her front door, frenzied at the prospect of spending a half hour with a freckled puppet and a grown man who calls himself Buffalo Bob.

She dusts her palms as best as she can, then wipes them on her gray flannel robe, her anniversary gift from Pete, $2.99 on sale at Nachman's he announced when he handed her the box. The gray slippers—real fur, he had said—well, those weren't on sale but he bought them anyway.

"Mom, pleeeeze!" Cassie whines. "Everybody's outside already."

Well, too bad. Lorena shuffles out of the kitchen, her slippers making a *wshhht wshhht* sound. "Sorry, kids," she says in her Nice Mommy voice. "Not today."

"Well, then, *when*? We've had the set a whole week already." Cassie fixes her with a hateful glare. "I wish you were Mrs. Powell." She storms out, slams the screen door behind her, yells, "I'm going to watch at the Powells'. They like kids."

The Powells live across from them and have a TV, until now the only TV on the block unless you counted the MacDougals, an older couple who never invited anyone over to watch. Maybe Peggy Powell didn't mind every kid in the neighborhood hanging out at her house, swarming like termites while she fixed dinner. They had to watch *Howdy*, had to watch *Kukla*, had to watch every puppet show that popped up on the screen. Well, Lorena wasn't Peggy Powell, handing out Kool-Aid to those sticky-faced kids. She didn't want them crammed into her living room, sucking on Tootsie Pops, putting their feet on the couch. That's not why she got a television set.

The idea of owning one had once seemed a fantasy, like owning a box full of stars. Lorena had wanted her own TV since she first saw one, a mirage that shimmered from a circular screen on display in the window of Peninsula TV Sales. Soon afterward, her best friend Della invited them over to watch on her brand-new set. Lorena had sat transfixed, mesmerized by its magic, spellbound in its glow. Pete practically had to drag her out the door before she'd leave Della's that night.

When they got home, she had lain awake, obsessed. She had to have a TV. Captured like black-and-white butterflies inside that box, awaiting release with just the click of a knob, were all of her favorite stars: Bob Hope. Red Skelton. Jack Benny. Groucho. Uncle Miltie. And Lucille Ball—*her* Lucy, as Lorena likes to think of her. She knows if she could meet Lucy, they'd become the best of friends.

But seeing stars is not enough. Lorena wants to be one. The June Taylor dancers have triggered her fantasies of fame—for Lorena dances, too. The first time she watched the dancers open *The Jackie Gleason Show,* her methodical consumption of a Hershey bar slowed to a nibble. She studied each step of their kaleidoscopic choreography with a hunger, a passion, a desire so strong that it twisted into envy.

She could do that. She could do better than that. A mantra began inside her head: I *will* do that, I *will* do that, and she silently chanted it all the way home. It hummed on the edge of her consciousness until Saturday came once again, teasing her anew with the June Taylor dancers. After that, Saturday nights at Della's became a ritual. Fueled by frustration and hidden anger, Lorena's mantra burned like a tiny flame that grew day by day, consuming her thoughts until little was left but desire.

Now that Lorena's got her own TV, the June Taylor troupe seems to dance just for her. Hidden beneath the coffee table, her feet tap in secret mimicry when the desire to perform overwhelms her. As the camera rises high above the dancers to capture their divine precision, she just knows that if life had taken a different path, she could have been a petal of that unfolding flower.

Before television, her vicarious performances were limited to Saturday matinees at the movies. She would sit in the dark sharing popcorn with Della and imagine herself mirroring the steps of Gene Kelly, *tappety tappety tap tap tap,* or descending a circular staircase on the arm of Fred Astaire. When the movie was over, the fantasy would end and she'd go home once again to real life.

Real life was once her fantasy life: a husband, a child, a home—

all the things she wished for until she got her wish. After that, the fantasy faded into a predictable pattern of cooking, cleaning, shopping, and mending that promised to repeat eternally.

Not that she complains, oh, no. She could have done worse. Pete's not a runaround like Della's ex-husband. Pete's a family man, always on time for dinner, always expects those biscuits. Before they got the television set, he'd stop by the bar near the shipyard to watch TV after work, maybe down a Ballantine or two. But now that they've got the TV he comes straight home—stays home, too. After dinner he parks his work boots on the coffee table alongside his beer and pretzels, watches wrestling or the Pabst Blue Ribbon bouts. He's a family man, yes, it's true. But mostly he's a company man.

He's worked in the shipyard since he was fifteen, part-time when he was in high school. He grew up here in Newport News, Virginia, wouldn't leave this place, he was born here just like his daddy. His whole family was Virginians, he bets they go back to Jamestown. That's the kind of tie he feels to this city, he tells her if she ever talks about moving someplace else. It's in his skin, his blood, under his nails and behind his ears, the grit and dust, the clang and roar of the shipyard. Even with his bum leg, he can scamper up those gantries like a monkey. It's just something he's done, something he'll always do, work with ships and steel, the music of the metal always singing in his ears.

Lorena grew up here, too. Her father worked in the shipyard. Almost everybody's father worked in the shipyard. It promised good jobs and steady work as long as there was war. War feeds this town. It makes it grow. With World War II, then with Korea, the shipyard crystallized into a geometry of cranes and gantries and angular ships that shadowed it all. The riverfront became a city of ships and the water grew still and black. And over it all rang a carillon of steel that played the songs of war.

Lorena is sick of it. She feels like she's in the bottom of a brown paper bag. Sometimes when she goes with Della to a matinee, she thinks that what she's watching is what's outside the bag, it's not all shipyard and the A&P and running the Hoover under the couch. It should be a Technicolor world, and she should be Doris Day. But then she comes out blinking in the sunlight and leaves it all behind her in the Paramount.

DELLA'S ALREADY IN line when Lorena huffs up out of breath from running across the parking lot. "Where did all these people come from?" she complains, flattening the top of her hair where the wind poufed it out. The line stretches before them and ends at the door of a bright yellow trailer—the very same trailer featured in the Lucille Ball–Desi Arnaz movie *The Long, Long Trailer*—parked smack in the middle of the A&P parking lot on its tour of the country.

"I told you we had to get here early," Della says, tapping at the face of her Bulova. "It's already nine-thirty."

"I didn't think there'd be such a long line." Lorena stands on tiptoe to peer over the crowd.

"A long, long line to see a long, long trailer," Della says, then, realizing she said something worth repeating, repeats it: "Long long line, long long trailer. Get it?"

"Yeah, yeah." Lorena is more annoyed than amused. She hadn't expected to wait, had itched with excitement ever since she tore the announcement out of the paper that the trailer was coming. She has seen the movie twice, could see it again and yet again. She just can't get enough of Lucy, her queen-of-hearts lips, her flapping lashes, her flawless flaming hairdo. Watching Lucy on TV was one thing, but seeing her flamboyance brought to Technicolor life on the big screen almost brought Lorena to tears.

The crowd shuffles patiently across the asphalt lot, disappears by twos and threes into one door of the bright yellow trailer, then stumbles out through the other. Dazzling as gold, irresistible as a magnet, the chrome-encrusted trailer draws Lorena and Della into its magical field. They pause in the doorway, dizzy with anticipation as the doorbell peals a musical hello.

"Oh my God," Della swoons. "Just like in the movie."

"They stood right here." Lorena's voice is hushed, reverent. "Lucy and Desi. Their fingers actually touched this door." She runs her fingers along the door, then reaches overhead to touch the door frame. "This is where Desi bonked his head. Remember?"

Their entry is blocked by a square woman in a striped dress who has affixed herself to the glass-doored oven in the kitchen. "Looka this, Delbert," says the woman, squishing her nose against the glass, "you don't even hafta open it to see in." But Delbert is mesmerized by the venetian blind in the window, opens and closes its slats repeatedly until Lorena pushes by to peer into the oven herself.

"Remember when Lucy made dinner while the trailer was moving?" Lorena asks Della as they jostle their way to the refrigerator. They open the very door that Lucy opened. "And how she made a Caesar salad, and it flew all over the place?" Lorena is in awe, that Lucy was covered in Caesar salad right where she is standing.

There's a real bathroom with a real shower. Everything matches: yellow drapes, yellow tile, yellow shower curtain. Lorena is overwhelmed. She caresses the pink satin quilt on the same twin bed where Lucy and Desi pecked a chaste kiss. Della sits on the other bed and sighs, "Wouldn'tcha love to live here?"

"It's so much better than a house," agrees Lorena.

"Much fancier."

"Remember how she wore that organza dress and flowers in her hair when she was moving in?"

"And how they ate by candlelight? And drank Chianti?"

"Yeah. Parked by a waterfall. In the mountains."

The low rumble of the crowd outside the trailer is punctuated by a hand whapping the window of the bedroom where they sit. "Hey!" yells someone. "Get a move on. There's people waiting out here."

"Just hold your horses," Della yells back. They take a last, longing look around them before leaving through the trailer's back door. The line now serpentines the parking lot, weaving in and out between cars.

"What'd you think you were doing? Moving in?" calls the same voice that accompanied the hand whapping on the trailer's bedroom window, a voice belonging to a peak-hatted soldier. Della and Lorena sashay off in a huff, barely sparing a glance at the soldier, who continues haranguing them from his place in line. "Where's your suitcase?" he calls. "Did ya give 'em a down payment?"

"Jeez Louise," Della mutters. "Some people." She opens the door of her car, a brand-new lime-green '54 Nash Metropolitan that she bought after her divorce was final, and slides in. "Wanna catch the matinee?"

"Can't. I should get groceries, long's I'm parked here." Lorena waves at the red-and-yellow A&P sign. "Mize well kill two birds, you know." She watches Della's car squeal away through the parking lot and finds herself wishing that she, too, had a car with that nifty continental kit on the back.

LORENA HEFTS THE grocery bag in one arm as she hurries from the A&P to her car. Her light jacket feels heavy and claustrophobic. She opens it to the weather, craves the brittle edge of wind on her body. The A&P was overheated, had this funny smell of dried beef blood and insecticide that always gives her a headache. The cold fresh air blows up her skirt and down her blouse. She throws her head back and lets the early May wind lift her hair off her face, away from her neck. A few strands stick there like seaweed.

The line still snakes through the parking lot to the trailer. Kids chase each other through the cars while mothers yell at them. Cassie didn't want to come along when Lorena invited her, and Lorena was hurt at Cassie's response: "What do you want to see an old trailer for?" Lorena just doesn't know what's gotten into that girl lately. She even turned down Lorena's offer to bake gingerbread men together, one of their favorite mommy-daughter things. Now Cassie doesn't even call her "Mommy" anymore.

What happened to the downy baby who curled like a shrimp on Lorena's shoulder, sucking her thumb and twirling strands of Lorena's hair between her fingers? When did she crawl down from that safe perch to become this scrawny fresh-mouthed ten-year-old who looks and acts more like Pete each day? Cassie's long green eyes are the only features left that Lorena can claim. The rest—short straight nose, angular chin, sullen pout of a mouth—belong to Pete.

There had been a time when Lorena felt that Cassie was her own, an extension of all her senses. When Cassie's infant mouth would close around a spoonful of strained spinach, Lorena could taste the metallic mush. When Cassie dug her toes into the soft sand of the beach, Lorena's feet tingled for them both. When Cassie wailed on the first day of school, Lorena cried tears for two.

What happened? When did her sweet Cassie erupt into this wild creature whose green eyes, once so trusting, now scanned her from beneath thick brown lashes as if Lorena were a villain on one of her TV shows? She only knows that Cassie isn't what Lorena was at ten, that maybe there's been some twist in time and ten isn't what it was twenty years ago.

Remnants of trash skitter across the parking lot—wrapper from a Baby Ruth, that waxy paper they give you with a doughnut. Where did she park? The lot's so jammed with cars, Lorena can't think straight, oh, there it is, way on the other side, sky-blue Dodge two-door coupe. Oh, no, she remembers, she forgot to get gas and the gauge is on empty. She'll have to stop at the Texaco. She trots across the parking lot, the heels of her flats scraping asphalt.

She's intent on fishing her keys out of the purse dangling from one elbow. A soldier shambles toward her, thumbs in his front pockets, hands curved toward his crotch, hat tipped over his fore-

head. Is that . . . no, couldn't be . . . the same soldier who was
yelling at her and Della when they left the trailer?

His hair is cut close along the sides, sidewalls, she thinks they
call it, and he walks with a loose lope that she recognizes from
somewhere, an unhinged walk that belongs to someone she once
knew. Does he know her? He must, because he quickens his step
and aims in her direction.

"Hey, Lorena, wait up," he's saying. "Remember me? Binky?"

Binky? Binky Quisenberry?

He looks different. Maybe it's the uniform. Or that haircut. Or
the skinny little mustache. But the nose over the mustache is the
same, broken just enough to give him that tough-guy Marlon
Brando look, and his eyes are still the color of rain.

It *is* Binky. She hasn't seen him since high school.

"Binky? Is that you?" Then, "Was that you, yelling at us outside the trailer?"

"Aw. If I'da known who it was I was yelling at, I wouldn'ta."
He looks sheepish, gives her a crooked grin. "I watched you walk-
ing to the A&P and it dawned on me, why, damn if that ain't
Lorena, so after I got outta the trailer, I decided to hang around."

Well, she thinks, the saying is true. There's something about a
man in uniform. Seeing Binky in these starched and pressed khakis
brings back memories of him in his football uniform, monumental
padded shoulders distorting the dark blue jersey with the number
"50" appliquéd in yellow across its back.

Now he wears the peaked cap low on his forehead and speaks
lazily of the army, how he's home, this time to stay. She leans
against the round fender of her car and shifts the bag of groceries
from one hip to the other. She wishes she had worn makeup,
combed her hair, something, but who knew she would run into
Binky Quisenberry in the A&P parking lot?

"You're still in uniform," she says. "Where've you been?"

He lights up a Lucky, his big hand curved to protect the Zippo's
flame from the wind. "Been everywhere. Been in the army since
WWII. Saw action in the Ardennes. I was there, right in the thick

of it, got wounded. Don't remember how, actually. It was all a blur. I remember ducking, then an explosion. I was in the VA hospital for a while."

"Wow," says Lorena, eyes big.

"Hey, you wanna see something?" He pulls his shirt open, shows her something jagged and white and lumpy going over his shoulder and down his back. "Got this. Wounded in action." Impulsively, she reaches out and runs her finger along it. It feels like cold Cream of Wheat.

"Wow," she breathes. Her finger tingles as if she had caressed something forbidden and exotic, and she shudders with the danger of it. "Did you get hurt in Korea, too?"

"Korea?" He buttons up his shirt again. "Well, I didn't exactly see combat in Korea. Actually, I never went to Korea, not that I didn't want to go but I was stationed at Fort Bragg and don't think that wasn't a challenge, working at the PX, keeping track of the stock, not to mention the shoplifting by the enlisted men's wives, you wouldn't believe what went on." He frowns. "It's not just battle that wins the war, you know, it's morale, too. That's part of the war effort, don't let anybody tell you different."

"That's right," she says. "I bought war bonds."

"I'm getting discharged this week," he tells her around the Lucky between his lips. He takes a long drag, pulls it out, crushes it beneath his army boot. "Don't know what I'll be doing then. Maybe work for my dad at the auto-parts store although it's been oh, 'bout ten years since I worked a regular job, not service-connected, you know."

Lorena nods, shifts the grocery bag to the other hip, combs her bangs to the side with two fingers of her free hand. As he speaks she watches his lips move beneath his carefully trimmed mustache, neat and thin, an Errol Flynn mustache that shelters smooth pink lips marred only by a fleck of tobacco stuck to the bottom one. Automatic as the miniature crane that grabs a toy in a carnival prize machine, her hand rises, plucks the tobacco from his lip, then lingers on its silken surface.

"Hey," he says. "Hey, Lorena." He grabs her hand and keeps it on his lips.

She is leaning against her car, one arm around the grocery bag, the other raised to Binky's mouth. She can feel his teeth hard behind the soft lips, feels her own lips part and her tongue circle them lightly. What is she doing? She snaps her hand away, shakes it as if something clung to it, something more than just tobacco, more than the softness of pink.

"I've gotta go," she says.

"Where?"

"I've gotta get gas," she says, ignoring his laugh. She flings the car door open, throws the groceries inside. "Gotta run." She starts the car, grinds the gears as she backs out of the space. She doesn't want to look at him.

"Hey, Lorena." Binky follows her, bending his head to talk to her through the window. "Can I see you again?"

She shakes her head no. "I'm married," she says, and shifts forward into first. The car shrieks, shudders, stops dead.

"Married?"

She nods.

"Who'd ya marry?"

"Pete. Pete Palmer." She starts the car up again and yells over its sputter, "You don't know him. He graduated a couple of years before us."

She can see him in her rearview mirror as she pulls away. He stands at ease, in his uniform. When she gets home, she remembers she forgot to get gas.

C A S S I E

WATCH THE test pattern while Mom's in the kitchen, keep the sound low so she can't hear the hum. The test pattern has changed. Slithery shapes slide in and out of the spokes, sometimes even in color. If I lean real close and listen well, I think I hear music and voices.

Today it's different. Something else is happening. The test pattern spins, fades to a blur, then runs together like watercolors. All of a sudden there's this pretty lady with yellow hair who's wearing a two-piece bathing suit that's way too small for her. She's got flowers and butterflies and words that don't make sense like "groovy" and "kinky" painted all over her skin. And she's dancing.

I turn up the sound. She's dancing to music I've never heard before, snappy and bouncy. She doesn't dance regular, just wiggles her arms and butt and giggles a lot. The best part is, it's in *color*. I didn't know they did shows in color.

"Mom!" I yell. "Come look at this."

"Look at what?" she calls from the kitchen.

"It's a new show, and it's in color, like the movies."

She hurries into the living room, gives the TV and me a funny look that makes her eyebrows almost collide. "What are you talking about?"

"Look! Isn't that a neat dance?" I get up and copy the giggly girl with the teeny bathing suit and the painted stomach, wiggle my butt, wave my arms. "Sock it to me!" I say.

Mom just stares. "Where did you get that from?"

"From the dancer with the dark hair, the one they're splashing with a bucket of water. She keeps saying 'Sock it to me.' "

Mom gives me one of her looks. "You telling me you see something besides the test pattern?"

"You bet your bippy."

"What?" Mom says, then snaps off my show. "And don't touch it until Dad gets home."

Sometimes I'd swear I was adopted.

I'M LYING ON my bed with my shoes on. I hate my room. Mom painted it brown. When I complained that I'm the only kid in the world with a brown room, she said, "Doesn't it remind you of a Hershey bar?" If I wanted a Hershey bar, I'd go get one at Al's newsstand.

I'm not supposed to go to Al's. I do, anyway, because he has penny candy and yo-yo's and comic books. But Mom says stay away from there because he sells dirty magazines.

Well, Dad has dirty magazines in his dresser drawer. I know because I explore sometimes, both Mom and Dad's dresser drawers, just to see what there is to see. He keeps naked-lady magazines beneath his undershirts. One has this lady on the cover who is wearing a frilly maid's apron and high heels and nothing else. She looks surprised. Her eyes are wide open and her mouth is making a big O. I study it for a while, and make that face in the mirror. I wonder what it would be like to have big titties. I think about that sometimes.

Dad also has rubbers. Those he keeps in the back of his night-table drawer behind some old newpaper clippings, one with a picture of him playing baseball in high school, others with obituaries and stuff. I know what rubbers look like because one of the boys in my class brought some called Trojans to school. He filled them with water and threw them at the girls. This, to me, is not romantic.

I know all about rubbers and romance and babies. My best friend Molly told me everything.

I remember exactly where we were. Sitting in the grass in front of my house, blowing dandelion fuzz into the wind last spring. Some guy was scraping paint off our house with this metal thing that made *scrrrt, scrrrt* sounds, and big white flakes fell on the bushes like ashes.

Molly was laughing at me. I had told her doctors give ladies shots when they want to have a baby, and that's how you got pregnant.

"A shot?" Her Bugs Bunny teeth poked out while she blew away a dandelion head. "Who told you that?"

I shrugged. It's just . . . that's what I thought.

"Didn't your mother tell you anything?" I shook my head no. "Remember that movie we had in school, where only the girls could go?" Yeah, I remember. "Yeah . . . well?" she said.

"Well?" I said back. I thought the movie was about menstruation, not babies. I want to have babies. I never want to have menstruation.

"You didn't make the connection?" She smacked one palm into the side of her round chipmunk face. "I can't believe you are so stupid."

"Well?" I asked. "What's the connection?" So she explained. About the man putting his Thing into the lady. About the seed being planted. About the baby being made.

"He puts *his* Thing inside *her* Thing?" I was stunned. It was too grotesque. "Why would she let him do that?"

Molly laughed again. Sometimes she laughs like a grown-up, a growly kind of laugh, maybe because she's eleven and has already gotten her period. Molly has titties and wears a training bra. "Because it feels good, stupid!" she said.

I've been thinking about what Molly said, but I can't figure out what would feel so good. When I look at the boys I know like Normie who wipes boogers under his desk, I wonder if I'd want their Things anywhere near my Thing and the answer is yuk, *no.*

But Molly may have been telling the truth, because the more I think about it, the more some things begin to make sense. Dirty magazines. Rubbers. Jane Russell.

"WHAT?" MOLLY SAYS when I tell her that somebody said "penis" on television. Her eyes get bigger than the surprised naked lady's on the cover of the magazine. And then I tell her the best part, where they talked about how this lady got so mad at her husband that she cut off his penis and threw it away.

"Oh my God," Molly moans, rolling back and forth over her ruffled white bedspread in her pink bedroom. We're wearing our new matching shorty pajamas because I'm spending the night. I have been saving up all week to tell her this, the news I heard on test-pattern TV.

"Yes!" I yelp, doubled over, holding my stomach. We both hurt from laughing so much. "Cut it off!"

"Penis!" she screams. "They said *penis.*" She sprawls out on the bed, panting, catching her breath. "What show was that?"

"My special show," I tell her.

"Your special show?" She looks at me. "Oh, no. You just made it up."

"No! No, *really.* Come on, I'll show you, there's all kinds of shows, in color even. They're on the test pattern."

"The test pattern?"

We tiptoe downstairs. It's late, so late that nothing is on regular TV. Her living room is quiet. I can hear the hum of her refrigerator in the kitchen. She flicks on their TV and in a few seconds the tiny round-screened Zenith blooms with the test pattern.

"You have to look at it a minute," I whisper. I stare at it hard. "Like this." Molly looks at me, turns back to the screen, and stares like I'm doing. I can see both of us in the web, our faces close as Siamese twins.

"Nothing's happening," she says.

"Wait," I say. "It will."

We wait. Nothing happens. I don't know what's wrong. "Maybe there isn't anything on tonight," I say.

"Yeah," says Molly, and I see her face leave the screen. She stands up. "Let's get some doughnuts. My dad got some from the bakery today." We skulk into the night kitchen, rustle open the grease-spotted bakery bag, nab a couple of jelly doughnuts.

"Penis." Molly giggles around doughnut bites.

I don't say anything. I only know it's true.

4

L O R E N A

BINKY QUISENBERRY. Lorena hadn't thought about him for years. In high school she would sit high up in the rickety wooden bleachers, shivering in her parka and pleated plaid skirt, and watch him practice as a hard cold autumn sun stretched long shadows on the field. She covered pages of notebook paper with his name, but his only acknowledgment of her existence was a mumbled "hi" in the hallways.

Now she thinks about him all the time, thoughts that transport her from what she is really doing, vacuuming dust from beneath the bed or rinsing out a gutted chicken in the sink or jamming clothespins into cold wet sheets that smack her arms as she hangs them on the line. All those things that were once so important to her, the touchstones of her day, don't matter anymore. She cooks, she cleans, she goes through the motions, but what really propels her through life these days is what goes on in her head.

What goes on is a movie. She is the star. Her hair is no longer mousy brown, but gilded in golden ringlets. No, no. It's flamed in russet, undulating in Rita Hayworth waves around her rouged and powdered face, her lust reflected in Binky's smoky gaze as he grasps her body next to his. She wears white satin pajamas—no, maybe a long red silk dress with a slit up the side. She decides on a lacy negligee with satin mule slippers. Something Rita Hayworth-ish.

Now they're dancing. She follows him as surely as a shadow, dipping, gliding, twirling, it's a Fred and Ginger night. They stop suddenly, frozen with passion. He bends her backward. Her shimmering auburn hair skims the mirrored dance floor. Their lips barely graze, and then he swoops her up into a spin, their movements as one.

Now they are lifting champagne glasses in a toast. Their glasses crash to the floor as they embrace. His mustache sweeps a path from her Revlon-glistened lips to her throat. Their bodies press together. Her bosom rises, a bosom held high by that expensive French bra she saw in Nachman's lingerie department the other day. Since it's her fantasy, she gives herself a real bosom: lace-encased, with Jane Russell cleavage.

"Mom!"

Huh?

"Della's on the phone. Didn't you hear it?"

Oh, good. She's been trying to reach Della to tell her about Binky.

"I'll get it upstairs," she says, and when she does, she's zapped by Della's electrified recitation of her Saturday-night date: "You can't believe what happened, he took me to the Crab Shack first, then we decided to skip the movie, you know this was our third date and for God's sake all we'd done was neck a little, and I didn't expect this but well he had gone and bought *rubbers* for God's sake so after he went to all that trouble what could I do, he's so good-looking, the girls at work think he looks like Alan Ladd and, to make a long story short, I think I'm in *love*."

Della's in love again.

Lorena is thrilled, thrilled to pieces for her, she says, but she's got her own news. "Guess who that soldier was?"

"What soldier?"

"The one who was yelling at us when we went to see the trailer."

"Who cares? He was obnoxious."

"Remember Binky Quisenberry?"

"No! That wasn't Binky Quisenberry. Binky was cute."

"He still is."

"How do you know?"

"He waited for me outside the A&P. He apologized, sorta."

"How does he look?"

"Like Errol Flynn."

"No! What did you talk about?"

"Just . . . stuff. The army. What he's going to do now."

"He's coming back here?"

Uh-oh, Lorena thinks. Della is on the loose. "Um, yeah. He says."

"Married?"

Funny. That never came up. "I dunno. I don't think so." After all, he had asked to see her again.

"Wow. Binky Quisenberry. Listen. If you see him again, give him my number."

"What about Alan Ladd?" It's not fair, Lorena thinks. Why should Della have Alan Ladd *and* Errol Flynn?

Della just laughs. "Hey. There's seven nights in a week."

When she hangs up, Lorena is envious. Della's life seems like an incredible journey with an itinerary based on whim. No matter which golden path she may choose, she'll still wind up in Oz.

LORENA HURRIEDLY DEALS out dinner, dropping each hot Swanson's tray with a tinny thunk on TV tables set up in the living room. She doesn't want to miss the commercial. She settles on the couch, knees trapped in the skeletal clutch of the table's metal legs, thighs pressed beneath its flimsy top. The dancing Old Gold cigarette packs tap across the screen of the Magnavox.

She pokes her fork around the aluminum tray, jabs at the thick, wet crust of a flaccid chicken thigh. The fork moves on, scrapes up a wad of mashed potato, inserts it between her lips, then pierces the reptilian hides of peas huddled in their own triangular compartment. Lorena chews absently, staring straight ahead.

On the luminous screen, Lucy is chewing, too. She's popping candy into her mouth, two hands at once, faster, faster, she can't stuff the morsels in quickly enough, her mouth balloons with chocolate, her eyes bulge out over candy-crammed cheeks.

"Ooooh, Looocy," Pete says as the show ends. He sucks on a desiccated chicken bone.

"Ooooh, Ricky," Cassie responds with a giggle as she mashes potatoes and peas into a paste. Cassie doesn't like TV dinners. Tonight she had watched mournfully as Lorena yanked three Swanson's boxes from the tiny freezer of the Frigidaire, then ripped them open to expose beige chicken parts rigid with frost, petrified swirls of gray potatoes, peas green and hard as dimestore beads.

"I want fried chicken," Cassie had announced. "*Real* fried chicken, not frozen." Lorena winced as guilt knifed through her gut, for she had once been proud of her fried chicken. Baptized in milk, enrobed in flour, each plump poultry part had been committed to Crisco as if it were an offering, sizzling and turning in the bubbling fat until the skin had turned to gold. Light, crispy, fragrant with spices, Lorena's chicken had yielded to the bite like the most delicate spun sugar.

But then frozen dinners appeared in the big white freezer of the A&P, Swanson's facsimile-TV-set cartons piled high next to the Birds Eye chicken pot pies. Lorena succumbed to the allure of opening a box, popping the tray into the oven, eating from it while watching TV, then just throwing it away. Everything she once slaved over was now encased in cardboard and aluminum.

Turkey. Meat loaf. Fried chicken. Why sweat over spattering Crisco when Swanson's made it so easy?

Pete had glowered suspiciously at the first TV dinner Lorena put before him, but since she accompanied it with her usual home-made biscuits, he was willing to compromise. Dinner was eaten more and more often in front of the TV, and complaints about the food were heard mostly from Cassie.

Cassie worries Lorena these days. When Lorena's not day-dreaming about Binky or mourning the dancing career she never had, she worries about Cassie. She's changed, gotten sassy, talks about seeing things on the test pattern that aren't there. And now she's gone from A's to F's in school.

"Miss Winkle sent home a note," Lorena announces.

"Baba-loooo!" Cassie howls, pounding on the edge of the TV table with both hands.

"What kind of note?" Pete says.

"Baba-loooo!" Cassie pounds harder.

"Cassie!" Lorena snaps. "This is important."

Cassie slumps down in the chair and stares glumly at her tray. "Miss Winkle says you're failing arithmetic," says Lorena. "She says you're not doing your homework."

"Failing?" says Pete.

"I'm not failing," Cassie mumbles.

"She says you've gotten F's on your last two tests. That's called failing."

"Miss Winkle hates me."

"Miss Winkle does not hate you."

"Well, I hate her."

"You haven't been doing your homework?" Pete asks, his face darkening into a scowl. "What's the matter with you?" He turns to Lorena. "Why hasn't she been doing her homework?"

"Maybe because she's been watching TV instead," says Lorena.

"Well," growls Pete to Cassie, "no more TV until you've fin-ished your homework." He turns his attention to *The Red Buttons Show*.

Lorena falls silent. She doesn't challenge Pete, especially not now. He's changed lately, gotten crankier, even snaps at Cassie, something he rarely did before. He and Cassie had always shared a special bond Lorena felt apart from. She even had little fits of hidden jealousy when Pete and Cassie would giggle over some silly secret. It made Lorena feel . . . well, she didn't know what she felt, except left out.

Now a vague guilt prickles the back of Lorena's neck. She senses that Pete is admonishing her as well as Cassie: What's wrong with her, not even noticing that Cassie had fallen behind in school? She hasn't been paying attention. Not to Cassie. Not to her wifely duties. Not to those things that she thought were so important to her just a few short weeks ago, before they got the TV.

When she's not settled down in front of the television for an evening of Lucy or Ed Sullivan, Lorena steals TV moments in snippets, sidling in from the kitchen to sneak peeks when Cassie is watching. It doesn't matter what's on—*Howdy Doody, Captain Video, The Lone Ranger*—as long as it's not obscured by snow, she'll watch. She is drawn to the light, the sound, the action, the *life* that suddenly exists in her living room.

When they got the TV set, something shifted in their lives. Lorena isn't sure what's caught her so off balance. Is it the rearrangement of the living room? Is it waiting to go to bed until *What's My Line* is over? Is it that every conversation now centers on television—the shows, the stars, the gossip?

Or is it because sometimes when she watches, she's sucked breathless by revelation: *She* could have been on that screen. She could have been the performer, not the audience. And she mourns for who she could have been and what she could have done, for she knows she has a gift.

She's got flying feet, a flip to her hips, a syncopated rhythm in her bones. When she danced the jitterbug at high school sock hops, her feet barely touched the shiny-slick floor of the gym. John Patrick would sling her like a wet towel over and under and through his legs, she was that limp and pliant. Bebop. When she got going the dance floor froze, they all stepped back and stopped mid-twirl to stare and clap in rhythm. Applause, applause—it fed some hunger deep down in her soul.

Her talent has lain dormant since then, but she was still a hoofer in her heart, a heart that beat to the rhythm of the greats: Eleanor Powell, Ruby Keeler, Vera-Ellen, Ann Miller, Ginger Rogers. When movie musicals were her only inspiration, her dream of dancing surfaced in the secret darkness of the theater, only to sink again when she came home to the obligations of marriage and motherhood.

But with the coming of TV into her living room, her need to perform gnaws at her on a daily basis. Bare feet tucked beneath her, Hershey bar unwrapped, she folds herself into a corner of the couch and imagines herself on the screen.

In the TV playing in her mind, she sees herself in satin shorts and tap shoes. She's taking her bows as the winner on *Ted Mack's Amateur Hour*. She's tap-tap-tapping to the top of the applause meter on *Arthur Godfrey's Talent Scouts*. Born to be a star, they shout over the applause. Born to be a star.

She doesn't tell this to anyone but Della. Della is her best friend, has been since high school. Della tells her everything. Della has a lot to tell these days. She's the only divorced person Lorena knows. It's a shame, people say about Della, a shame and a pity but mostly a shame.

Della doesn't care what people say, never did, didn't care that people knew she was stepping out on that swine of a husband she married the week after she graduated from Newport News High. Stayed married to Farley until he smacked her over the head with a turkey drumstick after she'd asked him to carve the bird last Thanksgiving and she just walked out right then, left him to explain to his whole family watching TV in the living room while they waited for her to serve them. Della did get custody of the TV.

Now Della struts her freshly painted self down to her new job at the shipyard to type letters for her boss. She's got a bunch of boyfriends, spends every weekend with a sassy smile on her face. Each day brings a fresh new drama; each night, the promise of lust.

Lorena tells Della about her dreams of being on TV, of dancing on *Ted Mack,* even confesses that she finds herself thinking about Binky. They tell each other everything, what they want and what they miss and what they dream about.

"Sometimes," Lorena tells Della, "I feel like I took a wrong turn somewhere and wound up in somebody else's life. Maybe there's another life for me. Not this one, but my real life."

She doesn't know what to say when Della laughs and says, "Sugar pie, this *is* real life."

When Della tells Lorena how lucky Lorena is, how she's got what Della doesn't—two people who really love her—Lorena doesn't tell her that two just isn't enough. She wants more: Hundreds. Thousands. Millions. She wants the *world* to love her.

And she's going to make it happen. She doesn't know how, yet. She only knows she will. After Pete leaves for work, she hauls her *Photoplay*s out of the closet and spreads them on the floor like she did when she was young. She leans on one elbow and turns the pages slowly, pictures herself on the cover posed by her pool in Hollywood, imagines herself featured in Hedda Hopper's column: "Lorena Palmer and Robert Mitchum caught smooching at the Stork Club."

Oh, she'll be such a good star. She'll faithfully answer her fan mail, she'll cheerfully sign her autograph. She will make it happen. Yes she will. All she needs is a break.

Della is wrong. This isn't her real life. Her real life is waiting to happen.

MORE AND MORE these days, Lorena wonders if she married too young. Twenty didn't seem so young when she was twenty. It even seemed old. Old maid. Such a terrifying label.

Most of her teachers were old maids. Lorena used to imagine their lives. Up at six, feed the cat, water the African violets. At night, listen to the radio: *Fred Allen, Fibber McGee.* Put out the cat. Climb into bed. Alone.

Miss Muncy, her fifth-grade teacher, never married. She wore black every day. No one knew why. Lorena and Della speculated and decided: a fiancé lost in the Great War. In mourning ever since.

At twenty, Lorena was unmarried, too. Too picky, her mother said. Old maid. That, she had decided on her birthday, must be her destiny. Then Pete came along.

She was typing when he came in. She had a job, the job she got the summer she graduated high school with A's in the only two courses that her mother said mattered—typing and short-hand. Her mother was right. Lorena landed a job at the shipyard typing memos and endless lists of numbers for her boss, who was head of accounting. Her mother nodded in satisfaction when Lorena got the job. "Well," she had said, "now you can support yourself."

The first thing Lorena noticed about Pete was his neck. It was thick and corded and dropped straight from his ears to shoulders that stretched the seams of his work shirt. That was all she saw of him at first—his head with its tumble of black, black curls spilling over his forehead, that neck, those shoulders.

"This the personnel office?" he asked.

He was lost. Had hardly been up here since he first started working the shipyard, oh, 'bout ten years ago. Had to fill out papers. First day on the new job, he explained as she left her desk to point the way down the hallway. When he got hurt, they moved him to an office job, just temporary, till he could work up high again. He slipped, that's all, just turned around and the plat-form wasn't there. Lucky he'd turned off the welding torch.

She noticed he walked with a slight limp, his right shoulder a little lower than his left. He was clearly a powerful man and his rolling walk intensified, rather than diminished, that effect, like a steamroller with legs. He peered at her with steel-blue eyes like ingots set above cheekbones hammered into planes by wind high up on the gantry.

"I'll be working that ship," Pete said, pointing out the grime-coated window at a battleship in dry dock for repair, stretching up high as a skyscraper. Pearl Harbor had been bombed, the country was at war and needed that battleship quick. "I can't climb yet, but soon's this leg straightens out I'll be welding up there again." She smiled up at him. She felt small, dainty. All around them rang the song of the shipyard, the rhythmic clanging so much a part of her life that it was theme music for her dreams.

When he asked for her number she gave it to him. And when he called and her mother asked who was he, what did he do, how did she meet him, Lorena described him but left out the limp. Maybe her mother wouldn't notice it when he came to pick her up.

"What happened to your leg?" her mother asked Pete when he walked into the house. She never was one for amenities. He was dressed up in his Sunday best, white shirt, brown pants, bow tie. Hair parted in the middle, greased with Vitalis, combed so the curls were flattened into shining waves.

"Broke it," said Pete. "Fell off a gantry."

"Will it keep you out of the army?" her mother asked.

Pete's face grew dark. He ran a hand over the top of his head, remembered the grease, looked at his hand. Wiped it on his pants. "That's what they tell me," he said.

"Good," said her mother. "No sense in getting killed."

THEY WERE MARRIED six months later. Lorena quit her job. Pete wanted her home. Wanted bacon and eggs for breakfast. His lunch bucket packed the night before. His Sunday shirt ironed. Dinner on the table at seven. He wanted biscuits.

At first it was exhilarating, being married. A married woman. Not an Old Maid. She had her own home, her own husband.

Their tiny first apartment was close enough to the shipyard so she could hear the noontime whistle. Now he's opening his lunch bucket, she'd say to herself when she heard the whistle's wail, now he's biting into the bologna sandwich she put in the icebox last night, now he's swigging coffee still hot from his thermos. Somehow that knowledge made her proud. She was a wife.

She became pregnant before their first anniversary. Not surprising, considering the time they spent in bed—every night and all weekend. But she liked that. She liked the feel of his muscular bulk rising above her, the way his black curls tightened up with sweat, the knowing that it was her lips, her breasts, her thighs, that brought him to this, this ecstatic falling away, this loss of control. It was sweet, the power she had.

As she swelled with baby, the days took on meaning, the waiting gave substance to her life. She was busy now growing a life, and that gave her own life focus. Dusting, baking, feeding bedsheets through the wringer of the washing machine—the motions of housekeeping became golden rituals, homage to hearth and home, the coming of new life.

"Your belly button's popped out," Pete noted one day as she stood at the sink brushing her teeth.

She looked down. There it was, her belly button, inside out. It looked like a dwarf's thumb, hitchhiking.

"Will it go back?" he asked. He seemed worried.

She mashed it in. It collapsed softly but sprang back. "I guess," she said. "After the baby's out."

"It better," he said.

After that, it was hard to feel pretty. The belly-button bump showed through the thin cotton of her maternity tops. She grew bigger and bigger and began to waddle, could never get comfortable at night, thrashed wildly, half-awake, dreaming of triplets.

"Ow! Stop flopping," he complained after she bopped him on the nose during a particularly frenzied night. "You're such a whale."

Well, she *was* a whale, she thought, lying on her back, her stomach rising pale and immense above the rest of her, crowned by that popped-out navel. She stared up at it in self-pity until her view fuzzed over with tears that trickled into her ears. "I'm *fat*," she bawled. He didn't disagree.

WHEN LORENA WAS in her ninth month the circus came to town. The Little Top Traveling Circus wasn't big, but it was big enough to have two tightrope walkers, a gorilla that rode a bicycle, and a bunch of either midgets or dwarfs, she never could remember which was which.

And it had a freak show.

She stood outside the freak-show tent and stared at the poster of the Half Lady and the Penguin Girl and the Alligator Man. "Come on," Pete said. "Let's look."

"I don't want to," Lorena said. She could smell sawdust, candy cotton, and the pork-rind breath of the man behind her who was pushing her in line. She felt her belly stretch and shift until it seemed to inflate and surround her like a life preserver. She felt very far away, as if she were floating above the shoving crowd. No, she didn't want to look at the freaks.

"Come on," Pete insisted, and propelled her inside, flipping a couple of quarters to the sideshow barker, who snapped off two red tickets from the big roll. Inside, the tent was murky and dank. When she became accustomed to the dimness, she realized she was standing right in front of the half lady, whose shiny satin dress ended at the hips and so did she. Even though she was perched on a stool, she came up to Lorena's chin.

Lorena planted her feet in the sawdust and gawked. The half lady's hair was rigid with ringlets, rather stylish for a freak. She lifted her face to Lorena's, a face that could have been anyone's face, nothing special, nothing strange. Wide flat cheeks flamed with dots of rouge. Small pointed chin, its dent a shadow in the weak spotlight. Her soft dark eyes focused on Lorena's belly as she reached out and touched it with tiny, rosy fingers. Lorena felt the baby move.

Suddenly the half lady sprang from her perch and landed on her hands on the sawdust-scattered floor. Lorena shrieked, grabbed at Pete, who staggered backward. "Jeezus!" he said. The half lady pranced around on her hands a bit, did a flip, and bounced back up on the stool, where she calmly patted her ringlets back into place.

"Let's go," Lorena said to Pete, yanking on his sleeve.

He ignored her. "Look! Baby Thelma!" he said. Baby Thelma weighed 655 pounds. "Six HUNNERD and FIF-ty-five POUNDS!" bellowed the barker, his undershirt translucent with sweat. Baby Thelma was piled into a chair that sagged dangerously beneath her. She wore a dainty nightie of a dress sprigged with flowers and lace, and flipped it flirtatiously above pale fleshy thighs. She had a sweet face, small, benign features embedded into a bow-topped global head that tipped and nodded just slightly at Pete's astonished comment: "Jeezus!"

"I want to go. Now." Lorena tugged at Pete as she waddled toward the exit, but he yanked his arm away to stare at the lobster boy's hands, the monkey woman's beard, the alligator man's skin, the porcine features of the pig-faced boy. He steered Lorena to the front of the crowd, where a child with a crusty scalp burrowed between them until he was the only thing between Lorena and Herman the Human Blockhead.

The Human Blockhead was preparing his instruments on a little table just beyond the rope that separated him from the crowd. Precise as a surgeon, he laid out a screwdriver, a six-inch steel spike, and a silver mallet. As he did this, he told a joke, something about a dog in a bar, then picked up the screwdriver, tipped his head back, stuck the screwdriver all the way up one nostril and plucked it out again in a graceful swoop.

Lorena felt her knees melt. "Pete," she whimpered, but the Human Blockhead had more in store. "Just warming up," he said with a grin. He looked like a marine with his close-cropped head, his square-set jaw, his blocky little body. He picked up the spike and stuck it in one nostril. Then with the silver mallet, he banged the spike up his nose.

BONK. BONK. BONK.

He drove that steel spike all the way up his nose until it disappeared into his head.

Afterward, when they laid Lorena flat on a tarp outside the freak tent with a cold towel over her forehead, she said it was more the sound than the sight of that spike disappearing into the Human Blockhead's nose that made her throw up.

She went into labor before they got home. She had the baby the next day. The hospital was four blocks from the shipyard. All day long, she could hear its sound, metal on metal, the tattoo rhythm of the shipyard.

Bonk. Bonk. Bonk.

THEY NAMED THE baby Cassandra, after Pete's grandmother, and called her Cassie. Lorena deflated rapidly, lost almost all the weight except for a soft roll just above her waist that never went away. Her belly button went back in, folded into a stretch-mark-scarred pocket, star-shaped. Pete poked it with his finger. "Now stay there," he said, and it did.

Cassie grew and life settled into a rhythm. She and Lorena fused into one, each dependent on the other, while Pete seemed to exist in a parallel world that touched theirs only when he needed to eat or sleep. After dinner he would listen to the war news as it spilled from the cathedral-shaped Philco radio, muttering to himself, Boy I'd show those Krauts a thing or two, damn this bum leg, I'd mow those Japs down, too, if it wasn't for this bum leg. Then he would fall asleep, mouth open, snore rattling deep in his throat, head thrown back against the lace doily that protected the lumpy green chair.

Lorena had crocheted doilies for each piece of furniture in the living room, even the ottoman where Pete's feet, splayed out into a V, rested, one toenail threatening to knife through a threadbare sock. She crocheted doilies for her mother, her aunts, for the neighbor lady who waved to Cassie when she took her for walks in her buggy. Snowflakes that would never melt, the delicate webs of lace spun from beneath her flying fingers as she listened to Helen Trent on the radio. Her days were filled with useful toil. Still, something was missing.

It started like a hole in her stocking. Tiny, barely there. She didn't even notice it at first, the void that pervaded each moment. It was there each morning when she opened her eyes to the spiny ridges of Pete's back. It was there when she spooned back an eruption of oatmeal from Cassie's toothless mouth. It was there when, sated from lovemaking, she rolled up like an anchovy in her husband's arms.

What was it? She had everything she was supposed to have. A husband. A baby. A cozy apartment full of doily-topped furniture. She used to wonder, What more could she possibly want?

Now, after all these years, she knows the answer. She found it on TV, right in her own living room. She's no longer alone with her dreams, for television is her mentor. It beckons, it teases, it tempts her with her future. Look, it says as she stares at the screen, see who you can be: You can be a dancer. You can be famous.

You can be . . . a star.

TAPPETY TAPPETY TAP TAP TAP. Lorena is testing tap shoes. The rejects are piled like shiny black beetles on the floor of the dance studio shop, this pair too tight, this too loose, this too clunky, this too flat. "Jeez Louise," says Della. "Make up your mind."

Lorena does an energetic shuffle-ball change in a gleaming patent pair tied with big black grosgrain bows. "What d'ya think? Would Ann Miller wear these?" she asks, twirling in the mirror to catch a rear view. Her sinewy legs look like Pinocchio's, ascending pale and wooden-looking from the tops of the shiny licorice shoes to the hem of the red satin tap pants she's also trying on.

"She'd wear 'em to bed, she'd love 'em so much," Della answers irritably.

"Hey, come on. You're the one said, 'Stop talking all the time about what you want to do, and just do it.' So here I am. Doing it."

"I meant pursue your career, not shop for shoes."

"Well, this is the first step. Putting together my costume." She poses in front of the mirror, one arm stretched over her head, the other reaching down past her cocked hip. "I need a top hat."

"I need a drink." Della slumps back on the folding chair and is enveloped in tulle and gauze from costumes jammed together on a rack above her. "I'm getting claustrophobia in here."

Tappety tappety tap tap tap. "I'll take 'em," Lorena decides as she performs a final test run. "These, too," she adds, wiggling her red satin-clad hips and shimmying her faux-tuxedo-shirted breasts.

"Woo WOO-o-o-o," she suddenly wails, to Della's alarm. "Woo WOOOO," she sings to her image in the mirror, arms and legs flailing in near unison. " 'Pardon me, boy (chug chug) is that the Chattanooga Choo Choo? . . .' "

The ancient saleswoman napping behind the register wakes up with a start. "Busby?" she asks.

"She wants it all, shoes and costume," Della announces. "Pay," she orders Lorena, and, fighting her way through tulle, stalks outside to wait.

"C'mon. I'll buy you a drink," Lorena says, happily clutching her new purchases as they walk down the street. "Let's be ladies and drink martinis." She steers Della into the dim and dusty lobby of the Warwick, right into the mahogany-paneled bar, empty now in mid-afternoon. "My treat," she says as they wriggle into seats around a toy-sized table.

Della's lips curl around the rim of the cone-shaped glass as she sips daintily between grimaces, explaining, "I hate the taste of gin."

"Me, too," says Lorena with a wince, "but I like the olives." They order another round. Lorena props her chin on the heel of her hand, leans conspiratorially across the tipsy table. "Y'know, if it wasn't for you, I wouldn't have the guts to do this."

"Hey," Della says with a salute of her refilled glass, "you're the one with the talent."

"Sure," Lorena agrees, "but talent just takes you so far. You need inspiration, someone who believes in you. You're the very very best friend anybody ever ever had." She dabs at her brimming eyes with a crumpled cocktail napkin.

"Here's to best friends," Della says, and downs the rest of her martini.

"Yup." Lorena fishes out her olive, pops it into her mouth. "By the way," she asks, "what do you think of my routine?"

"What routine?"

"My 'Chattanooga Choo Choo' routine."

"*That's* your routine?"

"Well," Lorena huffs, "I have to perfect it."

Della examines the toothpick-impaled olive she's been nibbling. "Well . . . I think, maybe it needs a little . . . work."

Lorena's eyebrows clash momentarily above her long green eyes, then spring up in revelation. "Tellya what," she says, tottering to her feet as Della rescues the glasses that wobble dangerously on the tippy table, "you tell me where it needs improvement. Now be honest," she adds. "Best friends can always be honest."

And she's off. Accompanying herself "WOOOO-WOOO-ooo, *chugga* chugga *chugga* chugga," arms swinging in great circles, " 'Pardon me, boy, is that the Chattanooga Choo Choo . . .' " gaining momentum, feet tapping, faster faster, echoing on the terrazzo floor of the cocktail lounge. ". . . When you hear that whistle blowin' eight to the bar, Then you know that Tennessee is not very far . . ." The bartender gazes in mild distraction as he wipes glasses, then politely patters applause at her finale.

Della is weeping, pounding on the table, her eyes streaming tears of laughter. "Oh, Lorena," she moans, "you just tickle me so."

"What's so funny?" Lorena asks, panting as she catches her breath.

"Uh," says Della. She wipes her eyes, puts on a serious expression. "Nothing."

"You were laughing at me."

Della looks bewildered. "Wasn't I supposed to?"

Lorena slumps down in her chair. "It needs a lot of work, doesn't it?"

Della reaches over and pats her arm. "Just practice, sugar pie. Just practice."

"Honest?"

"Honest."

C A S S I E

MOLLY'S FATHER HAS a beard. He must have the only
beard in Newport News. He talks what Mom calls
New York Loud out of lips so red it looks like he's
wearing lipstick. He's big. His shirt spreads a little bit around the
buttons, and curly chest hairs peek out. He's jolly and nice, and
when he smiles his eyes smile, too, soft mushy eyes, brown like
Molly's, with black eyelashes all around.

Over the couch in Molly's house is a huge painting of her
mother naked. Molly doesn't seem to care that it's there, that it
covers the whole wall. I try not to look at it when I go over there
but I can't help it. I stare at it when Molly's not looking. I don't
know anybody else whose father painted their mother with no
clothes on.

Mr. Finkelstein is an artist. They used to live in New York, but
they moved here when he got a job with the shipyard drawing
plans. I guess it must be boring for them after living in glamorous

New York, but this is where they live and where he paints, at a crooked wooden easel in their dining room. There are lots of his paintings all over the house, crowded together, signed in big loopy letters "Max Finkelstein."

Molly pulls me over to one painting he finished last month and she tells me not to touch it, it's still wet. He didn't even use a brush on this one, she says. It's his new style, all the colors squished right on the canvas out of the tube. I can't tell what it is, it's just big blobs of juicy colors, red and blue and orange sitting there like toothpaste. Molly says nobody else paints like this, squishing blobs right on the canvas. She says that someday her father will be famous for it.

When Molly isn't looking I stick my finger in the paint to see if it really is wet. It is. I wipe my finger on my dungarees and hope she doesn't notice the red smear. I think it's pretty neat that he paints blobs, but what I really want to look at is the naked painting of her mother.

When we go into her living room again to play Sorry on her coffee table, I sit on the chair across from the couch so I can look at the painting. While Molly is setting up all the pointy-headed pieces on the Sorry board, I pretend to care about whether she is yellow or I am blue. What I'm really doing is looking over her bent head to stare at her naked mother on the wall behind her.

She looks a lot like Molly. She is small and round and freckled, with curly reddish hair. She is lying on her side, leaning her head on one hand, looking at me like she's sleepy. She is smiling. Her lips make a crooked V shape like they do when she's asking me if I want some cookies, and I look toward the door that goes to the kitchen like she's going to pop out any minute.

I'm embarrassed to look at the rest of her, but Molly is still deciding what color Sorry piece she wants, so I do. Her mother's titties are round and white, and the nipples are big and pink. Down There, there's hair. It's reddish, like the hair on her head. I can't stop looking now, it's like somebody took my eyes and wired them to the painting, and I can't even look at Molly when she says "Come *on*. It's your turn."

Finally I force myself to look down and make my move, but my eyes keep jumping to the painting. It's not like I've never seen a naked lady before, because I've seen Mom when she's taking a bath or when she's wiggling into her bathing suit at the beach. She covers herself up quick, though, so I never get to study all the parts. I can't think of a time when I've ever been able to take a really good look.

Because of naked Mrs. Finkelstein up there on the wall, I start thinking about what I saw yesterday on test-pattern TV and wondering about men and women and the things they do together. "You know," I say, sliding my yellow man down the board and bumping Molly's, "I saw on my show—"

"Oh, no, not your show again." Molly rolls her eyes.

"There's a show on where people sit up on a stage and yell at each other about sex. Then people in the audience get up and yell at the people on stage about sex."

"Made it up."

"Did not."

"Made it up. Nobody talks about stuff like that. Especially on television."

"Cross my heart, there are shows where people yell about sex. Sex with each other. Sex with their daughter's boyfriend or their husband's mother or their neighbor's kid. Sex sex sex. I've seen *lots* of shows like that. They all have leaders who run around in the audience with a microphone so people can yell at the people on the stage."

"No such thing."

"Yeah there is. And there's another kind of show where people just talk and nobody yells, but a *colored* lady is the leader."

"Now I know you made it up. There's no colored ladies on TV except for on *Amos 'n' Andy*."

"Well, there are," I say because there are, "but what I want to know is, do people really do those things? You know, have sex with people they're not married to? Is that allowed?"

Molly scowls at the Sorry board, then moves her man and bumps mine. "Ha!" she says.

"Well?" I need to know.

"I guess," she says. "Why not?"

I don't understand any of this.

MR. FINKELSTEIN COMES home while we're playing Sorry, clunks through the door with a big roll of canvas and a bag from the art supply store. He dumps the bag onto the dining-room table and tubes of paint spill out. "Hello, ladies," he says in his voice that sounds a little like Groucho, a little like the Great Gildersleeve. "Why are you inside on this gawdjus sunny day?"

"I'm winning," says Molly.

"Well, that's a reason," he says. He starts picking through his artist's case, throwing rolled-up, squished-out tubes into the empty bag and filling the case up with the fat new tubes he just bought. "They must think I eat paint at Allen's Art Supply," he says. "I keep that place in business."

"Cassie says she sees TV shows that talk about sex," says Molly. She shakes the dice. It comes up double sixes. I want to disappear without a trace.

Mr. Finkelstein looks at me and his beard seems to bristle. I'm afraid to look at him, but when I do, he's laughing. "So what channel is this sex show on?" he says.

I don't say a word.

"She watches shows on the test pattern," Molly answers for me. "The other day they said 'penis.'"

"In what context?" asks Mr. Finkelstein. I don't know what he means.

"Cassie says they said a lady got mad at her husband and she cut his penis off." Molly says this like she's telling him she had toast for breakfast.

Mr. Finkelstein's face scrunches up like he's in pain. I don't know what to say, so I say, "I did *not!*" I can't believe how much I hate Molly right this very minute.

Mr. Finkelstein recovers and smiles at me. "You certainly do have a vivid imagination," he tells me. "What else do you see on your shows?"

I'm so embarrassed about the penis thing that I start babbling. "The World Series was on. The Los Angeles Dodgers won the pennant."

"Brooklyn. The Brooklyn Dodgers," he says. "And the World Series was over last fall. They didn't win."

"No, I'm sure it was the Los Angeles Dodgers," I say. He gives me a funny look, like I don't know baseball or anything, which I do, for a girl. "Maybe it's a different team," I say so as not to be rude, but I know that I saw what I saw. It was the Los Angeles Dodgers.

Molly folds up the Sorry board, puts it away. "Come on," she says. "Let's go to Al's and read comic books." I put my finger to my lips to shush her up but her dad doesn't get mad and say "You're what?" like Mom would do.

I'm so mad at Molly for telling the penis story that I don't even care whether we go to Al's or not. All I want to do is get out of their house and disappear from Mr. Finkelstein's sight.

When I think about the mothers I know and ask myself which one I would pick if I could, I'd choose Mrs. Finkelstein. She's different from other mothers. She has long, long hair that hangs down to her waist. She wears flowy dresses down to her ankles and goes barefoot inside, even in winter, and she walks smooth, like she's on wheels. Sometimes I think she's not home when I'm over at Molly's, and then she'll kind of glide down the stairs to the kitchen to make herself a cup of tea and then glide on back up. I used to think maybe she was sick but Molly says she's always up in her room writing poetry.

"Poetry?" I say. "You mean, roses are red violets are blue?"

"No," Molly says, "not like that. She writes books. She's going away this summer to a writers' colony where all she'll do is sit in a house in the woods and write all day." And then she gets this skinny book out of their bookcase which has real books in it and not just magazines, and shows me one of her mother's poems.

Well, I'll tell you, I never saw a poem like that. It doesn't even rhyme. Or even make sense, something about "the wild weird piglet of your passion."

"What does this mean?" I ask Molly.

She just shrugs. "Oh, she always writes stuff like that. She reads it to Dad after dinner. He really likes this one," she says, flipping to a poem that starts out "bursting forth from womb a snarl defied O woman woman woman."

"Yeah?" I say, trying to figure it out.

"She writes a lot about women."

"Yeah?"

"About how strong we are and stuff."

"Strong?" I think, Maybe she's right. I can beat Tommy Taylor in arm wrestling, and I always get picked first in kickball.

"She says I can be anything I want when I grow up. Not just a secretary."

"Like what?" I say, thinking, Mom was a secretary before I was born. Was that bad?

"Like a doctor. Or a judge."

"Or a welder in the shipyard?"

"Well, yeah, I guess." She looks at me funny. "Is that what you want to be?"

"No," I say, even though it's something I've thought about, how neat it would be to use the welding torch like Dad does, climb high into the sky and make sparks fly like the Fourth of July. "I was just wondering."

There are lots of things I think about being, but the one thing I don't want to be is a secretary, just typing up other people's letters all day. Unless I could be a secretary who uses this really neat typewriter I saw on test-pattern TV the other day. It looked like a typewriter, only it had a TV screen on top, and it didn't just type words but pictures. In *color*. If I had one of those type-writers, then I wouldn't mind being a secretary so much.

But if it's true like Mrs. Finkelstein says, that if I want, I can be anything, then I can think of a whole bunch of things I would rather be. A welder, maybe. Or a drummer in a band, like Gene Krupa. Or maybe a pilot—or even a space cadet, like Tom Corbett, so I can go to the stars.

I think Mrs. Finkelstein is just dreaming, like Mom dreams about being a famous dancer. There's no such thing as lady doctors or judges or welders. But what I like about Mrs. Finkelstein is that she thinks about stuff like that, things I never even thought about before.

6

L O R E N A

BUBBLING AND BOILING in black-and-white, the mushroom cloud fills the screen of the Paramount as a sepulchral Movietone News voice intones facts about the H-bomb test: Firestorms. Radioactive rain. An entire island vaporized.

"Did Binky actually fight in Korea?" Della whispers to Lorena, reaching over to claw a buttery handful of popcorn.

"He's got a real scar from World War II," Lorena says, bypassing the fact that during Korea Binky worked in the commissary at Fort Bragg and never, not even once, crossed the Pacific.

"Well, I'm glad the war's over," Della says around kernels of popcorn that squeak as she chews. "I never understood much what that was all about. North Korea. South Korea. Turn on TV news and what's on? Korea. Who cares?"

"Well, somebody cares. It's in the paper a lot." Lorena feels around the bottom of the popcorn box, fishes up a couple of unpopped nuggets, tosses them and the box on the floor. "We wouldn't send soldiers all the way over there if it wasn't important." She looks sidelong at Della's profile silhouetted in the dark, light from the belching bomb on-screen pinging off her upturned nose and mobile chin. She hopes people don't think she's as dense as Della just because they're good friends.

"Still and all," Della says, "I don't know what we were doing in a place with all those weird names, Panmunjom, Seoul, whatever. I mean, I thought we were finished after World War II and then what happens? Korea."

"SHHHH!" says a man with tall fuzzy hair two rows in front.

Lorena thinks about war all through the movie, maybe because it's *From Here to Eternity*. When she comes out, she picks up the war theme like a dropped stitch.

"Rosalind, the kid down the block, only eighteen, she married this guy before he shipped out," she says, squinting in the midday sun. "Her mother didn't want her to marry him but she did anyway, had to, I heard, because the guy was leaving for Korea and she was in the Family Way."

Della nods knowingly. "The Family Way. That'll do it." They pass their reflections in a storefront window. Della takes out a comb, fluffs her bangs, checks her teeth.

"Next thing we know, we hear his ship got blown up." Lorena waits as Della slathers a fresh coat of Tangee on her full lips in the window's reflection. "I didn't go to the funeral but I heard it had flags and drums and all. Shoulda gone, I guess, 'cause I've known Rosalind since she was about Cassie's age."

Lorena senses that Della isn't really listening because a couple of sailors lounging against the wall of Harley's Hardware have caught her eye. Della's pillowy little body becomes increasingly animated, accelerating into feverish gyration as they pass by the sailors.

Unfazed, Lorena continues: "Turns out she wasn't in a family way after all. She was just in love. I see her sometimes, sitting on her porch. Sometimes she'll walk down to the water and stare over at Norfolk. I guess that was the last place she saw him, when she said good-bye. Her husband was a sailor."

Della perks up at the word, seems to pay attention. "Yeah?" she says.

Lorena glances over at Della but Della's head is turned around and Lorena knows she's giving the sailors a wink. "She seems lost now, even walks different," Lorena persists, "not like that little bounce she used to have. I want to go up to her sometimes, tell her I know how she feels, but I don't. I can't imagine what it's like to be a widow."

Della has clearly signed off of Lorena's story, but Lorena continues it silently, asking herself, Was I that much in love with Pete when I married him? I think I was. He was nice-looking, seemed like he knew what he wanted. Seemed like he wanted me. We were happy. I liked being married, being half of a couple.

When Cassie came along, Pete liked playing with her, buying her toys, talking baby talk. But when she got older, he got bored with it all, with the crying and tantrums and stuff kids do. Once when Lorena accused him of treating Cassie like some Cracker Jack toy that broke, his sudden tears of denial startled her. Sometimes he'd do that—cry, and she wouldn't know why.

Pete was stingy with emotion, but those tears were coming more often these days. When she saw them, Lorena was more stunned than dismayed. She felt oddly powerful, as if Pete had shrunk down to her level. He was weak. She was strong. Now would be the perfect time to give him an ultimatum: She wasn't just a housewife anymore. No more vacuuming, no more biscuits. She was going to have a career. She had to practice, get her act together, do what she had to do. With or without him, she would dance her way to fame.

And then a nasty nightmare would intrude on that threat: Suppose he said no? Suppose he left? Suppose she had to work? She'd be typing, not tapping. That would be her future: typing, typing, endlessly typing the days away, just as she was doing the day Pete walked into her life. The thought of those days made her fingers wiggle and stretch in involuntary mimicry of the rhythm and movements of typing. She could feel the tapping of her fingers on the keyboard, hear the musical clatter of the keys—*tappity tappity tap tap tap*. Then cold panic would grip her and still her dancing dream, and just for that moment she'd be glad she had Pete.

"Cute, huh?" Della's scratchy voice jolts Lorena back. Now that they're out of range of the sailors, Della's walk has decelerated to its normal swing and sway. "Don'tcha love those adorable little sailor hats?"

Lorena, Rosalind still on her mind, says, "Why would you be interested in somebody who could be shipped out any day?"

"Well," says Della, pouting, "it's not like we're still at war. Didn't they sign a peace treaty or something?"

"It's called an armistice," says Lorena. Honestly, she thinks, Della can be such a dingbat. "We still got all kinds of problems with everybody, Russia, China, I don't know who-all else," she informs her. "Now that Russia's got the bomb, we got to worry about whether they might try to hit us here, what with the shipyard and all."

"The shipyard? They'd want to bomb the shipyard?" Della's eyes go wide.

"The shipyard. Norfolk, the naval base. Fort Eustis. Fort Monroe. Langley Field. All kinds of places around here they'd like to blow up. Where have you been? Don't you know we live in a target zone?"

"Jeez Louise! I *work* in the shipyard."

Lorena rolls her eyes. "Well, it wouldn't matter if you worked at Chicken in a Bucket if the H-bomb hits. It would scoop out a crater from here to Richmond." She doesn't know that, but it sounds terrifying enough to warrant Della's horrified gaze.

"Jeez Lo-*uise*!" says Della.

*　　*　　*

THE ROOM IS dark except for the first faint glow of early morning that seeps around the edge of the window shade. Lorena tucks her head farther under the covers. She feels herself rise a little as Pete's weight shifts. Now he's sitting up. Now he's up and out, she can tell because the bed feels lighter.

She burrows into the nest she's made of sheets and blankets, flannel nightgown scrunched high around her waist. She waits until she can hear the bathroom door shut, the flush, the knocking of the pipes as the shower shudders to life. She ducks back under the covers. Warm and dark, musky odor of bodies, sweat, stale sex. She pulls her pillow in after her and curls her body around it.

She thinks of Binky's lips. How she tingled when she touched that pink and tender surface, how they felt like the skin that forms over chocolate pudding after it's cooled. She mentally runs her fingers once again over his Cream of Wheat scar, follows it down his back, lower, lower . . .

Oops. Pete's out of the bathroom. He plunks himself on the bed, jarring her. Flicks the light on his side of the bed, tips the tiny pleated lampshade to a rakish angle, examines the frayed toe of one sock with a probing finger before he pulls it on. "My mother darned socks," he says.

Lorena doesn't answer. His mother darned socks. His mother scrubbed clothes on a washboard. His mother canned tomatoes and nearly wiped out his family with botulism. Her image shadows Lorena at every domestic turn. Last Sunday she came for dinner and hovered at Lorena's shoulder while she fixed apple pandowdy for dessert. His mother had a stake in its preparation since it, as well as her biscuit recipe, was handed by her to Lorena with great ceremony after the wedding.

"Slice those apples *thin,* dearie," his mother had admonished in her Pall Mall–rattled voice. "Pete doesn't like them thick and chewy, and that crust should be crunchy, you know he's picky about his crust."

When Pete's mother did that, Lorena's mind transported herself right out of the kitchen, straight to the hall closet. She saw herself rummage through winter coats and mildewed umbrellas and bowling shoes; saw herself pull out Pete's mail-order Red Ryder BB gun, load it with pellets, turn with the gun heavy under her armpit. She saw herself point it at her mother-in-law and shoot her right between those bullfrog eyes.

"What's for lunch?" Pete's asking. Lorena pops her frilly-capped head out of the covers.

"It's in the Frigidaire." Why does he always ask? She's been packing his lunch bucket the night before for the past twelve years, same thing, never changes: two bologna sandwiches on white, heavy mayo; big dill pickle, bag of chips, piece of fruit, slab of cake, thermos of black coffee left over from breakfast.

He makes the coffee, thick and sludgy, she makes it too weak for him. He's already down the stairs, calling, "Coupla eggs sunny-side, and gimme some bacon to go with that." She hears him rummaging around in the cabinets, banging doors, clanging pots. She crawls out from under the covers and stares at the ceiling. Shoves the mound of blankets and sheets away from her. She is not, never was, never will be, chipper in the morning, and she starts her day as she always does: loathing the fact that he is.

She shuffles into the bathroom, pulls her nightgown up around her waist, sits on the cold seat, yawns. She's up, and to prove it, she looks into the mirror. Yep. Her eyes are open. She must be up.

She digs her arms into the sleeves of the gray flannel robe, shoves pink feet into her slippers, flaps down the stairs to the kitchen. He is jazzed, got that Maxwell House perking, the glass knob on top of the coffeepot jumping with dark brown juice, the smell of it curling under her nostrils just like it does in the TV commercial. He's tossing Wonder Bread bags out of the bread box, some empty, some holding a fuzzy green heel or two. "Well," he says. "I guess this means no toast."

A pair of eggs stares cross-eyed at her from the pan as she shoves the spatula under them, jostling their mucous gaze until the yolks run into the whites. He sees what she's doing. "Hey! I hate that, yellow in the white. And where's my bacon?"

"We're out."

"Jeez." He's not so chipper anymore. She feels better now.

THE HOUSE IS empty, like somebody knocked the wind out of it. Cassie's left for school, Pete's off to work, and the house suddenly, blissfully, rings with silence. Lorena scrapes the remains of breakfast into the garbage pail that gasps open with a stomp of her fur-slippered foot. It's eight twenty-five.

A cold gray day. She looks out the kitchen window at a stone-colored bird hopping on the clothesline in the backyard. Beyond that are the back doors of another row of houses. She's surrounded by houses, rows and rows of wartime housing called Stuart Gardens, an overnight development built for the influx of shipyard workers and servicemen.

For unbroken blocks, identical white frame row houses trimmed in dark green face each other across scraggly squares of grass and weeds called "courts." The main feature of the court in front of Lorena's house is a dusty diamond of dirt defined by somebody's worn-out cushions that serve as bases for kickball or baseball, depending on the season. A sidewalk runs from the street past all the houses, linking them and framing the court in white.

In summer, people pull out metal lawn chairs, set them on their little patches of front lawn, and wave at each other across the court while the kids play ball or catch fireflies. Each house has its own front porch, just big enough to stand beneath when it rains. Each house has a ligustrum bush under the front window. In spring all the bushes bloom with white flowers and the court smells just like honey.

Many houses have a view of the water, the flat gray bay of Hampton Roads which laps at the narrow beach just down the hill from the court. Ships of all sizes—fishing boats, aircraft carriers, freighters—doggedly crisscross the water. Norfolk sprawls on the horizon. Dim forms of distant buildings visible in daylight become a carnival of lights at night. Lorena hasn't been there for years.

She pulls her robe around her, steps onto the front porch. A gust of wind from the water balloons her robe. She clutches it with one hand while the other shades her eyes from the eastern sun as it brightens the morning sky. She smells the musky odor of brine, of rotting sea life snared in tattered remnants of nets washed up on shore. The fragrance somehow thrills her. She's drawn to the water, always has been. But now she fears it, too.

Polio. You can catch polio from the water. That's what she's heard. She's warned Cassie to stay away from it, not even to dip a toe. The warm and milky water she splashed over Cassie's baby body a few short years ago has become as polluted and poisonous as witches' brew.

Lorena stares at the water from her porch, then from her bedroom window as she gets dressed. She finds herself walking across the court, down the hill, over the patchy grass of the so-called park to the beach. Flat black sandals hanging from two fingers, bare feet sinking into brown-sugar sand, she gazes across the opaque water at Norfolk.

And then she remembers: She had the dream again last night.

IT STARTS WITH light, the dream always does, a pinpoint pulsating faintly against the black. The light expands, kaleidoscopes into fragments across the infinite vision of dream. Brighter than lightning, the dreamlight shatters and multiplies, splinters of a galaxy brilliant against fathomless dark.

Deep in the burrow of sleep, she knows this is a dream, knows she experienced it all before the first time that she dreamed it, knows it wells up from the deep place where dreams are born. It's an answer without a question, so she welcomes the dream and watches.

The lights drift and settle into a glittering band that stretches along the horizon of her vision, a blinding faceted rainbow. She reaches out to embrace it and, when she can't, realizes that the shimmering vision she is trying to grasp is Norfolk with its myriad of lights.

In her dream, this is what she does:

She stands on the edge of the water, afraid. Her house is behind her, invisible in the darkness, swallowed up by the night. She could turn and walk back, retrace her path over the hard sand of the beach, the coarse grass of the park, the rocky protrusions of the hill. She could go home. But the lights are too compelling.

Inky waves wash over her feet. She walks into the water. It envelops her, soft, soothing, a veil of black silk that caresses her body, and she descends, sinking slowly, drifting downward in a lazy spiral. To her surprise and pleasure, she can breathe underwater. She takes great gulps of—not air, but a strange elixir that revives her and makes her feel alive. The water, once so forbidding, is transparent as glass. Columns of light dance through it like golden ballerinas.

Colorful shapes of mysterious creatures float past her as she drifts. They seem friendly. She reaches out but they escape her touch, pass through her grasp like ghosts. Now and then one seems to be familiar, but who or what it is eludes her. They speak to her in the language of shells, burbling syllables on the edge of comprehension, sounds she understands but can't articulate herself. The creatures seem to be leading her toward the city's glow.

In her dream, she remains inert, drifting this way, that way, this way again, venturing neither forward nor back. Norfolk's phosphorescence dims and fades as she watches. She sees, but never touches, its light.

LORENA TAKES A deep breath of auditorium air, a redolent blend of sweat and dust and springtime flowers that bloom outside the propped-open windows. It's still light outside, a rosy twilight that washes the ocher walls of the high-school auditorium with pale pink.

"Can you smell it?" she asks Della, who sits next to her on the hard wooden seats. They are the only occupants of this row. The other competitors for roles in the Community Theater production of *Guys and Dolls* sit in a nervous clot in the front row.

"Smell what?" Della takes a nostril-dilating sniff.

"Show business." Lorena closes her eyes. "The excitement. The applause. The blood, the sweat, the tears."

"Smells like mold to me."

Lorena pulls her knee up to her chin and rests one shiny black tap shoe on the seat to retie its bow. "I've been practicing like you said. I really think I've got my routine down. It's different from when you saw it."

"Yeah?" Della asks. "How?"

"You'll see," Lorena says with a teasing smile. "I've added a lot of new steps I've seen Cassie do."

"Cassie? I didn't know she could dance."

"Me, either, but I think she's got my talent. She imitates these steps she sees on TV, steps I've never seen before." Lorena stops herself. She doesn't want to get into how she catches Cassie dancing in front of the test pattern, how just yesterday she saw her doing some dance that involved her arms arcing over her shoulders, then holding her nose like she was swimming. And another step where she scratched under her arms like a monkey.

"What's that?" she had asked Cassie, who responded by pointing to the test pattern as she gyrated and sang "Come on baby, do the locomotion." Startled, Lorena turned the TV off, but then asked a sulking Cassie to show her the steps she just made up.

"I didn't make them up," Cassie protested, but showed her anyway. Lorena quickly added them to her routine, a last-minute but, Lorena was certain, impressive addition sure to wow the director of the production of *Guys and Dolls* she was auditioning for tonight—her first step on the road to stardom.

A parade of hopefuls sings and dances across the auditorium stage, few of whom present any competition that Lorena can see. She and Della suppress their giggles at the chunky ballerina who staggers dizzily offstage after her third pirouette. They sneer openly at the off-key baritone whom Lorena recognizes as her dry cleaner.

"Ne-ext," calls the director in a nasal whine. "Lorena Palmer," he reads from a list. He's wearing dungarees and a little beret and it's rumored that he once had a bit part in a Hitchcock film—a nonspeaking part, but you could recognize him in the crowd. "Lorena Palmer," he repeats. "Where aaa-re you?"

"Here, here." She scrabbles sideways out of the row into the aisle, adjusting her tap pants as she goes. Before she ascends to the stage, she hands a green record to an assistant, who plunks it atop the 45 player.

"Dancer?" asks the director. He sounds bored. From the stage, all Lorena can see of him is the top of his beret, round and red with a little stem coming out of the top like a pumpkin. "You bet," she says, flashing what she hopes is a dazzling smile before she takes her position. The auditorium looms like a musky cavern before her. She sees Della—tousled curls bright in the gloom, face turned upward expectantly—give her a thumbs-up. Lorena nods at the assistant, then waits, trembling, as the needle drops onto the record.

WOOO-WOOO-ooo. Slowly at first, her arms rotate to the relentless rhythm, picking up the pace, churning churning chug-*a-chugga*-chug-*a-chugga,* now the feet, a subtle tap, then faster, faster, she gets into the groove, she's moving to the music, she's bopping with the beat, *yes* this is what it's all about, and she flings herself into the new moves she learned from Cassie, arms crawling in that swimming motion, a quick segue into the monkey scratch. She throws the director a saucy wink; his reaction is a bug-eyed stare. She can tell that he's in awe.

"So Chattanooga choo choo . . ." Revving up for her grand finale . . ."Won't you choo choo me ho-o-ome." And . . . split!

down she goes, legs splayed, arms high, big smile. Della's enthusiastic if solitary applause echoes through the auditorium.

"Thank you," says the director in a strangled voice. He hunches over his list. "Next!"

"Thank *you*," sings Lorena to the top of his beret.

"How'd I do?" she asks Della as she plops into her seat.

"Um. You were just . . . spectacular. No, really. Just spectacular."

A lithe blonde is nervously taking her place onstage. Lorena elbows Della. "Falsies," she says. But she's wrong. As the blonde begins her routine, it is clear that her bounce is authentic, a gentle rise and fall that synchronizes with each perfectly executed leap and twirl. Worse, she has hair that undulates in waves, a golden curtain she uses as a prop, sweeping it before her face, flinging it back dramatically, running her fingers through its shimmering strands in a gesture that seems choreographed.

"She looks like Veronica Lake," says Della.

Lorena slumps in her seat, arms folded. "Veronica Lake isn't a dancer."

The blonde winds up her routine with a precise pirouette. The director's beret is tipped back, he gives a little patter of applause. "Thank you," he says. "Very nice. And you are . . ." He checks his list, "Miss Ellenson?" She smiles prettily, nods. "Very nice, Miss Ellenson."

Miss Ellenson is chosen for the cast. Lorena is not. She and Della slog out of the auditorium accompanied by the plunking notes of "Luck Be a Lady Tonight" and the nasal voice of the director assigning the coveted roles.

"It was the hair," says Lorena. "The way she flung it around and all."

"Yeah," says Della.

"Men like that kind of hair. Long and blond. I bet that director woulda paid more attention if I didn't have such straight mousy hair."

"You have nice hair," Della says. "Nothing wrong with your hair."

"Was it my dancing?" Lorena stops and turns to Della. "Is that it? My dancing wasn't as good as hers? Tell me the truth."

"No, no." Della hesitates. "She was pretty good, though. But," she adds at Lorena's stricken look, "not as . . . exciting as you, all those new moves and all."

"So what did I do wrong?" Lorena wails. "It's the hair, isn't it? Be honest now."

"Well . . ."

"So what should I do?"

"Maybe take some dancing lessons?"

"YOU KNOW I hear stories all the time, every day, Lawdamercy, everybody's got a story and it's always bad." Maybelle gives Lorena's hair a mighty yank as it disappears into the last of the metal rollers. Lorena is captive in the pink plastic chair at Maybelle's House of Beauty, imprisoned in rollers attached by rubber-coated wires to the permanent-wave machine above her.

Maybelle grabs the big black plug of the machine, rams it into the wall receptacle. Lorena can almost hear the sputter and zap of electricity flowing into the rollers, frying her hair into the curls and spirals men go crazy for. As she sits, she envisions one man in particular: Binky Quisenberry. She closes her eyes, imagines herself the star of a Flash Gordon movie, prisoner of the space aliens, her brain connected to the machine. Binky would come, her handsome soldier, and rescue her.

Maybelle rants on, chunky arms crossed, her stumpy body in its pink beautician's uniform planted in front of Lorena as her hair cooks in the machine. ". . . a buncha whiners, that's all I hear, their husbands did this their husbands did that, well I say like President Truman said, If ya can't stand the heat get outta the kitchen. Get outta the kitchen, you dumbbells, y'all got better things to do in life, just don't come whining to me. Look, I don't need a man in my life, I got my byooty parler, I got my own business, what do I need a man to tell me what to do?"

Lorena nods agreeably, the rollers and wires nodding with her. They burn her scalp but she doesn't want to whine, not to Maybelle, not to this bastion of womanhood whose tough little face would knot up even more if Lorena confesses that the reason she is enduring this torture by perm is not only to advance her wished-for career but to enchant the enemy: men.

She's done. Maybelle releases her from the machine. Lorena's hair sproings out in hard little curls and she lets Maybelle steer her first to the washbasin for a shampoo, then to her chair for a pincurl set, and finally to a seat beneath the helmet of the dryer to laminate the twisted coils into submission. Exhausted, Lorena sinks into the chair in front of the mirror for her comb-out. Maybelle wields comb and brush in a frenzy, poufing Lorena's perm out to a mammoth puffball, foreign and frizzy. Lorena reaches up, touches it. It feels like mesh.

Maybelle steps back, beaming. "Like it, honey?"

Lorena feels like crying. This is not her hair. She wanted waves, big deep Veronica Lake waves, a swoop over one eye, sexy. Not this dandelion head. She looks like Nancy in the funny papers.

"Will it go down?" she asks, fearful of Maybelle's wrath.

"Nah, honey, don't worry," Maybelle reassures her. "That's the beauty of these perm machines, not like those newfangled cold waves. These are *permanent* perms."

"Not even a little?" Lorena's voice breaks. "Even if I wash it a lot?"

"Sugarplum, you've got curls till you cut 'em off."

Lorena stares at herself in Maybelle's mirror. And in a tiny voice she says, "I want to look like Veronica Lake."

"Well," Maybelle says, scurrying for her appointment book, "I can fit you in next Tuesday for bleach."

1

C A S S I E

MOM WENT TO Maybelle's and came home looking like Harpo Marx. She got a perm, a perm so huge it looks like she'd have to jump to touch the top of her head. I hate it when people see her with me. She didn't like the perm either, at first, but since Della told her it made her look taller she thinks maybe it's not so bad.

The worst part is that now Mom wants to curl *my* hair. She wants me to look like Shirley Temple, who was her favorite movie star when Mom was my age. Ever since she saw me doing some dance steps, Mom thinks I inherited what she calls "her talent." When I told her I learned those steps from test-pattern TV, she got mad, but she still wanted me to show her how to do them. I've caught her practicing in front of her mirror. It's enough to make you want to curl up and die.

I'm sitting on the wicker hamper and she's twisting my stringy brown hair around strips of torn rags, trying to make it curl in corkscrews like Shirley Temple's hair in this picture Mom tore out of an old *Photoplay*. She propped the picture up over the sink, keeps checking it to see which way to roll the rags so I'll have Shirley Temple curls instead of my own ugly hair.

I hear the kids outside yelling in the court. When I look out the window, Normie and Weezie and Ginny Sue are chasing each other with water pistols. What am I doing inside when they're having fun outside? I want to squirt Normie with my water pistol, get him back for the last time he got me. When I try to escape Mom, she grabs me back. First I have to be beautiful. Mom knots the last rag to my scalp. I feel as though a thousand bees have landed on my head. I hate this. I start pulling at the rags. I want them out.

"If you take them out, you won't be beautiful," Mom says. "You won't look like Shirley Temple. Don't you want to look like Shirley Temple for Della's May Day party?"

I don't want to go to Della's stupid May Day party. What I really want to do is blast Normie up the nose with my water pistol like he did to me the other day. I could run out and get him while my hair is setting, but I'm not about to go outside and show my rag-knotted head to the kids in the court. Besides, Mom won't let me because if I jiggle the rags loose I won't have curls and I won't look like Shirley Temple.

BOING-G-G. MOM UNWRAPS the first curl. It hangs like a chocolate spring next to my cheek, where a Shirley Temple dimple should be. I smile wide trying to force the dimple out, and Mom unwraps the next curl. It looks like a twin to the spring on the other side.

Mom is happy. She hums "On the Good Ship Lollipop." As she unties each rag, another curl boings down, and when she finishes, my face is buried under a wiggly forest of curls. Mom smiles. "See?" she says. "You *can* be pretty."

I don't feel pretty. I feel dopey. Mom makes me wear my pink party dress. It's such a baby dress, with a big bow tied in the back

and smocking all across where I should have titties but don't. I'd
rather have clothes like some of the people on test-pattern TV.
They dress different all the time.

Lots of times they just wear regular clothes like anybody. But
other times they wear these great costumes. Sometimes the men
don't wear suits. Sometimes their pants fit tight and then get real
wide below the knee, or else they're so droopy they look like
they're going to fall off. And girls wear pants a lot, all kinds of
pants. Skinny pants, wide pants, stocking pants, dungaree pants.
Or else they wear skirts so teeny they might as well be shorts.

Sometimes kids wear funny hats and neat shoes, not just Buster
Browns or Mary Janes, but boot shoes, or shoes that look like
they're on blocks, or huge tennis shoes that everybody wears in
some shows, not just kids but ladies and men, too. I'd like some
of those big fat shoes myself.

But no, I have to wear my stupid party dress and Mary Janes.
When I'm all dressed, I go outside to wait for Mom and Dad. I
slide my yellow water pistol into the pocket of my dress. I stand
on the porch of our house and watch while Normie pins Weezie
on her back and squirts water all over her face. She's screaming
and Ginny Sue is yelling at me, "Come on! Let's get him!"

I jump up and the two of us attack Normie, pull him off Weezie, and blast him with our water pistols. I give him a great nose
shot which makes him so mad he wrestles my pistol away. He
gives it to me with both barrels, squirting and squirting until my
face is dripping and my hair is flopping like an old mop against
my cheeks.

Here comes Mom out the door in her new shirtwaist dress and
white gloves and her good hat with the plastic cherries. Dad is
dragging behind her. She's made him wear his suit.

Mom looks at me like I grew another head or something.
"What happened to your hair?" she squeaks.

"What?" I say like I don't know.

"Five minutes! You're outside five minutes and look at you!"

Her hand is crawling over my head like a tarantula. "How did you get so wet?" She spins like a top on one high heel and heads back for the door. "Come on, we've got to fix you in a hurry. Criminy," she mutters under her breath, "she's hopeless." She drags me to the bathroom and I stare at the hopeless person in the mirror.

"I didn't do it." I sniff as tears roll down my undimpled cheeks. "Normie did it."

She doesn't say anything, just grits her teeth, grabs a towel, and rubs my hair really hard. She tries to twirl some life back into it, but it hangs in strips like flypaper. Only the ends bend up, just a little, to remind me they were curls a few minutes ago.

"Straight as a stick," Mom grumps. "Like trying to curl raw spaghetti." She shakes her own head, carefully, so she doesn't mess up her Harpo hairdo. "Looks like you've got Gramma's hair."

Oh no! Not *Gramma's* hair. Straight, thin, gray, such awful hair she had to wear it in a bun. I see myself doing what Gramma did, braiding her waist-length hair over one shoulder, her stubby fingers weaving over under over under until the last little wisp disappeared into a tail that she strangled with a rubber band. Then she reached back and twisted the braid around one finger, round and round on the top of her head, jabbing it with U-shaped hairpins she took one at a time from where they were clamped between her lips. She twisted and jabbed until the braid became a hard gray lump that didn't move until nighttime when she let it tumble like a snake down her back.

I start crying, I can't stop, I watch my tears roll down until my face is wetter than when Normie squirted it. I'm crying for my hair, for what it is and what it will be. "Well, it's not *that* bad," Mom says, like she's trying to make me feel better. "Maybe next week I'll take you to Maybelle for a perm."

"No!" I shriek. "I'll kill myself. I don't want Maybelle to give me a perm."

So the next day, when I see the box of Lilt Party Girl Children's Home Permanent she's bought for me, I throw the whole thing in the trash even though it cost a dollar fifty. I don't care about curls. My hair will be forever straight, and I will never be Shirley Temple.

L O R E N A

ELL, THIS HAIRDO is better. It even has a name: the Poodle Cut. Lorena pats her newly shorn curls, turns her head this way, then that way, looks at herself as Maybelle holds the hand mirror up so she can see the back. "Honey," Maybelle says, "you look just like Faye Emerson. The spitting image. People will stop you on the street and ask, 'Didn't I see you on TV last night?'"

Cutting was the only solution to the puffball head Lorena had acquired when her hair was fried in the perm machine, then bleached to the color of corn niblets. She couldn't wear a scarf everywhere, and her good hat with the red plastic cherries looked silly unless she was dressed up with gloves and all. So she had skulked back to Maybelle to throw herself at her mercy, pleading ignorance as to the care and feeding of her head. "I just can't do a thing with it," Lorena had whimpered. "I don't have your talent."

Maybelle had preened a little at that, nodded sagely, then of-fered her solution: cut it. "Hon, you got body now. All's you need is shape so's you can just wash and wear, like Mary Martin in *South Pacific*." Then, snapping her scissors in great sweeps, she snipped and clipped until all that was left was a tidy little cap of curls.

When Lorena gets home, she surveys her poodle head in the bathroom mirror. Her face looks round, her ears stick out, and with her bangs curled tight like that, her forehead seems to go on forever. She has no chance of being mistaken for Faye Emerson.

EVERY TIME LORENA does something to her hair, she has her Hair Dream. In the dream, her mother is shearing Lorena's hair with giant scissors, just as she did when Lorena was four and stuck chewing gum in her hair.

She remembers the knotty clump hardening, stuck like a stone near her scalp. Her mother yanked at it with a big black comb, pulling and pulling while Lorena screamed in pain. But the gum remained rigid, so out came the sewing scissors, blades clacking sharply like the bill of an angry bird. Chunks of Lorena's shiny brown hair fell around her feet until she could hardly see the tile on the bathroom floor.

But her mother wasn't finished. She took Poppy's shaving brush, scrubbed it furiously in his soap mug, grabbed Lorena's patchy head, and lathered it up. Ignoring Lorena's cries, she drew the straight razor across her head, around the ears, over the crown, down the back to her neck. Lorena screamed the whole time, No no Mommy no, but her mother held her tight between her legs, locking Lorena's head in the crook of her elbow.

When she was finished, her mother picked Lorena up so she could see herself in the mirror, shiny-head bald, her ears big and pink as a rat's. Lorena ran into her room, threw herself on her bed, and cried until she fell asleep without dinner. When she woke up in the middle of the night, she reached up and felt her slick smooth head and cried again until morning.

She still has the dream, even now, almost thirty years later. In the dream she feels the straight razor as it is drawn across her head, scraping the skin over the ears, across the crown, down the back to her neck. She sees her ears like pink parentheses on either side of her tearful face, feels the slippery smoothness of her head. And she still wakes up crying, sobbing into her pillow as she did when she was four years old.

"YOU GOT A poodle cut." Della's nails, pink and oval as Jordan Almonds, pick at Lorena's curls as they walk into the Paramount for the Saturday matinee. "You're getting so daring!" They lean back in the worn plush seats and chew Jujubes while they wait for the lights to go down.

Jujubes, Jujyfruits, Sugar Babies, Good and Plentys: like popcorn, Lorena eats those only in the movies, never anywhere else. Movie food is food to be eaten one piece at a time, from a box, in the dark. When food she has relegated to a certain place or time—turkey at Thanksgiving, candy corn at Halloween, hot dogs at the beach—is eaten out of context, it never seems to taste the same.

Gentlemen Prefer Blondes is playing. Jane Russell, Marilyn Monroe. "She's getting divorced, you know," Della says.

"Who?" Lorena asks, poking her finger at a Jujube stuck on a back molar.

"Marilyn Monroe and Joe DiMaggio. Louella Parsons said so in her column."

"Awww." Lorena is genuinely dismayed. It seemed like such a perfect match, the glamorous movie star and the famous baseball player. "Why?"

"She was making this movie where she stands on a subway grating and the wind blows her skirt up and her underpants show. All these people were watching while they were filming and he got really upset, and they had this big fight." Della shrugs, pops a Jujube in her mouth. "Seems like a dumb reason to get divorced."

Lorena nods. It sure does. She could think of lots of other reasons to get divorced, like having to make biscuits every night, or not being allowed to talk when *Cavalcade of Sports* is on, or being so bored you could scream. But mostly only movie stars get divorced unless you're someone like Della. Della isn't afraid of anything. Not of being talked about, or of having to work, or of being alone. Della is the bravest person she knows.

"Bobo Rockefeller got divorced from Winthrop and got five and a half million bucks," Della is saying. "Now, *that's* a good reason to get divorced."

"Why did *you* get divorced?" Lorena blurts. She knows Della walked out on Farley when he smacked her with the turkey leg, but Lorena had shied away from asking if it wasn't something more. People didn't get divorced unless it was so unspeakable that they never spoke of it. "I don't know if I could do that, just walk out."

"Well, sugar, why would you? You've got a kid who needs you and a guy who doesn't beat up on you—"

"He beat up on you?" Lorena interrupts.

"Yeah," Della says with an embarrassed shrug. "I didn't want to tell anybody, not even you, Lorena. The turkey was just the last straw. So leaving Farley was easy, 'specially since I don't have kids. Now I'm thirty-three, no husband in sight, and even if one shows up down the road, that'll be kinda late to start having babies. So what's left but to have a good time?"

And that she does. Della never seems sad, never stops laughing her big neighing bray that makes people turn around and raise their eyebrows. She moves like she knows where she's going, attracts attention with dresses a size too small for comfort, doesn't care that people call her The Divorcée.

Lorena examines Marilyn Monroe as she appears breathless and bosomy on the big screen. Well, she figures, there's somebody won't have a problem finding herself a new husband.

*   *   *

LORENA AND DELLA are sharing a banana split at Peoples drug-store after the movie. The dust-encrusted ceiling fan buzzes over-head, ruffling lipstick-imprinted paper napkins that clutter the tabletop of the booth where they're sitting. Two partially smoked Chesterfields lie cold and contorted in the ashtray, remnants of Della and Lorena's latest attempt at smoking, with which they have experimented since high school. Neither enjoys it, but both are determined to emulate Bette Davis's sophisticated technique. Della has mastered the art of inhaling smoke through her nostrils after exhaling it through her mouth, a feat Lorena envies and practices when alone.

Della points to the profile drawing of a girl on the matchbook cover over the words "Draw Me." "I did that," she says.

"Did what?"

"Drew her. If you draw her exactly like that, the Famous Artists School will let you sign up for correspondence classes where they teach you how to paint."

"You want to paint?"

"I guess. I know I can draw okay. Look. I practiced a lot." Della digs out a pencil and painstakingly copies the girl's profile on a napkin, halting with each movement of the pencil to check what she's done against the matchbook cover.

"Hey," says Lorena when Della displays her finished product. "That's pretty okay. I bet you get in."

"Yeah. I hope so. I always wanted to be a famous artist." She tucks the matchbook into her purse, then looks at Lorena with a sly smile. "Guess who I ran into when I was mailing my drawing at the post office?"

"Who?" Lorena licks her spoon with a chocolate-coated tongue.

"Binky Quisenberry."

Lorena gags on the ice cream she has sucked into the back of her throat.

"Are you okay?" Della asks. Lorena nods, speechless. "Any-way," Della blithely continues, "he was real friendly, told me he's out of the service now. Looks real cute in his uniform."

"If he's out of the service, why is he in uniform?"

"Different uniform. He's working for the post office."

"He's a mailman?"

"I guess that's what you are if you work for the post office."

"Did he ask you out?" Lorena very deliberately carves into the banana with her spoon, drags it through the chocolate sauce, lifts it to her mouth. She avoids looking at Della.

But Della is looking at Lorena. A little smile separates her tiny curved lips, exposing teeth that seem too big for her mouth. "No-o-o," she says, "but he did ask about you."

"Me?" Lorena interrupts the journey of her spoon to stare at Della. "How did he know you knew me?"

"I told him I was with you that day we went to see the trailer, when he was so rude. And then he remembered that we were best friends in high school."

"Oh." Lorena is all out of words.

Della isn't. She tips her head, separates a coppery coil from her nest of natural curls, twirls it around one pink-tipped finger, and says in a singsong voice, "Somebody's got a crush on someone."

Lorena feels her face flame red. "Don't be silly."

"Na-na-na-na-nana," Della sings.

"Well, so what? It doesn't matter anyway. I'm married."

"Never stopped *me*," Della says.

"Well, it stops me."

Della nods, agreeing. "Yeah, it woulda stopped me, too, if I had a real family like you do. You're lucky."

Lorena busily wipes her mouth with her napkin, takes out her change purse, counts out twenty-five cents for her banana split. "Come on, it's getting late, I've got to get on home."

"Oops, you're right. Big Saturday night." Della gives a Betty Boop wink. "Dinner at my house with Alan Ladd to watch *The*

Jackie Gleason Show, then"—she yawns and stretches—"it's early to bed." She winks again. "And away-y-y we go!"

"Away we go," repeats Lorena. And, with a wave at Della, away she goes.

LORENA LEAVES THE A&P with a bag of groceries, her flats scuffing as she crosses the barren parking lot. No long, long trailer is in sight, just a sticky stretch of asphalt dotted with cars that glint in the springtime sun. She swings open the car door, half hopes to see a soldier loping toward her, hat tilted over his forehead, hands hanging by their thumbs from his pants pockets.

But all she sees is a box-shaped woman in wide plaid shorts yank a screaming toddler through the parking lot, and a couple of ponytailed teenage girls sneak a smoke as they straddle the bumper of Lorena's car. Red-faced, they shuffle away in matching saddle shoes, leaving two squashed butts and a crumpled Pall Mall pack in their wake. Lorena tosses the bag of groceries into the car but doesn't get in herself. Standing here in the parking lot has twanged something deep within her: memory, desire, a compulsion to buy makeup. She slams the car door and hurries back to the shopping center.

She's in Woolworth's. She bypasses her usual stop, the candy counter, its bins overflowing with M&M's, Hershey's Miniatures, Mary Janes. She ignores the alluring aroma of chocolate, the meaty promise of peanuts, the smooth seduction of butterscotch. It is the cosmetics counter that beckons: pots and jars and tubes of goo to smear all over her face.

Lately she's felt drab. The hairdo didn't help, even if Della insisted she looked perky. "Perky" was not in Pete's vocabulary; "goofy" was. "Why'd you go and get that goofy haircut?" he had asked when she came home with her poodle cut. "First you frizz it out to there, then you bleach it till it's dead, and now this goofy haircut. Why don't you just leave it alone?"

She pokes around the makeup display. She needs Della. She examines an eyebrow pencil. What goes with Harpo hair? She unscrews a square bottle: Hazel Bishop Complexion Glow. This color is Rachel. She once knew a girl named Rachel. She smudges a dab of it on her wrist, holds her wrist to her cheek, stares into the warped aluminum that passes for a mirror over the counter. A little pink, but it'll do.

Party Puff powder, a dollar, she'll take it. She streaks her hand with three Westmore "kiss-tested" lipsticks: Rose Petal, Red Flame, Tangerine Dream, fifty-nine cents. Red Flame, she'll take that, she likes the name. And that cute black pot of crimson rouge. Ring it up: cosmetics, jar of Odo-Ro-No 24-hour Protection Cream, Woodbury Soap for the Skin You Love to Touch.

She can hardly wait to get home to try on her new face. With exquisite precision she lays out her purchases on her dressing table, pausing to savor the pristine virginity of each item as she tears off its cellophane: powder puff still white and unsullied, lipstick pointed in a crisp salute, rouge smooth and red as a stoplight. They so perfectly accessorize her dressing table that she almost wants to take a snapshot with her Brownie before she musses them all up.

It is a lovely dressing table. When she saw it in Nachman's furniture department, she just had to have it, had to have its kidney-shaped top, its froufrou lace skirt, its teeny tiny drawer with the cut-glass knob. Most of all, she had to have its great big egg-shaped mirror with the movie-star lights all around that made her feel like Marilyn Monroe whenever she turned them on.

She seats herself on the pink tufted cushion of the dressing-table chair and unfolds a Maybelline ad she cut out of *Life* illustrating Three Quick Tricks to Eye Beauty. As she uncaps her sharp new pencil in preparation, she reads: "Step one: Draw a narrow line around your eyes with your eyebrow pencil, then upstroke at the outer corner."

She draws a wobbly line. It goes down, not up.

"Step two: Do beautiful, expressive brows." The model has two perfect black wings flying above her upstroked eyes. Lorena pencils in brows that expand to Groucho dimensions.

"Step three: Apply mascara, holding the brush to set upswoop." OW. Lorena pokes herself in the eye with the miniature brush she had dampened with her spit before scrubbing it across the ebony cake. OW. *Damn*. Her eyes look like Dempsey's after a losing fight.

Long minutes later, her dressing table is a shambles. But Lorena's skin is pink, her cheeks are crimson, and her Red Flame'd lips are all aglow.

She hears Cassie's footsteps coming up the stairs. When Lorena opens her bedroom door, Cassie's face is a mixture of shock and delight.

"Hey," says Cassie. "Clarabelle!"

LORENA IS HUNCHED beneath the kitchen sink with a can of Old Dutch cleanser and a brush, scraping gunk that has accumulated since she cleaned it out last spring. She's on her hands and knees in an old pair of pedal pushers with a rip in the seat. Making this rusty glop disappear has become her focus, her purpose, her mission in life.

Spring cleaning: the dreaded annual ritual, relegated to the attic of her mind until Harriet Nelson reminded her that she had neglected her housewifely duty. On last night's show, Harriet, tidy in her Peter Pan collar blouse, announced to tie-and-jacketed Ozzie, Why, it's spring-cleaning time! Whereupon Ozzie, jubilant at the chance to do windows, ensnared the equally compliant Ricky and David to clean out the garage. This they did with manic delight, never mussing a hair of their rigid crew cuts.

Why, Lorena wondered as she watched the Nelson family buff up their already perfect home, wasn't Pete like Ozzie? Ozzie wouldn't put his feet on the coffee table and flick ashes on the rug. Ozzie would say, "How did your day go, dear?" and compliment her on her pot roast. Ozzie wouldn't blow his nose in the shower.

Lorena swore when she got married that her marriage would be different from that of her parents, who sat across from each other at the dinner table like two warring eagles with their talons out. She would never let her husband catch her looking frumpy, dinner would always be on time, her children would be charming and say "yes, ma'am" and "no, ma'am," her daughter would wear pinafores and have Shirley Temple curls. Weren't they supposed to live an Ozzie and Harriet life?

But here she is, a frump who has dinner on time but not to their liking ("What is this? Snot?" Cassie had asked, poking the okra with her knife), and her child was neither charming nor curly-headed. Lorena felt cheated.

Instead of having tea at the Ritz, she's on her knees under the sink, scrubbing away like the maid she could have had if only she had planned her life better. As she scrubs away at the stubborn sink gunk, she lets her mind graze in far-off pastures. She'll take tap lessons. Perfect her routine. Try out for *Arthur Godfrey's Talent Scouts*. She's humming "Tea for Two" when she hears the doorbell. She sticks her head out from under the sink, wipes her hands on the pedal pushers, yells "Just a minute," before she unkinks herself and goes to the door.

"Can Cassie come out to play?" Margaret and Ginny Sue gaze at Lorena with pathetic eyes.

"She's at her dancing lesson," Lorena hisses. She knows what the next question will be.

"Can we watch TV till she comes home?"

"There's. Nothing. On." How many times will she have to say that before she's entitled to rip their grubby little throats out?

"Can we watch when there is?"

"We'll have to see," she says, her effort at control betrayed as she slams the door.

She trudges back to the sink and crawls back underneath to

resume scrubbing. And there's the doorbell again. She tries to ignore it, but its persistent buzzing penetrates her resolve. She clambers out from under the sink and storms to the door.

"Go home!" she shrieks as she flings the door open, and immediately slams it shut again.

It's Binky. In uniform. Her hands fly up to her hair, then down to the seat of her ripped pedal pushers. She opens the door a crack, peers around its edge. "Binky," she croaks. "What are you doing here?"

He's holding out her mail. "Surprise! I'm your new mailman. I finished my training. I asked for your neighborhood for my route. They let me have it since I'm just out of the service and all. You gonna invite me in?"

"How did you know where I live?"

"Phone book. Looked it up. Pete Palmer, right, that's what you told me?"

"Oh," she says from behind the door. She doesn't want him inside, not the way she looks with her frizzy hair and ripped pants. All that makeup, sitting unused on her dressing table and not on her face. "Well," she says, reaching her hand around the door for her mail, "thanks for delivering it."

"That's my job. That's what I do. Rain, sleet, shine, blizzard, hail, whatever, I forget how it goes. You gonna invite me in for a lemonade?"

"Lemonade?"

"Nehi? Co-Cola? I don't care."

"Um," she says, "I'm doing some . . . cleaning." That's smooth, she thinks, mentally beating her head against the wall. She shouldn't have answered the door, why did she answer the door, she knew what she looked like, why did she answer the door? "I'm not really dressed."

"You look fine to me."

"Wait a minute," she says. She shuts the door, drops her mail on the coffee table, runs upstairs. Bangs open a drawer, pulls out shorts and a halter top. Rips off the pedal pushers, changes. Dips her pinky finger into the rouge pot, smears quick crimson circles onto her cheeks, scrawls Red Flame lips onto her mouth. Runs back downstairs. Opens the door. "I think I've got a Coke around somewhere," she says, panting. He comes in, drops his big leather mailbag by the doorway.

He does look handsome in his uniform. Snappy, as a matter of fact, those gray pants with the stripe down the side, that braided cap with the visor, so official-looking it just makes you want to stand and salute. His military haircut has grown out and it looks like his brown hair has been combed back with something gooey—Brylcreem, Vitalis—beneath his cap. He has kept his pencil-thin Errol Flynn mustache.

His lips are still soft and pink. She remembers how they felt when she touched them in the A&P parking lot that day, tender as the plush of the Paramount's chairs. Her fingers tingle at the memory, setting off a tremor through her body that erupts into a nervous giggle.

"Something's different." He tilts his head quizzically, appraising her. Then, "Your hair," he says.

Her hands fly up, fingers stretched over the springy mass of poodle-clipped curls. "It was supposed to . . . Maybelle said . . ." she sputters.

He reaches over and twangs a curl. "You look like, whatshername, Mitzi Gaynor."

Mitzi Gaynor?

The movie star? She looks like Mitzi Gaynor the movie star?

"Well," she says. "Hardly." But she is flattered, and she turns just so, looks pertly over her shoulder before she heads toward the kitchen calling "Ice?" in what she hopes is a Mitzi Gaynor voice.

"Nope," he calls back. "I like my Cokes warm and fizzy."

Please don't say "Like my women," she thinks.

"Like my women," he says.

She's glad he doesn't want ice because Pete didn't bother to fill the tray and there's one lonely cube left. She brings two warm fizzy glasses of Coke into the living room, where Binky sits sprawled out on the sofa as if he'd been there all week. "Here," he says, patting the cushion next to him. She complies and detours around the undulations of the coffee table to sink into the couch right next to him.

"Well," she says.

"Well," says Binky.

"So you decided not to go into business with your dad," she says to make conversation.

"Bad idea." He takes a noisy slurp of Coke. "It's never a good idea to go into business with a relative. Especially when that relative is my dad. Auto parts, that's not my field anyway, I like cars and all but the parts, well, they're not the same thing. As the whole car."

"Well, I guess." She's not even sure what auto parts are. Carburetors. Brakes. Door handles. "Your dad must have been disappointed."

"I don't know. He didn't actually, you know, ever *ask*."

"Didn't ask? If you'd go in with him?"

"Not actually."

She looks at her glass. She's left a big greasy red lipstick smear on the rim. She feels a burp welling beneath her rib cage, a gassy Coke bubble rising, rising until she can't suppress it and a growly "bor-r-r-rk" escapes, puffing out her cheeks and making her eyes water. " 'Scuse me," she mumbles, humiliated.

"BRAAACK," he responds in kind, a manly belch whose explosion momentarily deflates him until he puffs back up with a contented sigh. "Boy, nothing like a warm Coke to get your innards going."

"Can't argue with that."

"I saw your friend Della the other day, she mention that? Funny, I didn't remember her right away, but she knew me, came right up, said 'Hi.' Then she mentioned your name, and alluvasudden I got this picture of you two walking down the hall at school dressed in those sailor blouses you used to wear. She was kind of fat then, wasn't she?"

"Fat?" She never thought of Della as fat. She was voluptuous, that was the word Della used to describe herself after she heard Jerry Lester use it to describe Dagmar on *Broadway Open House*. Voluptuous. It had a nice, round sound to it. It conjured up images of the Venus de Milo and Mae West. Voluptuous was what Lorena always wanted to be and never was. "Della's not fat," she said in defense of her friend's poundage.

"Hey, no, I don't mean she's fat now. She's thinned out, lost that heft. Not my type, but looks pretty okay."

Good. Della's not his type, so Lorena magnifies Della's virtues. "She looks great," she says, "and she's real independent, she's got a real job."

"She told me, said she was divorced from that guy she went with in high school, Farley Something, wasn't that his name? She said she didn't have kids but you did."

"I've got a girl, Cassie. She's almost eleven."

"Just one?"

Lorena doesn't feel like telling him that they just never got around to having another one, even though Pete wanted a son, not that he didn't want a daughter, too, but he always pictured himself playing catch with a son, taking him fishing and crabbing, doing all that stuff that girls don't do.

But all she says to Binky is, "Just one."

"So, where is she?" he asks.

"She's at her dancing lesson."

"Dancing?"

"Yeah. Tap. She just started. I think she's got talent."

Binky gives another belch, smaller, more discreet this time. "I used to take accordion lessons."

"The *accordion*?" She can't picture Binky pushing that serpentine instrument between his big square-fingered hands, playing "Lady of Spain wah-wah-wah-wah . . ." "I don't remember anybody playing the accordion except for Winnie Wachholder, who used to play during assemblies."

"I was little when I played. Eight or nine. My mother made me." He looks crumpled when he says this, as if his mother is standing over him right now. "And then I threw it out my bedroom window into the driveway and my dad drove over it." He's distracted by the memory but snaps right back. "So she's at her dancing lesson now?"

"Yeah. Her lesson's on Thursdays. Takes the bus, gets home around four."

"She any good?"

"Not yet. She hates it. But she's got real talent, that's what I think. She's very original, makes up her own steps. She just needs to get the basics down."

"But if she hates it . . ."

"She just thinks she hates it. She has to give it a chance, develop her talent." Lorena sighs. "I wish *I* had had a mother who made me develop my talent."

"Talent? What's your talent?"

She looks at him, pushes her bottom lip out in a pout. Doesn't he remember? "I dance," she says.

"Dance? What kind of dance? Jitterbug?"

"Well, yeah." Doesn't he remember everybody standing around clapping when she was on the dance floor? How good she was? "But tap dance is my specialty. I'm working on my routine. I'm going to try out for one of those amateur-hour shows on TV. You know, Ted Mack, Arthur Godfrey."

"I got a cousin does that."

"He dances?"

"Naw. He finds people. For Arthur Godfrey."

"He's a *talent scout*?" Lorena clutches her hands and flings them to her chest. "For Arthur *Godfrey*?"

"My cousin Wally. He's from Norfolk. Always was kind of . . . different, you know, showbizzy like. Ran away to Hollywood when he was sixteen but my aunt Edna made him come home and finish high school. Now he lives in New York, travels all over looking for people to go on *Arthur Godfrey*. That's his job."

"Oh my God," says Lorena.

"Well, he's not *that* special," Binky says, his voice tinged with annoyance. "He's more weird than special."

"Can I meet him?"

"What?"

"Can I meet him? *Please!*"

Binky shrugs. "Well. I dunno. He's hardly ever around anymore. I mean, I don't even know if he'd remember me, it's been so long—"

"Listen," Lorena interrupts. "You track Wally down and meanwhile I'll perfect my routine so that when you do find him, I'll be ready."

"Sure. Sure thing," Binky agrees, snaps his wrist to his face, looks bug-eyed at his watch. "Oh boy. I'm late. I gotta get going. First day on the route, got to stay on schedule."

Lorena leaps between him and the mailbag as he reaches down to retrieve it. "I would be forever, and I do mean forever, indebted to you if I could meet Wally," she cries, and grabs his hand.

"Hey," he responds with a grin. "My turn," and he pulls her hand to his lips. "Remember? In the parking lot?" he murmurs, and she feels his lips on her fingertips once again, wet and slick. The tip of his tongue reaches out like a fat pink worm and licks the space between her fingers, zinging her whole body as if he had licked her all over. Her lips part, and before she thinks to stop him, he has planted his face on hers and she can't remember when she's felt like this, fusing, melting, surrendering . . .

He stops abruptly. Backs away from her, picks up his mail sack without looking. "Don't move," he whispers. "I want to remember you just this way." Before he shuts the door, he adds, "See you tomorrow."

Lorena feels paralyzed for long minutes after he's left. She stares at the pile of mail on the coffee table. Binky kissed her. She hasn't been kissed by another man for . . . what? Thirteen years? Unless she counts Uncle Rudy, who may he rest in peace used to try when Aunt Lula would have them over for Sunday dinner.

She feels different now. Sexy. Sensual. Desirable. Does it show? She staggers upstairs to look in the bathroom mirror. Her hair looks electrified. Her ears are sticking out. Her face is smeared from nose to chin with lipstick. She looks as if she just finished a cherry Popsicle.

But Binky kissed her. And not just a kiss. It was a seal, a promise, a pledge to her future.

It's destiny, she whispers to the face in the mirror. It's written in the stars. Soon you will meet cousin Wally. Soon you will *be* a star.

9

C A S S I E

I REALLY WANT to go back out to the pool, but no, we have to sit here in the dumb coffee shop even though I've finished my hamburger and I'm bored bored bored with all their talking. This is supposed to be my special treat, to have lunch and swim at the Chamberlin Hotel, but Mom and Della act like I'm not even here except when Mom says "Stop that!" if I make the table move with my knees or slurp my straw in the bottom of my glass.

And then I see him. Snooky Lanson. I know it's him, I can tell all the way across the coffee shop. It's not just somebody who looks like him, kind of pale and freckle-y, hair combed high in a pompadour. It's Snooky Lanson, the TV star. I know his voice. It booms all the way across the room, even though he's not singing like he does on *Your Hit Parade,* one of my very very favorite TV shows. He's sitting at a table with a bunch of ladies in bathing suits covered with frilly robes and men dressed in cabana sets, bathing trunks with matching shirts like the kind Dad took back to Nachman's after Mom bought him a set.

I've never seen a real live famous person before, not in the same room with me. "Mom!" I say, but she's so busy yakking with Della that she's not paying attention. "Mom, Mom, look!" I pull at the sleeve of her striped beach jacket and she says her usual "Stop that," until I say the magic words "Snooky Lanson" and she looks at where I'm pointing.

"Don't point," she says, smacking my hand down, but she's craning her neck to see for herself. "He looks older in person," she says to Della, who has unstuck her bottom from the plastic seat of our booth and is half standing for a better view.

"Snooky Lanson?" asks Della. "Isn't he on *My Hit Parade?*"

"*YOUR Hit Parade,*" I say, and roll my eyes around. Most times I really like Della, a lot. She's funny and nice and treats me like a real person, not just a kid, but sometimes she can be such a dumb Dora, as Dad would say.

"You know the show," Mom says to her. "The one where they sing and dance to the top hits of the week. And at the end they sing that song." And then she sings it in her Minnie Mouse voice: "So long for a while, that's all the songs for a while . . ." I would like to die. Just crawl under this table and die.

"Mom! *Stop* that." I cover my face with my hands. "He can hear you."

She laughs. "No, he can't. He's too busy talking." I look over at his table. He's laughing, his big TV teeth open wide, his little squinty eyes almost shut. Every time he says something, the lady next to him in the floppy straw hat laughs and squeezes his knee.

"I want to get his autograph," I say.

"Don't bother the man," says Mom.

"I want to!"

"Well . . ." She starts pawing through her beach bag. "Do you have something for him to write on?"

I think fast. My napkin. It's not really dirty, just a very faint chocolate smudge, he'll never notice. "I need a pen," I say, smoothing out the creases in the napkin. I'm nervous he might leave before I can even ask. "Hurry, hurry. Don't you have something to write with?"

"Just hold your horses," Mom says. She sticks her arm in the bag all the way to her shoulder and scrabbles around until she comes up with this short yellow pencil stub, like the ones she and Della use to write down their canasta scores. "Here."

"That's all you've got? How can I ask Snooky Lanson to write his name with something so stubby?"

"That's it, kiddo," she says. "Take it or leave it."

I take it and the napkin and walk slowly over to the table where Snooky is sitting. The closer I get, the slower I walk. Nobody looks at me, they just keep talking and laughing until I'm standing close enough to touch him. It's strange to see him up close. He has very pink skin, peeling in patches from the sun, and orangy-yellow hair that sticks up funny. I always think of him in black-and-white, and here he is in color. His shirt is all bright with palm trees, flamingos, sailboats. His hamburger has just one bite out of it. He's holding a french fry, waving it around while he talks.

When he looks at me, I am afraid because his eyes are so pale, blue and pale and blank as the stationary Della gave me for Christmas to write thank-you notes on. I want to write on his eyes: "Dear Mr. Lanson, How are you, I am fine. Thank you very much for signing my napkin. I am sorry about the pencil. Thank you very much. Yours truly, Cassandra Palmer."

That way I wouldn't have to talk. But I open my mouth and out comes a squeak. "Could I have your autograph?" The straw-hat lady next to him bends down to me and says with her juicy pink lips, "Isn't she sweet?" I don't feel sweet. I feel dopey. The napkin has gotten all wrinkled and sweaty, and I don't even want to think about the pencil.

But I hand them both to him anyway. He smiles his wide Snooky smile and doesn't seem to notice the stubby pencil or the dinky napkin. "What's your name?" he asks.

"Cassie," I mumble. And then he writes. The napkin tears a

little as the pencil digs in, but when he hands it back it's still in one piece and below where it's printed "Chamberlin Hotel" in swirly blue letters, he's scribbled "To Cassie, best regards, Snooky Lanson."

I don't know what to say. Thank you doesn't seem to be enough. "I will treasure this," sounds goofy. So I curtsy. I haven't done that since kindergarten, but I remember how. I dip low over one bended knee and stick the other leg way in back of me, and say the only French words I know: "Mercy bocoo."

The straw-hat lady applauds, and Snooky and his friends all laugh. Then he leans over and gives me a kiss on my cheek. I can feel his stubbly whiskers, white, almost invisible against his pink and scabby cheeks. And then I turn and run back to my mother and Della, who are sitting with their eyes and mouths round and surprised.

"What was that all about?" Mom asks.

"He wants me to go on his show," I say. "He likes the way I curtsy."

Mom and Della look at each other. "See what I mean?" my mother says. "She tells the most fantastic stories with such a straight face."

"Sometimes," I say, carefully folding the napkin and tucking it into the pocket of my terry robe, "they're true."

MOM'S MORE EXCITED about Snooky's autograph than I am. She won't let me just paste it into my scrapbook, like I want to do. Oh, no. She has to get a frame for it at Woolworth's and hang it in the kitchen.

I think she's sorry she wasn't the one who went up to Snooky to ask for his autograph. She probably thinks he would have discovered her, like he would have asked her to tap-dance or something. She saw me watching her when she was practicing her routine and instead of getting embarrassed like a normal mother would, she tried to show me how to do it, saying with each step, "Brush, brush, shuffle-ball change, lunge and pullback." The loose skin on her arms jiggles all around when she does that.

One night when we were watching TV, Mom got this brilliant idea that she and I could try out to be the dancing Old Gold cigarette packs in the commercial. She would be the big pack and I would be the little pack. Then she got up and tried to follow the steps the Old Gold packs were doing until Dad got mad and told her to sit down, she was blocking his view. She said It's just a commercial, and then they started fighting and I went up to my room to read Nancy Drew.

But she won't let go of the dancing Old Gold packs idea, so now she's making me take dancing lessons. I hate it. I like to dance, but not when I *have* to. I dread Thursdays, getting on the bus with my tap shoes in a shopping bag, climbing the stairs to the dusty studio that smells like feet, tapping while Miss Fritzi plays that tinny old piano and counts ". . . and a one-and-a-two . . ." until she loses her temper and squawks ". . . *together*, ladies, you're not a herd of cows." This is not fun.

Mom thinks I have her talent. It's all my fault for showing her the dance steps I learned from test-pattern TV. The dancing there is different from anything on regular TV. I like the way the painted ladies in bathing suits dance, not just with their feet but with their arms and heads and butts. And there's a show where a bunch of teenagers do dances with funny names like the twist or the swim or the monkey.

Once I saw this neat guy with tall greasy hair dance the hootchy-cootchy while he sang about somebody being a hound dog. When I told Mom I saw him on Milton Berle's show, she said she never saw anything like that on Milton Berle, I must have made it up, like I made up the story about the four English guys with long hair on *The Ed Sullivan Show* who sang about wanting to hold my hand. People in the audience screamed and screamed while they were singing, just like they did for the hound-dog guy.

It would be fun to sing and dance and have people scream for you, but it's not something I'd really want. After I saw something on test-pattern TV about this princess who got killed in an accident because she was so famous that these guys chased her to take her picture, I don't know why *anybody* would want to be famous.

I AM WEARING the most beautiful dress imaginable. It is silver, made by Mom from Christmas-tree tinsel she found in the back of the hall closet. It moves when I move, brushes my legs like crystal feathers when I walk. Each strand catches the blue rays of the footlights and shimmers like neon. I walk across the auditorium stage and take my place.

I am the star of the fifth-grade play. I am the month of May. I get to wear the dress of lights, the dress that looks like rain.

All the mothers are looking at me. My classmates are in the wings, watching. I hear somebody hiss at me, "You only got the part because your birthday's in May." The lights are warm and bright and all the mothers' faces blend into a pink blur, except one: my own mom, sitting in the front row.

I want to make her proud of me, like she was when I was little. Then it didn't matter what I did or said because I was so cute. That's what Mom says—"Wasn't she cute?"—when she shows people the picture of us taken a few years ago, where we're dressed alike in our mother-daughter sundresses. You can see Dad's long shadow on the grass as he held the camera. "Wasn't she cute?" Mom always asks. I don't remember being cute. I just remember that day, Mom cuddling me close on her lap, her smell of roses and powder, the soft squishy feel of her cheek on mine. "Wasn't she cute?" I guess that means she doesn't think I'm so cute anymore.

I listen nervously for my cue from Dewey Puckett, who is dressed in a big pointy hat and his mother's bathrobe. He is Father Time. "Mother's Day!" he spits at me through the space in his teeth. "Memorial Day! What boring holidays. If I had known May would be such a dull month, I would have left it out of the calendar altogether."

I am supposed to get mad, stomp my foot, and say, "Dull? Never! May is the month of flowers." Then Tony Fanelli in a green crepe-paper beard will leap from the wings and throw pink paper streamers at me while I say, "And don't forget May Day."

". . . out of the calendar altogether." My cue. The air is thick in the auditorium, as heavy as the black velvet curtain I can touch behind me. I smell the ham and collards cooking for lunch in the cafeteria. I look at Dewey, hands on his hips, sneering like the little snot he is, waiting for my line. I stamp my foot and tinsel rainbows flash around my knees.

"Dull?" I say. "Never!" Mom gives me a big grin. I glance toward the wings at Tony Fanelli, who is standing there like a blob. "May is the month of my birthday!" I say all wrong because I'm thinking about Tony and how I just know he's not going to leap when he's supposed to. What's my next line? Something about flowers. "And don't forget to bring me flowers," I say, but Miss Winkle, crouching offstage like a toad, croaks in her Froggy the Gremlin whisper, "No, no! It's 'Don't forget *May Day*.' " I hear a giggle, then another, and then the whole audience is tee-heeing.

I glare at the sea of pink faces opening like clam shells to laugh at me. "Don't forget my birthday," I say, wrong again, but it startles Tony Fanelli enough to leap and throw pink streamers at me. One streamer doesn't unroll. It bonks me on the nose and makes me so mad I do a Whitey Ford windup and pitch it back hard into Tony's butt. Now the audience laughs even more.

Mom's frozen grin is the last thing I see before I stomp off-stage. I want to vanish, me and my beautiful dress of rain, just disappear into a tinsel puddle like the Wicked Witch of the West. I swear I'll never do that again. I swear this is the last time I'll ever get up on a stage in front of people and make a fool of myself.

Mom doesn't say too much on the ride home. She doesn't even get mad when I braid strips of the tinsel on my costume while we drive. And tonight when we're watching TV, for the first time all week Mom doesn't bring up the Old Gold dance thing.

L O R E N A

TODAY LORENA FEELS —well, perky. She washes her hair, sets the frizz in pincurls, and it does indeed look like a poodle. Spends an hour with her new makeup, lines her eyes in a fairly successful upswoop beneath brows that hover black as crows' wings, rouges her cheeks into perfect circles.

She has a hard time choosing the right dress. The shirtwaist with the cinch belt, or the princess dress with the low-cut neckline? She decides on the shirtwaist with her patent-leather high-heel shoes, polished up with a little Vaseline so she can see her blurry reflection in their toes.

Lorena is vacuuming. It's a little awkward in heels, but if the housewife in the Hoover commercial can do it, so can she. Not a one of those models in ads is doing housework in a robe or raggy clothes. You sure don't see Betty Furness wearing torn pedal pushers when she flings open the door of the Westinghouse, no sirree. She looks like she's Cinderella on her way to the ball—blond hair

in an updo, gold hoop earrings—instead of demonstrating how
crispy the cabbage stayed in the Humidrawer.

Lorena is vacuuming, shoving the Hoover back and forth over
the same spot on the rug. It's three-thirty. About this time yesterday, Binky delivered the mail. She assumes he'll deliver it the
same time today. Oh! she'll exclaim when he rings the doorbell.
You caught me vacuuming. What a *surprise*.

Three forty-five. She's worn a path in the rug, sucked it limp
with the Hoover. Where is Binky? Cassie is outside playing and
could walk in any second. All Lorena wants is a few minutes
alone with Binky, let him see she doesn't always look dowdy in
torn pedal pushers, that she usually looks, well, perky.

Four o'clock. Where is he? She gives up vacuuming, starts dusting, whaps the feather duster over the shelf of knickknacks, over
the ceramic Hummel boy tooting his horn, the snow-globe sou-
venir from their honeymoon at Virginia Beach, the sepia-toned
photograph of Pete's mother in its dimestore frame, the wooden
Dutch shoe planted with a plastic tulip. *Whap, whap*. The knickknacks haven't been so free of dust in months.

Now what? Her heels hurt. She slumps down on the sofa and
stares glumly at the vacant screen of the TV. Nothing on to watch
right now, just the test pattern, and then she starts thinking of
Cassie, wonders why she has fixated on the test pattern, decides
she's just devised those stories to torment Lorena. And then the
doorbell rings. She leaps to her feet, minces precariously to the
door.

It's Cassie. And Molly.

"Can we have something to drink, we're dying." Cassie brushes
by Lorena and heads for the kitchen, followed by Molly, who
adds, "And something crunchy to eat, I need crunch." They are
both damp and dirty from the kickball game going on in the
court, and exude a faint aroma of banana Popsicle.

"Didn't you get something from the ice-cream man?" Lorena
asks, annoyed that the doorbell signaled this invasion rather than

a visit from Binky. "I gave you a nickel for a Popsicle. Isn't that enough?"

Cassie emerges from the kitchen with a package of strawberry Kool-Aid. "Can I make this?"

"Make it," Lorena sighs.

"How come you're so dressed up?" Cassie asks, suddenly noticing. "You going somewhere?"

"Yeah," Lorena says. "Upstairs."

She strips off the dress, throws the shoes in the closet, goes into the bathroom. As she sits contemplating the tile, she hears the doorbell ring. She leans forward, opens the door a crack to catch what's being said, finishes up quickly, and throws open the door.

"Who is it, Cassie?" she calls in her most melodious voice. She hears the slam of the front door.

"Nobody," Cassie yells upstairs. "Just the mailman."

Lorena scrambles back into her dress and heels, skitters down the stairs. Cassie stares at her, a Kool-Aid stain giving her frowning mouth a clown's grin. "Where you going now?" she asks.

"Damn," Lorena mutters.

"You said I couldn't say that. How come you can?"

Lorena doesn't answer. She throws open the front door, spies Binky way down the row of houses. "Forgot to mail something," she mumbles as she scurries past Cassie and teeters down the sidewalk calling "Yoo-hoo." When he turns around, she slows her trot to a sashay and waves.

"My, my," he says as she approaches. "Don't we look nice today." His eyes roll like marbles up and down her shirtwaisted shape.

"Oh, this old thing. I wasn't expecting you or I would have answered the door myself."

"That your kid?" he asks.

She nods. "Cassie."

"Cute. Looks like you, huh?"

Lorena shrugs. "Some say." She bats mascara'd eyes, tosses

poodle-cut hair, says in what she hopes is a Mitzi Gaynor voice, "I'd ask you in for a Coke, but with Cassie there . . ."

"Sure, sure." He ponders that. "When didja say she has her dancing lesson?"

"Thursdays. Gets home at four," she says, attempting nonchalance.

"Oookay. Thursdays." He pokes at his temple with a forefinger. "Gotta remember that." He flashes a crooked grin and contemplates her with rain-gray eyes half-hidden by lowered lashes. "I'll see you then, then."

He slings his mail pouch over one shoulder, gives her a little salute before resuming his rounds. She imagines his legs, pictures them firm and furry beneath those clinging gray pants, as they carry him away up the sidewalk. She saunters slowly back toward her house, hopes he's turned to notice the sway of her skirt, the tap of her high heels.

Cassie looks up from the Monopoly board she and Molly are setting up on the floor as Lorena comes back into the house, kicks off her heels, and plods up the stairs. "What's going on?" Cassie asks. "Is there a party or something?"

Lorena doesn't know what to say, so she says nothing, just shuts the door to her room. Stares into the mirror. Turns her face this way and that. Looks pretty good, she decides, good enough for Binky's approval. All that work wasn't wasted after all. She reaches for the Pond's to erase the upswept eyes, the crow's-wing brows, the gleaming cheeks and lips, but as she dips her fingers into the pearlescent cold-cream pudding, she hesitates. She looks *too* good. She decides to wear her face a little longer. Maybe see if Pete appreciates her efforts.

PETE DROPS HIS lunch bucket on the kitchen counter with a clang, reaches into the Frigidaire, extracts a Ballantine. "What a day," he complains, flipping off the cap with a bucktoothed bite from the remover screwed to the wall. "I dunno about the new foreman. Like to snap my head off today. Seems like he's got it in for me or something." He tips his head back to suck on the Ballantine, Adam's apple bobbing beneath plucked-chicken skin.

Lorena plants herself in his line of sight, pouts painted lips, bats licorice eyelashes. She emits a mew of sympathy for Pete's plight. He finishes his beer, bangs the bottle on the counter next to his lunch bucket, belches. "What's for dinner?" he asks.

"Meat loaf." She won't give up. "Notice anything?" She moves until she's standing right in front of him.

He allows her a quick glance, then a grimace. "Not your hair again."

She gives a puff of exasperation. "I haven't been back to Maybelle since last week."

"You're wearing lipstick," he tries again, impatient now.

"So? I wear lipstick. It's not like I never wear lipstick."

He squints. Tips his head. Then, "What's that stuff on your eyes?"

"Like it?" she asks.

"What is it?"

"It's eye makeup. Mascara. Eye shadow. Eyeliner."

"I don't like it."

"You didn't even notice it."

"You look like Della. All that paint and stuff. I think you been hanging out with Della too much."

"Well, I think Della looks good," she says, remembering Della's gyrating prance before the sailors, a neon-plumaged parakeet outshining Lorena's brown wren self. "There's nothing wrong with accentuating your assets," she adds, echoing Della's advice.

"What?"

"Never mind. You wouldn't understand."

"Listen. I got problems at work *you* don't understand. I come home, all's I ask is dinner on the table, a little peace and quiet, and what do I get? Bozo the Clown."

Clarabelle, Harpo, now Bozo. She just wanted to look pretty

again. Didn't he remember? How she looked when he saw her that first time, asked her out, wanted her to marry him? Didn't he remember?

"I used to be pretty," she says, pouting. "I was Miss Buckroe Beach 1938."

"Yeah, yeah. Miss Buckroe. How many times you gonna remind me of that? You'd think it was the highlight of your life."

Well, she thinks, it was.

LORENA WAS SEVENTEEN that summer, a summer of long, lack-adaisical days spent baking in the sun at nearby Buckroe Beach. Facedown on an old frayed blanket redolent of suntan oil, sweat, and mustard from hot dogs bought at the stand, she lay immobile for hours, lulled by the throbbing pulsation of waves and the bubbling music of the merry-go-round calliope.

From the vortex of darkness behind her closed eyes a recurring fantasy would emerge: being tapped for stardom by a Hollywood talent scout. "You are magnificently gorgeous," exclaimed the phantasmagorical scout of her imagination, "but can you dance?" And she dazzled him on the spot with her Ginger Rogers footwork.

Prone on her blanket, lost in her dream, Lorena was so certain that fame would come to her that her baby-oil-and-iodine-basted body shivered with anticipation.

It was Della who suggested that Lorena enter the Miss Buckroe contest. Della would have entered herself, but she had broken her elbow doing a swan dive off the high board trying to impress some guy at the Community Center pool and had to wear a cast for most of the summer. She wouldn't be able to perform her baton twirling for the talent part of the competition. But, she pointed out, Lorena could tap-dance.

"Miss Buckroe?" Lorena's round nose wrinkled in dismissal at the suggestion. "They don't care about talent. Besides," she sighed in a fit of candor, "I'm too flat-chested for any beauty contest."

"Socks," said Della.

"Socks?"

"Everybody does it. We'll stuff socks in your bathing suit."

So, sock-stuffed chest held high on the Fourth of July, Lorena lined up with nine other sweating girls on the flag-draped plywood platform in front of the balloon-dart concession. Although she could tell from the wide grins on the faces of the judges that her tap-dance routine had gone flawlessly, she knew that her appearance in a bathing suit was what really counted.

Clutching her cardboard with the number "3" painted on it, she posed like the others: front toe of her high-heel shoe angled forward, hips tilted one way, head tipped the other. Mayor Gupkie, Councilman Bunting, and the editor of the *Daily Press* made notes, chewed gum, and studied with narrowed eyes the rigid bodies of the contestants.

She felt their gazes scrape over her body like a trio of razor blades, peeling away her white Jantzen from the top of its argyle-plumped bosom to the bottom of its modesty-paneled skirt. She gritted her teeth, froze her smile, and stared way, way up at the Ferris wheel. It turned slowly against a sky blackening with carbuncle clouds, lumpy and rumbling with muted thunder.

She looked down. Behind the three huddling judges was Della, waving at her with her cast, giving her the okay sign with her good hand, thumb and forefinger joined in a circle. Della—corkscrew curls escaping from a wide headband, soft round bosom mounding over her bathing suit like generous scoops of ice cream over a cone—Della, Lorena thought, should be up here, not I. And she felt a sudden rush of love for her friend who was smiling and waving bravely, cheering her on.

Lorena's frozen smile broke into a grin; her whole face beamed and melted. In that instant the three judges looked at Lorena, her eyes soft with affection, her mouth wide with love, and they knew who would be Miss Buckroe Beach of 1938.

When they called her name and she teetered out from the line of girls with their quivering smiles to slide under the shiny red winner's sash, her grin was genuine, a twin to the grin of Della, who stood on tiptoe to applaud, her cast swinging wildly. And when the crown of paste and glitter was placed upon her head, Lorena felt as though time had stopped and she had been transported to another dimension, a realm of singular adoration where she would reign as queen.

Big bullying clouds eclipsed the sun as Lorena shone in all her royal splendor. It took the cosmic crack of thunder to startle her back to reality. Judges and audience disappeared in a rumbling stampede for shelter as a curtain of rain closed the show. Lorena remained alone on the platform, staring numbly at the suddenly vacant arena where just a moment ago she had been the star.

She felt the crown crumble like a cookie in her hair, now streaming water and sticking to her face. She looked down and thought she was bleeding. The red sash hung limply from one shoulder, the color leaching onto her new white bathing suit, mottling it with pink. The argyle socks bunched into multicolored lumps visible through the soaked-through fabric of the suit. Her golden moment had been reduced to a flash of glory, now just a memory seen through mascara-tarnished tears.

Later that summer, she relived her crowning moment when she saw *The Wizard of Oz*. Forever after, she identified with the good witch Glinda, who, glitter crown and all, ascended to the heavens in a bubble. In the theater, Lorena wept as she longed to recapture that feeling of enchantment, that magical moment that had eluded her ever since.

LORENA PULLS THE blanket over her head, blocking out the light from Pete's side of the bed. He's studying a worn newspaper clipping he keeps in his night-table drawer. He takes it out sometimes when he's feeling blue, rereads the account of the home run he hit during his junior year of high school, the bases-loaded run that won the league championship. Lucky hit, he once confessed to Lorena. Lucky hit. Never got a hit before, usually warmed the bench, but for some reason the coach put him in that day and pow, he smacked it right into the stands.

Never did that again. But there was the proof he did do it once, right there in the paper. PALMER DRIVES IN WINNING RUN. His picture, too, sliding into home, kinda cute he was, straining, tongue out to one side, legs reaching like a pair of tongs for the plate. He didn't have to slide, he told Lorena when he first showed her the clipping. It being a home run he coulda just trotted in, but when he heard the crowd's cheers he got so excited he just slud in there, riding in on a red cloud of dust.

Never got another hit. The next few times he got up to bat he was so nervous he whiffed, swung so hard he spun. The coach had mercy and put him back on the bench. He didn't even go out for the team his senior year. He could tell his daddy was disappointed he was just a one-shot fluke, but, he told Lorena, "Like my daddy said, You can't make a living offa baseball anyway. He said anybody can hit a ball, but there's only a few of us strong enough and brave enough to weld a big ol' hunka metal into a ship that floats."

So Pete started hanging out at the shipyard after school, rode up on the elevator behind his daddy like a shadow, not really all that scared, not really, the side of the ship dropping sheer as a cliff beneath them. He'd stand off at a safe distance on the metal grid of the platform, watch his daddy clamp on his face shield, pull on his leather gloves, then hook the torch up to the generator chugging and panting like some prehistoric beast.

His daddy pulled a stick from the bunch of electrodes stuck in the back pocket of his coveralls, clamped it into the torch, and lit it with a striker. Pete knew at the sudden hiss to look away. The blue flame touched steel, exploded into a blinding shower of sparks that filled the sky with a thousand stars too bright for unshielded eyes. Metal joined metal until it all flowed sweet and pure, a river of steel that glittered bright as silver in the sunlight.

The first time his daddy let him use the torch, Pete almost passed out, he confessed to Lorena. His daddy thought it was from the excitement. Pete wasn't sure himself, but from the moment the helmet was placed on his head and tightened with a twist of a knob, he felt funny. He pulled on the gauntlet gloves and leather bib, flipped the face shield down with a jerk of his head like he saw his daddy do.

Then his daddy fired up the torch. It looked like a green tornado through the black glass window of the face shield. Pete touched the flame to steel. He didn't know if it was the rush of heavy metal fumes trapped beneath the face shield or the banging, clanging noise of the generator that swelled between his ears, but he felt himself grow giddy, then dizzy, then felt the cold metal grid of the platform pressing into his knees.

"You'll get used to it, kid," his daddy had said as he helped him up, and his daddy was right. Once he had the proper training, he did get used to it, but he never felt he came close to his daddy's talent.

"He was an artist, my daddy was," Pete would tell Lorena. "He loved what he did. That's why I know he died happy."

Lorena didn't know how anybody who fell ten stories off a platform to land headfirst in a slipway could be said to die happy. Every time Pete retells the story of his daddy's skill and daring, and then the accident, she says the same thing she said the first time she heard it, shortly after they met: "How do you know he was happy?" And every time she asks that, his answer is the same: stony silence.

She figures Pete's silence is a manly trait, a stoic acceptance that the possibility of stepping into air off a very high place is real but worth it when your work is noble and true. But Lorena has noticed that Pete's pride in his job has soured. He's been coming home from work all crabby, grumping about his new foreman, talking about how the shipyard has changed now that Korea's over and done with, studying the editorials in the *Daily Press* about how there might be layoffs.

"How we gonna protect ourselves from the Commies," he wants to know, "if all we build is ocean liners like that S.S. *United*

States? S.S.," he snorts. "That stands for sissy ships. Sissy ships for fancy people."

Sure, they're still building aircraft carriers like the *Forrestal*, and don't think he's not proud to be part of that, part of creating what's going to be the biggest warship in the world, but then what? There's talk of layoffs, too many workers, not enough work. Not that he's worried they'll lay *him* off, he's proven his skill, his value, his loyalty. It's clear he'd give his life for the shipyard, just like his daddy did.

But these days, when he talks about the shipyard, he seems deflated, like some of his innards were sucked out. Sometimes, Lorena thinks, Pete seems shorter at the end of the day than he was when he left for work.

Aside from Pete's problems at work, they hardly talk about what they've done all day. Used to be, when they were first married, they'd share silly stories about things that happened and people they knew, but now all they talk about is what's on TV. Pete never asks about what she's thinking or doing. He doesn't know that Lorena tried out for the Community Theater and didn't make it. He doesn't even know she has a tap costume.

Well, she thinks, maybe she can perk him up by telling him about her plans. After all, Binky was interested, even offered to introduce her to his cousin Wally the talent scout. Surely her own husband would want to know about her new ambition. She'd leave out the part about Binky and Wally.

"You know," she begins, "I think I can make a career with my talent."

"Talent?"

"I dance, remember?" She pouts. "Don't you remember how much I like to dance?"

He shrugs. "So? I like to eat. I'm not making a career of it."

"Well," she says, ignoring that. "I've been getting up a routine. So I can try out for *Arthur Godfrey's Talent Scouts*." Excited now, she goes to the closet and pulls out her costume and tap shoes. "Don'tcha love this?" she says, holding the red satin tap pants and tuxedo top up to her body, turning this way and that.

Pete blinks. "Where do you think you're going to wear that?"

"For my audition, silly." She feels flirtatious now. Just the sight of the flippy pants puts her in a dancing mood. "Wanna see my routine?"

"No. No, I do not want to see your routine." He falls silent, scrutinizes her as if she were a mutant. "You're nuts," he concludes. "I don't know what's happened to you lately, but I swear you're getting as crazy as your aunt Lula."

"Crazy? Because I have plans? Lula didn't have plans. She just saw things that weren't there, flying saucers, stuff like that. That's *different*."

"Crazy is crazy. Lula. You. Sometimes I think your whole family is nuts."

"Are you calling my mother a nut?"

"You're *all* a buncha nuts."

Lorena slams the bedroom door, takes her costume to the bathroom. The silky slide of the tap pants soothes her as they shimmy over her hips; the crisp tuxedo top makes her feel perky and proud. She stares at herself in the mirror, adjusts the top hat to a sassy tilt.

She'll show him. Crazy? Nuts? Someday he'll eat those words.

11

MISS FRITZI WAS once a Rockette. There's a picture of her in a long line with other Rockettes on the wall of her dance studio, kicking really high like the June Taylor dancers. The Rockettes all look alike with tall fluffy feathers sticking up out of these sparkly caps they wear, so Miss Fritzi put a big red arrow pointing to herself in the picture so you'd know which one she was. She's about halfway up the line that goes from the stubbiest Rockette to the real tall one in the center.

She's not a Rockette anymore because she got married. Her husband is an officer stationed at Fort Eustis. Mom said, "Can you believe she gave up dancing in Radio City Music Hall to get married?" Sometimes I think Miss Fritzi feels the same way.

Like today. She has us all in a row and she's demonstrating a new step. "Cassie," she chirps in her parakeet voice, "wake up!" because it's my turn and I'm looking out the window thinking about stuff.

"I'm up," I say, but I don't know what I'm supposed to do, so

Miss Fritzi shows me, hop-shuffle-hop-step-heel-toe, but my tap shoes won't do that, they feel heavy and clunky like my feet belong to somebody else. The tops of Miss Fritzi's ears go purple, which happens when she gets upset.

"You must pay attention," she peeps. "Think of dancing as teamwork. Now," she says, shaking herself like a ruffled-up bird that's smoothing its feathers, "all together now, and a one-and-a-two-and-a-hop-shuffle-hop-step-heel-toe."

The other five girls do that, sort of, but I'm a step behind because I watch to see what Melanie, the girl next to me does, and then I do it. *"Cassie,"* Miss Fritzi caws, really frazzled now, "if you don't pay attention, you won't be ready for recital."

Recital?

"You mean we have to do this in *front* of people?" I ask.

The girls in line with me twitter nervously except for Melanie, who wears her hair like Miss Fritzi, pulled back into a tight bun like a ballerina. "We get to wear costumes," Melanie announces. "Flower costumes."

Not me.

"I can't," I say.

"Well, of course you can." Miss Fritzi's shoes tap impatiently on the scarred wooden floor. "Everybody gets to wear a costume."

"I want to be a rose," says Melanie.

"I don't want to be anything," I say.

Miss Fritzi holds her head with both hands like it's going to come off. "Please God not now," she says to the ceiling. To me she says, "Your mother has already paid for your costume." She leans her birdy body over my head. I can hear her teeth scritching together. "All you have to do is . . . *dance*." The word comes out like a squawk. *Day*-ance.

So I dance. One step behind Melanie, shuffle-hop-step, I dance without caring because it's my very last dance. I won't be a rose, I won't be a dope. And now I know for sure that I won't be back.

* * *

I STARE OUT the open window of the bus as it carries me home, away from Miss Fritzi and Melanie and dancing forever. The window rattles like maybe it'll clonk down any second on my elbow but I don't care because if it breaks my arm it'll be a perfect excuse to never dance again.

The bus is hot. The black plastic seat is torn and itchy and sticks to my skin. I'm sitting right behind the bus driver, looking at the dark splotch of sweat on the back of his gray bus-driver shirt. I can see his eyes in the mirror above him, just his eyes, nothing else, sly and shadowy. Every now and then they look at me.

Usually I sit in the back of the bus when I ride to school with Molly, even though that's where the colored people sit. We like to ride there because it's fun to kneel on the long backseat and make faces out the rear window at the cars behind us. One day Molly asked, "Why can't the colored people sit up front?" I had never thought about that before but after that I thought about it a lot.

Even when the bus isn't crowded, colored people have to scrunch together in the back seats. Like now, the front of the bus is pretty empty, just me and a couple of ladies in flowered dresses carrying shopping bags from Nachman's and this old guy who's sleeping. But in the back the seats are full, mostly colored ladies who must be maids. Once when the back of the bus was really full, I saw a colored lady standing up, so I pointed at the empty seat next to me for her to sit down and she just looked at me funny, shook her head no, and watched the ceiling of the bus the rest of the way.

Something else I don't understand is why colored kids go to a different school. I never thought much about that, either, even though our bus passes right by their school on the way to ours. I used to look out the window at the colored kids walking to school, wonder things like How did the girls get their hair all braided like that, what kind of houses did they live in over in colored town, did they have to list the products of Brazil like we did in geography, stuff like that.

Then one day Molly asked, "How come they go to a school that's closer to where we live, and we go a school that's closer to them?" And then I started thinking, Yeah. Why is that? Molly said that in New York, colored and white kids are allowed to go to the same school. Of course, I wouldn't want to go to their school, being as how it's all falling apart. It's just this old wood building with broken windows and flaky paint, instead of brick like ours.

When I asked Mom why we go to a different school from the colored kids, she said, Well, it's the law. That's the way things have always been, and that's just the way things are. But a couple of weeks ago I saw on test-pattern TV where the Supreme Court made a new law that said white and colored kids were going to *have* to go to school together. When I mentioned it to Mr. Finkelstein, he looked surprised and said, Well, it's about time, but then he asked How did I know that? because he hadn't heard it on TV or read it in the paper. When I told him I saw it on the test pattern, he looked at me funny like he did when I told him about the Los Angeles Dodgers.

And then yesterday it was big news on regular TV: the Supreme Court said that from now on we'd go to school with colored kids, and it was the law of the land. I asked Dad if that meant I'd have to go to that broken-down old colored school, and he said, "No way is that ever going to happen." And Mom agreed with him for once. I didn't even try to tell them about the colored guy I saw on the test pattern who is running for president. First of all, they'd never believe that he was a general, like Ike.

Late last night I saw on the test pattern that a bunch of colored kids were trying to go to a white school in this town called Little Rock. I remembered the name because the white people there were throwing rocks at the colored kids. When I told Mom that it was true about colored and white going to the same school, that there were even soldiers with bayonets to protect the colored kids, she looked at me like I was crazy and said I was making it up. She thinks I make everything up. She never listens when I try to tell her things.

She doesn't listen when I tell her I hate dance class, that I don't want to dance in front of everybody, and that I want to quit. She just says I can't because "I already paid for your lessons through June and I paid for your costume for the recital and you are not quitting." When I ask for a real reason, she tells me the same thing she said when I asked why colored kids have to go to a different school: "That's just the way things are."

But now I know that just because she says it, it doesn't mean it's true. There's no law that says I have to dance, or wear a flower costume, or make a fool of myself in front of people again. It's *not* the way things are.

12

L O R E N A

PETE IS BURNING the hot dogs. He always burns the hot dogs but he doesn't care because that's the way he likes them, coal black and splitting on the outside, pink and frigid on the inside. Nobody wants to eat them, but since he's in charge of cooking the dogs for Cassie's birthday party, there isn't much choice. He's planned Cassie's birthdays since her first one, when his mother baked the cake and he dressed up like a clown. One of their few family rituals, Pete's beloved, silly clown had made its appearance every year until this one.

"Uh, Dad," Cassie had said when, the week before her birthday, Pete still hadn't mentioned any plans. "For my birthday, maybe you don't need to be a clown this year."

"Birthday? Your birthday's already?" He looked bewildered, lost.

"Yeah. You forgot?" Cassie shot a worried look at Lorena, who bit her lip in guilt. She had forgotten, too.

"No. No." He smiled weakly. "You don't want the clown?"

"I'm too old for a clown, Dad."

"Sure you are." He drew her close to him in an awkward gesture. "Too old," he had said in a faraway voice. "You're too old now for a clown."

So here they are—mostly kids except for Della and Molly's dad, Max, who walked Molly here and then stayed—standing around the barbecue pit in the shelter on the beach, eating cold hot dogs and birthday cake as the wind kicks up sand all around them.

Pete's a little drunk from the several bottles of beer he's downed. He's in charge, bought the weenies, bought the drinks, fixed the beans. Lorena baked the cake. What's left of it after the starved guests demolished it is a few crumbs and eleven burned candles embedded in a smear of blue-and-white icing. Cassie huddles with Molly and a couple of girlfriends, giggling over something.

Lorena has invited Della to keep her company and they sit, heads together at a picnic table, whispering like schoolgirls. Lorena ignores Pete when he raises his bottle in their direction and slurs, "Look at her over there, sipping grape Nehi like it was champagne, so dainty with that little pinkie of hers raised high." He takes a swig of beer.

Lorena is indeed drinking a grape Nehi, holding the sweating purple bottle right at the spot where her breasts disappear into her off-the-shoulder blouse, a peasant thing with smocking and a red drawstring. She's wearing shorts. Her skin is the color of iodine. Her eyes are ringed in white where her sunglasses had perched when she baked in the sun at the Chamberlin. She tilts her head as Max shambles up to say hello.

"Well, hi, Lorena," he says, "and who's your friend there?"

"This here," she says, "is Della. Della, Max Finkelstein. He's an artist. He's Cassie's best friend Molly's father. Cassie says he's got paintings in his house that'll be in a museum someday, they're so covered with paint. Just gobs and gobs of it, right out of the tube, she says, just squishes it out, bam, right on the canvas."

"That right?" says Della. "I paint, too. Got me one of those

Picture Craft kits where you paint by number. I did mountains the other day, hung it in my living room, makes the whole place just sparkle, it's so pretty." She reaches up to retie the scarf holding back her tumble of auburn curls, reaches down to tug at the bottom of her shorts.

"I just started another one called *Twin Scotties*," Della says. "It's dogs. For my bedroom." Then she gives Max her full display of big and brilliant teeth, a smile so startling that it still amazes Lorena that so many teeth could fit behind those heart-shaped little lips.

It's moments like this that Lorena wishes Della would disappear. Sure, she's her best friend and all, got a good heart, a soft spot for kids, and you got to admire her standing up to Farley. She does have her good points. Most times it's like it was in high school, hours of gossip, chatter about hair, makeup, men. But times like now, Lorena feels that talking to Della is like eating cotton candy. There's nothing there but air.

"Max doesn't paint by numbers," Lorena says. "He's a real artist."

Della lifts her eyebrows. "Well," she says. "I'm going to enroll in the Famous Artists School. What kind of art do you do?"

Max plunks his big body in its paint-spattered dungarees down on top of the picnic table, rests his sandal-shod feet on the seat, drains the last of his Ballantine. "What I do," he says, "is relate the pigment directly to the canvas so there is no intermediary such as a brush. The shock of pure color. The existential experience of the moment of creation. I feel that I am on the brink, the cutting edge, of the next direction art is taking, a free fall from the figurative into the abstract.

"So why am I in Newport News instead of New York? you may ask. A legitimate question. I need to work in isolation. I need anonymity to develop my skills. I need this job at the shipyard or I won't be able to pay the rent.

"But I'm not complaining," he says, shifting his bulk backward as the picnic table begins to tip beneath his weight. "I like it here.

I grew up on the rough-and-tumble streets of the Bronx, the asphalt jungle. Knives and shivs. Stickball in the street. I was a
delivery boy in the Fulton fish market while I went to CCNY.
That smell. It never leaves you. This beach here on a hot summer
day at low tide, it reminds me of my youth, fish wrapped in newspaper, guts in the gutter, that silvery sheen on your hands you
can't wash off for days. Call me sentimental, but when you carry
that with you, home is home wherever you are."

"I think I'll get a beer," says Della.

"So," says Max, sliding into Della's seat when she leaves.
"Your Cassie and my Molly are like Siamese twins these days,
right?"

"Seems so," says Lorena. "Molly's a real . . . unusual girl.
Sweet, too," she adds, not wanting to indicate her discomfort
with Molly's precocious pubescence, or her worries that, thanks
to Molly, Cassie was more familiar with sex than any eleven-year-
old had any right to be. She declined to mention that she had
walked into the kitchen while Molly was stretching one of Max's
rubbers over a cucumber to demonstrate for Cassie how it works.
"Very sweet," she repeats to Max.

"Cassie is quite unusual, too," says Max. "They seem to be
well matched."

"How do you mean?" asks Lorena, wondering if Cassie was
stretching rubbers over cucumbers, too.

"She says she watches some interesting shows on the test pattern," he says with a chuckle.

Oh, God. She's telling everyone. "She's always had a good
imagination," Lorena says, hoping that will explain it all away.

"That's good. That's good," says Max, nodding. "I always en-
courage imagination in children." He pauses. "Have you ever
thought that, well, maybe . . . she's really *seeing* something
there?"

"You mean, for real?"

He shrugs.

"No. Well, no. I mean, what is there to see?" Lorena wishes he would drop this subject. It makes her think about Aunt Lula again, Lula who swore she saw flying saucers, saw them with her own eyes, spinning like tops over Chicken In A Bucket while she was waiting for her bus across the street. Lula was so amazed, so transfixed, that she let that bus just pass her by. The next one didn't come for fifteen minutes, so she sat on the bus bench and watched those saucers spin and swoop, watched their metallic incandescence dance across the sky. So clear was it, she said, she could see tiny green faces in the windows. And, she added, it wasn't the first time.

Lorena doesn't see any point in mentioning Aunt Lula to Max, although mention of a family defect might induce him to discourage Molly's friendship with Cassie—something Lorena's thought of herself since the cucumber-and-rubbers thing. But she rejects that option and tries to dismiss the subject with a laugh.

"Ha, ha," she says. "Kids."

But Max is not so easily dismissed. "The reason I mention it is that the other day when I asked her what other things she had seen besides the Los Angeles Dodgers win the pennant—"

"Um. Aren't they from Brooklyn?" Lorena isn't quite sure.

"Yes. Anyway, she very reluctantly shared some other things she had seen, all very curious. She thinks Ronald Reagan was elected president, and of course, he was just *acting,* as I told her, even though she insisted it wasn't a movie.

"But when she told me about the Supreme Court's decision on integration a week *before* it happened, it made me wonder, How could she know that?"

Lorena looks puzzled. "She told you about it before it was on TV?"

Max nods. "Intriguing, huh?"

"Well." She looks thoughtful. "You sure it was *before*?" And then she brushes it off with a little laugh. "Maybe you got your days mixed up. I do that a lot myself."

Max runs his hand down his beard several times as if he's petting a dog. "It makes you wonder, though, doesn't it?" He looks intently at Lorena. "So. What do you think?"

Lorena doesn't know what to think.

"WHADDAYA THINK?" DELLA is asking Lorena. "Should I drop him like a hot potato or give him another chance?" Lorena's lying on her back in bed, twirling her finger around the phone cord while Della's latest saga pours through the black receiver cupped to her ear. Pete is downstairs watching the Roller Derby. The crowd's cheers seep through the floorboards in a rumbling chorus.

"And, hey," Della says, "what's with your friend Max? You two seemed pretty cozy there today. Kinda cute, that way he talks, fancy New York talk, although I sure don't get what he was saying about fish and guts and stuff. What *was* he talking about?"

"Well . . ." Lorena hesitates. Ordinarily she tells Della everything, but she's embarrassed by what's happened to Cassie, her obsession with the test pattern, her crazy talk. How did she get a kid like this? Lorena wonders. Maybe she had no business being a mother. She just doesn't understand kids at all. Filled with remorse, she blurts out her problems to Della.

"Max was talking about Cassie," she confesses. "She's been acting strange. I'm worried she's gonna be like my aunt Lula."

"Lula?" Della asks. "Crazy Lula?"

"Well," says Lorena. "I don't know if I'd call her *crazy*." Although she did.

"What's going on with Cassie?"

"She's seeing weird things. On the test pattern. Things that aren't there."

"Big deal. Kids make things up. Remember the stuff we used to make up? Like when we told everybody Miss Muncy's fiancé died in the war?"

"We made that up?"

"Well, *yeah*."

Lorena falls silent. She had thought it was true. Maybe she, too, was like Lula.

Lorena pictures Lula at her kitchen sink, cleaning up after one of her Sunday dinners so many years ago. Lula, her feathery wisps of hair frozen in place by an elastic-bound net, scrubbing a hopelessly burned pan with Brillo, pausing now and then to wave the rusty pad airily about her head as she spun one of her fantastic tales.

"Tell me about the flying saucer," Lorena had said to Lula, wanting to believe. "Tell me again how you saw their green faces."

"Well," Lula had drawled. "Not much to tell. Just saw them clear as I'm looking at you right now. But then," she added, "they never came back. And they promised they would."

"They talked to you?"

She nodded. "In their own way." She scrubbed vigorously for a minute, then said, "You know, things pop into my mind all the time. I don't know where they come from. People tell me they're not there, but it don't matter because to me they're real all the same."

"How can you tell what's real?"

"Well," Lula said after a thoughtful pause, "true to tell, I can't. Sometimes I don't know what's inside my head and what's out. It *all* could be inside for all I know." And then she had flashed her false teeth at Lorena in a blue-white grin.

"Hey," Della is asking into the phone. "You still there?"

"Huh? Oh yeah. I was just thinking."

"Well, if you ask me, sometimes you think too much about what might happen, and don't pay enough attention to what's happening right now. I always say, unless thinking's going to get you somewhere you wanna go, maybe it's best not to do too much of that."

Lorena thinks on that a moment. "I guess I do tend to worry a bone to death," she agrees, and hangs up. Sometimes, she has to admit, Della is really smarter than she looks.

*   *   *

"COMMIES," PETE MUTTERS around a mouthful of peanuts. "Commies are everywhere." Feet sprawled in a V on the coffee table, he glares at the TV and echoes the accusations spit through Roy Cohn's curled lips at the army's counsel. The camera pans over to Joe McCarthy, who smugly sneers his approval of his protégé's outburst. Pete is rooting for McCarthy as if the Army-McCarthy hearings were a football game. Lorena hasn't chosen sides yet, although she thinks Joseph Welch is making the army's side look pretty good.

"Close your eyes and just listen to him," she tells Pete. "Doesn't Welch sound like you think Abraham Lincoln must have sounded?"

"Now *there's* a Commie for you."

"Lincoln?" She always liked Lincoln, even if she was from the South.

"Well, he started it all."

"Started what?"

"All this *Comm*anism."

Lorena frowns at the TV set. She doesn't understand what it's all about, "Commie" this, "Commie" that. She knows the Rosenbergs were Communists, that they gave A-bomb secrets to Russia, but she figures they were caught and executed, so that was that. But McCarthy said that Commies were everywhere in the government, even in the army. She wonders if Binky knew any Commies when he was in the army.

Until the hearings were on television, she didn't follow politics much, just what she skimmed in the newspaper. All she knows is that it's Eisenhower and the army against Senator McCarthy, Roy Cohn, and Herbert Hoover. But she's not quite sure, now that she sees the actual people in front of her on the TV screen, which are the bad guys and which are the good. It was easier when somebody told you, like in a history book or the Bible. Then you could just take their word for it. Seeing real people gets confusing. Like Hoover. He's kind of cute in a Jimmy Cagney way, but he's on McCarthy's side, and McCarthy looks mean.

"I'll tell you who else is a Commie," Pete says, interrupting her musing.

She shrugs, not interested. If he thinks Lincoln was a Commie, he could name anybody.

"Max Finkelstein," he says.

"Max?" She grabs the peanuts away from him. "You're crazy."

"Think about it. He's an artist. A bo-hee-mian. From New York. I bet he believes in free love and all those Commie things. And," he says, hammering his point home, "he's Jewish."

"What does *that* have to do with it?"

"Commies are always Jewish."

"Roy Cohn's Jewish."

"Yeah, well," Pete says, "he's one a them *good* Jews. But most of 'em are like the Rosenbergs."

"Stalin wasn't Jewish."

"He was Russian. Over there, you don't have to be Jewish to be a Commie."

Lorena used to assume that everything Pete said was right, that he was smarter than she was because he was a man. But she's beginning to realize that that made as much sense as saying Max was a Communist. Matter of fact, there were some times she didn't even think Pete was as smart as she was.

She rattles the last peanut in the can, retrieves it, pops it into her mouth. "I like Max."

"I bet you do," Pete grumbles. "I saw him looking down your blouse at Cassie's birthday party."

"Oh, good grief," she says, but she's flattered anyway. Max was looking down her blouse? She hadn't noticed. He was neuter in her mind, a fuzzy bear person whose physical appeal was more of an invitation to pat and nuzzle than to perform even the remotest of sexual acts. Now that Pete had said that, about Max looking down her blouse, his image momentarily took on a more erotic cast in Lorena's mind. But the moment was fleeting. Max wasn't her type.

The mention of Max swings her thoughts to Cassie. Uh-oh, she corrects herself, there I go again. Thinking. Like Della said, if thinking's not going to get you somewhere, it's best not to do too much of it.

Still, she pictures the faraway look in Cassie's eyes that she's had since she was born. It still startles Lorena when Cassie stares at her as if she were looking at something beyond her. Well, Cassie's just strange and that's all there is to it, all that wondering about colored people and stuff. It's okay to wonder about those things, like you wonder if there's life on other planets, or if Hitler is still alive, or if the Communists are going to take over the government. But some things are just the way they are and that's the way they'll always be.

"TURN IT OFF," Pete is demanding as he waves his hands in front of his face. "I can't look at him. Her."

"What?" Lorena looks up from the *Photoplay* she picked up when the news came on. She glances at the TV. She sees a primly smiling woman wearing a head scarf over her blond hair. "What did she do?"

"It's that . . . that guy who turned himself into a girl. Christine Jorgensen. Remember? He had this operation in Denmark where they . . ." Pete grimaces. "Well, you know. *Operated*. And now he's this . . . *Thing*."

"Oh, yeah. I wondered what happened to her." Lorena studies the woman on the screen. She looks like a schoolteacher, heavy eyebrows lowered just slightly as if in admonition. Lorena wonders how she got her hair to make that little wave over her forehead. The voice-over is talking about the opening of Miss Jorgensen's nightclub act, her operation, her new life. "She doesn't look like a Thing," Lorena says. "She looks like a She."

"Makes me sick." Pete makes a throwing-up face.

"Why does Christine Jorgensen in a dress make you sick, when Milton Berle in a dress makes you laugh?"

"Jeezus, what a question." He heaves himself up from the couch to rummage through the refrigerator. "We outta beer?" he calls from the kitchen.

She hears him clanging milk bottles and cans around in his search. There is beer, but she forgot to refrigerate it and it's sitting beneath the sink, not his usual Ballantine but Hamm's.

"I bought some," she ventures. "I forgot to put it in the Frigidaire."

"Forgot? What good is warm beer?" he complains. Then, "Where is it?"

"Underneath the sink."

She hears him open the cabinet, then slam the carton on the counter.

"Hamm's?" he moans.

"In the land of sky-blue wa-a-ters . . ." she sings.

"Why Hamm's?"

"I like the song."

"I *hate* Hamm's." Now he's in the living room, brandishing a bottle of Hamm's.

"What's the difference?" she asks. "It all tastes the same."

"What do you know? 'Purity, Body, Flavor.' The Three Ring Sign. *That's* why I buy Ballantine. Not for some damn song."

"You buy other things because of their damn songs."

He looks puzzled.

"You'll wonder where the yellow went," she sings, "when you brush your teeth with Pepsodent."

He's out the door, bottle in hand. Stands on the porch, staring into the night. Then, "AAArrgh," he screams, and lets the bottle fly across the court. She hears it pop as it lands, a faint *whhhsht* exploding in the soft May air.

Holy mackerel, what's he so mad about? The beer? The Commies? Christine Jorgensen? Lately there's no telling what would light his fuse.

What would Harriet do if Ozzie behaved like that? she asks herself, although she can't imagine Ozzie ever flinging a beer bottle, especially in front of the neighbors. But if he did, what would Harriet do? Lorena thinks a minute, then decides: She'd probably ask him if he had a bad day.

"Did I have a bad *day*?" Pete explodes, repeating the question. "I've had a bad *year,* if you gotta know."

Lorena stares at him. What's been wrong with his year?

"My daddy'd never stood for this," he mutters. "He woulda crushed that little shit 'fore he opened his mouth one more time."

"What little . . . shit?" Lorena winces as she says the word. She can almost feel the ghostly *whap* of the switch her mother wielded when she had said that word decades ago. It had rarely passed her lips since.

"The foreman. My boss," he adds with a sneer. "Seems I don't work fast enough for him. Like I can't outclimb, outweld, outwork anybody with *two* good legs. Anybody's seen me up there, they know I'm twice as good, twice as fast as any a those twerps that drag ass once they're outta sight of that little shit."

"What'd he say to you?"

Pete's face folds into a childlike pout. "Said . . . I shouldn't work up high. Said I wasn't stable enough up there, what with my leg and all. Said I was a danger up there. A danger!" he shouts, pacing the floor in his uneven gait. "My daddy woulda punched him out if he heard that. Us Palmers been workin' that shipyard since there was a shipyard. We kept that place alive."

The Palmers kept the shipyard alive? Lorena is amazed. "How do you mean?" she asks, and is blasted by Pete's response: "*Because.*"

Well, okay. What can she say to that? "Can you transfer to another—"

"No!" He slumps down on the couch. "This is where I've always been. This is where I belong." He shades his eyes with one hand, looks down at the floor. "I shoulda been foreman myself by now."

Lorena chews at her upper lip with her bottom teeth. She is afraid to say anything more on the subject. So she changes it. "I'm making fried chicken for dinner," she chirps.

But Pete doesn't seem to hear. All he says is, "That little shit."

C A S S I E

QUIT MY dancing lessons. Mom doesn't know. I limped into class the Thursday after I found out there was a recital and told Miss Fritzi I hurt my leg and wouldn't be coming anymore. I don't know if she believed the leg thing. She didn't look very sorry even though she nodded her head up and down sadly as I was explaining, but I could tell she was trying not to smile. She even gave me money back for the lessons and costume that Mom already paid for.

So now I just trot myself out to the bus stop on Thursday like I'm leaving for my lesson, only I take the bus to Al's newsstand and read comic books until it's time to go home. I can't give Mom the money Miss Fritzi gave back to me because she'll know I quit, so I use some of it to pay for Cokes and comics and a couple of big dill pickles Al sells at the counter. The rest I'm saving to buy a training bra.

Mom says I'm silly to want one because I don't have anything to put in a bra, but I feel stupid wearing an undershirt because the boys can tell. Molly has a bra with elastic in the back that snaps when the boys pull it. Even though she pretends to get mad, it makes me feel like she's a grown-up and I'm still a baby.

I need to talk to Mom about some things but it's like she's someplace else. She just stares off over my head, or else she's fooling with makeup or yakking on the phone with Della. She's too busy for me now, not like when I was little. Then she'd play games with me, take me to the beach, let me dress up in her high heels and her hat with the veil. We'd make gingerbread men together. And biscuits, my special biscuits where I'd press my hand on top of the dough, and when they were done baking there would be my handprint, all puffy. The last time we did that, my hand had gotten too big and I mashed them flat. We haven't done it since.

Sometimes I pretend like Molly's mom is my mom. Mrs. Finkelstein talks to me like I'm a person. Today she comes downstairs while Molly and I are drawing fashion ladies which we do sometimes, dressing them in fancy styles we copy from magazines. My favorite ladies are the snooty ones in the "Modess . . . because" ads, even though I don't get what that means. Because what?

Mrs. Finkelstein leans over my shoulder. She smells like summer, grassy and clean, and really looks, not just pretends to look, at my drawing. "You're quite talented," she says.

I don't know what to say, so I say, "I'm not all that good." And then I think how bad I am at dancing and I confess, "I'm not really good at anything."

"Don't be silly," she says, smoothing my hair with her long fingers. "Everybody's good at something. The hard part is knowing just what that something is."

That makes me feel better. Maybe art is what I'm good at. And because Mrs. Finkelstein seems to like what I do, I guess I show off a little. I draw tiny little bows all over the skirt of the lady. I add lace ruffles on the bottom. I put a veil with dots on her hat. For good measure, I add a butterfly.

"How original," she says, looking at my drawing when I'm finished. "It's much more creative than Dior's designs." She picks it up, studies it some more. "You know," she says, "it's one thing to draw well, but quite another to have the imagination to go with it."

Oh, Mrs. Finkelstein, I want to say, will you be my mother? But I don't. I don't wrap my arms around her neck and give her a hug like I want to, even though I know she'd hug me back because she's always hugging Molly. I don't tell her I wish I could go home and get my toothbrush and move into her house. I don't tell her that lots of times when I come over, I pretend that she's my mom.

I don't do any of those things. I just say thank you.

When I come home, I pretend Mom is Mrs. Finkelstein. I can talk to Mrs. Finkelstein about things. Things like training bras. "Mom," I say, "I think it's time for me to get a training bra."

"You don't need one," she says.

"But—"

"You don't need it, and that's the end of that."

LATELY THE ONLY time Mom pays attention is if I tell her about something I saw on the test pattern. She gets this worried look on her face and asks me Do I feel okay? which makes me feel like some kind of freak. I don't understand why nobody else sees what I see, but that doesn't mean *I* don't see it. I think if they really tried, they'd see it, too.

Maybe for them it's like that puzzle where you have to stare hard at a drawing of a forest before you can see all the hidden animals. And then when you do see them, you wonder why they didn't just pop out at you in the first place because they were really there all along.

I don't talk so much about the things I see anymore because Mom and Dad don't want to hear it. They're too busy picking at each other about stupid stuff like the biscuits are burned or there's never any beer in the house or Mom's spending too much at May-belle's. They always fight during dinner, and I always get a stom-achache.

One night they were fighting about something and I started crying right at the table, just sat there with my nose and eyes all drippy. They didn't even notice until I started going huh-huh-huh, like I do sometimes when I cry. Then Dad leaned over and made his silly clown face—that cross-eyed wagging-tongue face that made me laugh when I was little. I didn't think it was so funny this time, but when he did it again, he looked so goofy that I made the silly face back. We started to giggle and Mom left the room, so Dad and I went to watch TV. He let me snuggle next to him. But later I heard him and Mom fighting again when they thought I was asleep.

There was this family on test pattern TV the other day where the mother was fat and loud and messy and her kids yelled at her and said things that I would get smacked for, but in the end they all listened to each other and it was okay. It was the best show because it was more real than Ozzie and Harriet, whose kids aren't like any kids I know.

I bet if I lived with the fat lady I could tell her I hated dancing lessons and didn't want to go anymore and she'd listen to me. The other night, Dad was grumbling about how bad work was and how he should quit, and I came this close to telling him that *I* had quit. But when I started out, "Hey, Dad, guess what?" he gave me this sad droopy look and I just couldn't tell him the truth.

Sometimes I don't even know what the truth is. I used to think that everything on TV was true. Well, not everything. I know some shows are fake and the people are just acting. I don't even think that wrestling is real, although Dad says it is. But are Ozzie and Harriet and Ricky and David a real family when they're not on TV? Do they get together in their real house and paint by numbers like they do in the Picture Craft ad? Or are they just pretending?

I don't even believe anymore that what I see on the news is

true, stuff like the Russians are bad and want to drop the bomb on us. I believed that until I saw on test-pattern TV that the Russians are really our friends, and we're even sharing a spaceship together. When I told this to Mom, she just rolled her eyes and said, "Would you keep your wild imagination to yourself? You want people to call you a Commie?" Now I don't know what to believe.

They say the Korean War is over, that we're in a cold war now, whatever that means. But I see all kinds of hot-war stuff on test-pattern TV, battles in places I've never heard of. You can tell the difference between real war and the pretend war you see in the movies. Real war is scarier. In the war stuff I see on the test pattern, people get hurt and killed right in front of you, sometimes in black-and-white, sometimes in color. There was one battle that was all green, bombs exploding and everything. That one looked pretty neat.

Maybe what I see on the test pattern isn't real either. Maybe it's all just magic, a trick like a dance I've seen this guy do—he's sort of colored and sort of not—where it looks like he's going forward when he's really sliding backward. Mom caught me doing that step while I sang along with him to this funny song that went "Beat it, beat it." I couldn't tell if she was mad or not, just had this strange look on her face when I tried to tell her about the guy dancing on the test pattern. She didn't believe me, so I just let her believe what she wants to believe—that I made up the dance myself.

The worst part is, she wants me to teach her that step. When I see her practicing in front of the mirror, it makes me wonder if I got the wrong mother by mistake.

14

L O R E N A

LORENA STARES UP from her bed at the patch of light thrown onto the ceiling from the porch light. You'd think it would have made a permanent imprint by now, night after night, the ragged patch of light that glows just above her head. It always surprises her in the morning that the patch is gone, that the rough-plastered ceiling is clean except for smoky wisps of cobwebs that cling in the corners like leftover dreams.

She can't sleep, can't stop thinking about Pete's reaction when she showed him her costume. It's keeping her up, stirring her anger, feeding the flame of ambition that's been smoldering in her gut. There she was, sharing her dream with him, how she wanted to try out for *Arthur Godfrey's Talent Scouts,* and all he had to say was "You're nuts." Well, she'll show him, she thinks, and then she remembers what else he said: "You're as crazy as your aunt Lula."

Aunt Lula. Now Lula's on her mind again. And Cassie. Could Cassie be crazy like Lula? Lorena pictures Cassie dancing in front of the test pattern. Singing along as if there were something there. That step—Lorena had never seen anything like it, backward and forward at the same time. Maybe Cassie had inherited Lorena's talent, but she also may have gotten Lula's nuttiness.

That thought makes her spring wide-awake. She looks over at Pete. He's making preliminary snurfing sounds that will inevitably accelerate until they erupt into a gut-rattling snore. "Pete," she says, and gives him a nudge.

"Wha?" he mumbles, turns, and settles into a fetal position.

"Cassie watches the test pattern," she says.

"Rrrmf."

"She stares at it for hours. I think something might be wrong with her." She nudges his back between the shoulder blades. They curl forward and he burrows farther into the blankets. "Are you listening?"

"Testpat," he murmurs. "Cass watches."

Lorena leans forward, folds her arms around her knees, stares into the darkness. She can make out her dressing table, sparks of light flashing from the mirror. Herself a ghostly form staring back at herself. "It worries me. She really believes she's seeing these things." She hears the beginning rumblings of a snore and gives him another nudge. "Are you listening to me?"

He rolls over on his back with a sigh. "Can we talk about this tomorrow?"

"No." She flicks on the bedside lamp. It bursts into light and they both squint against the glare. He puts the pillow over his head, moans, then pulls himself into a sitting position. His hair ruffles up in back like chicken feathers. His striped pajama top is open where a button has broken off. He yawns. She can see the dull silver ponds of his fillings.

"Okay," he says. "Cassie watches the test pattern. What's the problem?"

"There's nothing there. And she thinks there is."

"So? She's always made things up. Remember Pookie?"

"She only talked to Pookie until she was four. Then she stopped," Lorena says.

"Yeah. She stopped. What's the big deal?"

"This is different." Lorena reaches up and refastens a pincurl that spirals down from beneath her frilly nightcap. "She's seeing TV programs that aren't there. Some of them are in Technicolor, she says, like in the movies."

"Remember when you saw Uncle Rudy in the A&P?" Pete asks.

"She says she saw nearly naked girls dancing on tables," says Lorena. "She said they had words painted on their stomachs and bee-hinds."

"Uncle Rudy had been dead nine years and you saw him in the A&P, putting Grape-Nuts in his basket."

"She says 'Sock it to me.' She says that's what one of the naked girls says. 'Sock it to me.' What does that mean?"

"I remember I said to you, 'How can you see Uncle Rudy in the cereal section? He's *dead*,' " Pete says. "And you swore you saw him anyhow, wearing those baggy tweed pants he never had cleaned and the Hawaiian shirt he wore to our wedding. Picking his teeth with his little fingernail like he always did. I mean, you had details."

"Then she says some colored man in a robe comes out and says 'Here come de judge, here come de judge.' Where would she get that from?" Lorena pulls off the nightcap, rips the bobby pins out of her hair, and begins to repin the curls.

"Did I say you were crazy for seeing Uncle Rudy? No. All's I said was 'You got some imagination, putting Uncle Rudy in the A&P when everybody knows Aunt Lula did all the shopping.' "

"It worries me. Do you think Cassie might be like Lula? A little, you know . . . crazy?"

Pete yawns noisily and plops back on the pillow. "Wouldn't surprise me. It's in your family. You see Uncle Rudy. Lula saw Buddhas on refrigerators. Cassie sees TV shows that aren't there. Y'all just got it in your blood."

Well, she thinks, pummeling her limp pillow before settling back to stare once again at the ceiling, at least they never locked Lula up or anything. Why, she even got famous for that Buddha she saw.

Where was that clipping?

Lorena throws the covers off, sits up. Is it still in her treasure box? She creeps over to her dresser and reaches beneath some moth-eaten sweaters she's been meaning to donate to the Salvation Army. She takes the Whitman's Sampler box into the bathroom, opens it, inhales the phantom aroma of long-ago-devoured chocolate. Blinking in the sudden brightness, she rummages through sweetly scented mementos.

Dance card from her senior prom, scrawled with names long since forgotten. Pressed flowers from her wedding corsage, brown and crumbled as cornflakes. Faded few inches of torn red sash, the letters "Miss Buc" barely legible. Sepia-tone photo of her mother looking proud and stern beneath a hat decorated with a stuffed bird. Lorena stares at the crinkled photo, examines it for parts of herself although her mother always said, "You look like your father, that SOB, may he rest in peace."

Here it is. The clipping was beginning to yellow but the type was black and clear:

BUDDHA APPEARS ON KELVINATOR

Scores of curious onlookers gathered to see the image of Buddha which appeared on the refrigerator of Mrs. Rudy Willet of Phoebus, Va.

"Ordinarily you get Jesus on refrigerators. You get your weeping Madonnas on walls," said Phoebus's mayor, Andy Barlow. "This is our first Buddha. Couple of years ago, we got what we thought was a Moses, but since nobody knows what he looked like, that don't count."

The refrigerator, a Kelvinator, was just fine until Mrs. Willet put leftover Hawaiian Tuna Noodle Surprise inside after dinner last Tuesday. The refrigerator gave what Mrs. Willet describes as "a pitiful moan, just pitiful" and then broke out in green hives. As Mrs. Willet watched, she says, "The hives started to clump up and take a shape, and all of a sudden I realized it looked like this roly-poly statue my Rudy brought back from when he was in the Philippines. He said the statue was of Buddha, and over there he was just as famous as Jesus."

Mayor Barlow is unsure of the future of the Kelvinator Buddha. Due to a shortage of Buddhists in Phoebus, he says, there's no church to send it to.

Well, there you go, thinks Lorena. Not one word about Lula being crazy in that whole story. And who knows? Maybe she did see the Buddha. Maybe it really *was* there.

Pete hasn't started snoring yet. Lorena lies on her back in the darkness and listens to him breathe. She tenses as he turns in her direction. His hand scoots across the sheet, then plunks upon her flannel-covered breast. They haven't had sex in over two weeks. This is Pete's way of letting her know it's time.

When they were first married, she dressed for bed. Slipped into the bathroom and emerged in her bridal negligee, a gift from Aunt Lula. Draped in a floor-length robe and gown of silk and lace, she would allow Pete to peel away each virginal white layer, his hunger unchecked by her arm catching in a sleeve or the gown tangling between her legs. His panting frustration fueled her desire and she found that sex was her time to shine, her opportunity to star in whatever fantasy she chose to swirl through her brain: ravaged virgin, willing mistress, red-hot mama.

Time and action shredded the silken gown. Years later, it wound up at Goodwill, never to be replaced. Bed became a place to sleep, and gowns were bought for comfort. Now when Lorena dresses for bed, she sees her mother in the mirror. Fluffy cap over pincurls, Lollipop panties under her flannel gown, she crawls nightly under the covers expecting nothing more exciting than a groaning yawn from Pete as he rolls away from her.

Every now and then, Pete comes to life, as he is doing tonight.

She lies immobile as his hand starfishes its way from one breast to another, then plunges beneath her gown to snap the elastic waist of her Lollipops. Her compliance is tinged with pity for his problems, as well as fear of his cold withdrawal if she should deny him. She knows that as far as he's concerned, she could be anyone. He could be anyone to her, too.

She decides to make him Binky.

Oooo, Binky, she sighs to herself. Closing her eyes, she pictures Binky's face, those rainstorm-gray eyes, that Errol Flynn mustache, that snappy postman's hat set at a jaunty angle. Oooh, yes, yes, Binky, she moans silently, touch me there, as Pete grabs her, unceremoniously climbs on top, and begins to pump. Oh Binky Binky Binky, she begins, and then it's over. With a grunt, Pete dismounts and collapses on his side of the bed.

Lorena always felt a little guilty after sex, like her mother was listening on the other side of the door. Her guilt was compounded by her secret fantasies, the crowds of men she had visualized over the years once the initial thrill of early-marriage sex was gone.

At first she fantasized about people she knew—friends, the pharmacist, the chicken man in the A&P who cut up her fryers with loving care and then threw in extra livers. But as her parallel fantasy of becoming a dancer grew, the lovers in her sexual fantasies became more than mere acquaintances. She had moved on to the rich and famous. Fred Astaire, of course, and Gene Kelly, but her amorous rendezvous also embraced nondancing stars of movies and television: Clark Gable, Kirk Douglas, Julius La Rosa. She even conjured up a memorable threesome with Dean Martin and Jerry Lewis.

Binky is the first true possibility. The idea of an affair scares her. She could never really do it, no, really, she's a lousy liar. She'd wind up confessing, pleading guilty, spilling the beans. She had always been a good girl.

But this wouldn't be just any old affair. Sure, it would have passion and all, but *this* affair would also have meaning. It could change her life, take her somewhere—take her straight to Cousin Wally.

It's something to think about. Like Della says, unless thinking's going to get you somewhere, it's best not to do too much of it.

So she thinks about it. She thinks about it a lot.

THE INVITATION COMES in the next day's mail. "Tomorrow," it says. "Three o'clock. B." It slides, unstamped, through the slot, buried in a barrage of bills. She almost overlooks it. Just a slip of paper inside a plain envelope. She reads it over and over again, then tears it into tiny pieces and flushes it.

Tomorrow is Thursday. Lorena is flattered that Binky remembered that Cassie has dancing on Thursday. He cared enough to plan this. But tomorrow? So soon? She's not ready. She needs Maybelle. With a trembling finger, she dials.

"Sorry, sugarplum," says Maybelle. "I'm booked till next week. How's Tuesday?"

"Too late. Too late," Lorena mumbles, and hangs up. She fluffs her flattened curls in the mirror and sighs. She can't do this, no she just can't, it's not right. But then she thinks of Binky's slow gray eyes, remembers the way his lips felt, wonders what lies in wait beneath those black-striped gray pants. Oh yes.

She can barely cut out the biscuits for dinner, her hands shake so. The pork chops are overcooked, the mashed potatoes lumpy, but dinner is eaten in hurried silence without a peep of complaint. For that, Lorena is grateful.

The silence of dinner continues through the evening, broken only by *Perry Como* and *Arthur Godfrey and His Friends*. Cassie goes up to her room after Haleloke does her hula, and Pete and Lorena are left alone, the light from the TV washing their faces with silver.

She waits for the commercial, then asks, "How's work been?" On the screen a blonde swings impossibly shiny hair. A chorus sings "Halo everybody, Halo." Pete doesn't answer, not now, not during the entire half hour of *I've Got a Secret*, not when he gets into bed and rolls away from Lorena.

Lorena stares at the patch of light on the ceiling until she falls asleep, the patch imprinted on her brain. Indelible and glowing, it surfaces in dream, becomes a TV screen filled with the crew-cut image of Garry Moore, the host of *I've Got a Secret*. Next to him sits Lorena herself, whispering in his ear her secret, which is superimposed across the screen for the audience: "Having an affair with Binky Quisenberry."

The audience applauds. She beams at the camera. Garry Moore winks, adjusts his bow tie, calls first on Henry Morgan, who asks, "Does your husband know your secret?" She shakes her head no. Bess Myerson looks thoughtful, taps her beauty-queen teeth with a fingernail, then asks, "Does this involve some talent?" Lorena consults in a whisper with Garry Moore before vigorously nodding yes. The audience's applause is louder this time.

Garry calls on the next panelist. It's Cassie. She's wearing the dress of tinsel and her hair is a tangle of curls. She looks piercingly at Lorena, then asks, "Are you as crazy as Lula?"

Lorena's eyes pop open. The patch on the ceiling is gone. The room is dark and Pete is snoring. She lies and waits for morning.

BRA. BRA. LORENA paws through her underwear drawer looking for the least-frayed of her Maidenform Chansonettes, all identical: white cotton, 34-B. She holds each one up, looking for signs of wear, examines the cone-shaped cups for breaks in the concentric stitching. Oh, well, she sighs, and plucks one from the jumbled heap.

She showers, pulls on toreador pants and her peasant blouse, cinches her waist with a wide stretch belt, releases her hair from its pincurls. Mitzi Gaynor, Mitzi Gaynor, she pleads with the mirror, her hand trembling as she applies Seagreen eye shadow, Powder Pink lips, a spritz of Evening in Paris behind each ear. She's ready. She waits. Three o'clock. Where is he? Three-fifteen. She dabs on another layer of Odor-O-No, reapplies her lipstick.

Doorbell.

Oh God. She feels herself move down the stairs, across the living room. She peers through the glass square of the door, sees Binky's hat and matching gray eyes, opens the door, and shuts it quickly behind him.

"Lorena," he says.

"Binky."

She's not sure what's supposed to happen next. If this were the movies, he would embrace her and sweep her off her feet. But what he does is slap the leather of his mailbag before dropping it at her feet. "Weighs a ton," he says. "Makes me sweat like a pig."

Suddenly he's suctioning her lips with his, cupping his hands around her bottom, grinding his pelvis into hers. His tongue is snaking around her gums and she can tell he had tuna for lunch. They shuffle over to the couch, where they collapse, burrowing into each other with snurfing sounds. Binky grasps the elastic shoulders of her peasant blouse and pulls it to her waist, exposing the stiff cotton cones of her Maidenform. A look of disappointment crosses his face but he moves on, reaching behind her to unhook the bra.

"Wait!" She yanks her blouse back up. "Not here."

"Huh?"

"Upstairs."

He shrugs and follows her up the stairs, into her bedroom. At the sight of her marital bed, a wave of panic envelops Lorena. "Maybe we shouldn't . . ." she begins, but Binky has pulled her down on the bed and her blouse is back around her waist and he's grappling with the stubborn hook of her bra, which won't release, so he pulls it down far enough to nibble on her nipple.

"Oooh, Binky," she sighs to the top of his hat. Impulsively, she removes it, flings it off the bed, then runs her fingers through his Vitalis-slick hair. He's struggling with the zipper on her toreador pants, finally peels them down over her Lollipops. She kicks off her sandals, pedals her legs until she's freed the toreadors, and they pause, exhausted, she in her Maidenform and Lollipops, he still in full dress uniform. He reaches into his back pocket, pulls out his wallet, extracts a rubber, and turns his back for a brief but busy moment. His purpose accomplished, he plunks himself atop Lorena.

Despite sun which sizzles like melted butter on the bed, Lorena shivers beneath Binky, awaiting his caress. He leans over her and slides his gaze over her prone body. "Can you get that thing off yourself?" he says, and plucks at her bra. "Those, too," he adds, tugging at her Lollipops.

She complies, yanks the bra around so the hook is in the front, rolls the panties down into a pretzel at her feet. She leans back and shyly covers herself with her hands. She's never been naked in front of another man. She's hardly been naked with Pete.

"Take your shoes off," she murmurs, and she hears two thunks as they hit the floor. Then Binky surrounds her, a storm cloud of gray, all buttons and flaps and stripes in a blur of uniform, lips, tongue, fingertips slipping into places she had forgotten she had and she hears the *rrrrrp* of a zipper and feels the molten explosion inside and then Binky is flopped over on his back and sweating like a pig.

"Wow," says Binky.

"Wow yourself," she sighs as the throbbing ebbs like the tide going out. He's finished? She was just starting.

"No, I mean, Wow, it's late." Binky squints at his watch. "I skipped lunch to make up the time, but I'm really going to be off schedule."

"What time is it?" Lorena jumps up, starts pulling on her clothes. "Cassie gets home on the four o'clock bus."

"It's four o'clock." He wrestles the black oxfords onto his black-socked feet, gives her a quick peck good-bye, and hollers as he pounds down the stairs, "Next Thursday, okay?" She hears the door slam and, minutes later, open again.

"Mom?" Cassie calls. "I'm home."

THAT NIGHT LORENA lies in bed staring at the light patch on the ceiling as if awaiting some sign. She can't sleep. Something momentous has occurred, a shift in her consciousness more profound than the change she felt on her wedding night when she lay awake marveling that she was no longer a virgin, an event she had dreaded as well as anticipated. And when it was over and done with before she knew what was happening, she wondered why she had spent so many years fantasizing about such an insignificant moment.

But by sleeping with another man, she had crossed a boundary more daring than that of exchanging a maiden's innocence for marital experience. Why, she thought, this is like a *movie*. Illicit. Daring. Lustful. Well, maybe not that lustful, but it was probably because she had been so nervous, being an extramarital virgin and all. Next time she'd be better.

She did feel guilty. Oh, yes, she was ridden with guilt, but it was all mixed up with the excitement of being desired and admired, of being wanted. Being the object of such passion instilled a passion within her that overrode the pangs of regret she felt when she looked upon the faces of Pete and Cassie. She was wanted. She was wanton. She just couldn't help herself.

And if the side effect of this marital detour could mean fame and fortune, wouldn't the guilt be worth it? Once she was rich and famous, she knew she would be happy. She'd have everything she ever wanted and never worry about anything again. Not money. Not looks. Not love.

Because when you're famous, it means you've got it all.

CASSIE

DAD AND I are comparing feet. We always do that on the first warm night, lying barefoot side by side in the lawn chair that tips back so we can look at the stars. Dad and I have the same feet. The second toe is longer than the rest, longer even than our big toes. Dad calls it our "Lookout Toe." He says it sticks out like that so it can check around and see if there's danger ahead for the other toes.

Dad had a close call this morning when he went to put up the TV antenna. We get too much snow with just the rabbit ears, so he bought a big outside antenna and carried it up to the roof. Next thing I know I heard this big thump and Dad yelling *shit* and then another bunch of thumps and other words I can't say, and then I saw his feet dangling outside my window. He climbed down the chinaberry tree to the ground. It's lucky he caught himself on the gutter before he fell or he would have broken something for sure.

The air is soft, sprinkled with firefly light, buzzing with summer sounds. Crickets crackle in the soft dark, radio voices leak into the night—Fibber McGee, a ball game. I hear the kids playing, Margaret's voice way way off, "Ally-ally-in-free." We watch the lights of Norfolk over the water. We look in people's windows across the court. The Powells' and the MacDougals' windows are dark except for the silvery squares of their TVs. There's nothing on now we want to watch, so we sit outside between *Topper* and *Our Miss Brooks*.

I like snuggling with Dad, burrowing into his soft cotton shirt, sniffing his smoky smell. The webbing of the chair makes patterns of cold on our backs but he feels warm by my side. Tonight he's in a good mood and it's like it used to be when we'd sit out here until I fell asleep listening to him tell stories about when he was little.

"Mornings I'd lie in bed under the quilt my grandma made from my grandpa's old shirts, shirts he wore out from working on ships," he says. "I'd lie there and smell the biscuits and bacon my mother was fixing for breakfast."

Even though I've heard this story before, I like hearing it again. I close my eyes and see a little-boy Dad, like in the picture I have when he was six. It was taken at Virginia Beach, and he's wearing a funny striped bathing suit that covers him all the way up to his neck, all the way down to his knees. His face is scrunched up in the sun and his hair is wet against his forehead.

"And while I was lying so warm under the quilt, I could hear the sound of the shipyard," he says. I peek up at him and his eyes are closed, too. "That sound followed me around all day. To school, to the playground—it was like my heartbeat."

"I hear it, too," I say.

"You can't hear it the way I do," he says. "I hear it from the inside out."

He tells me how I was named after that grandma who made the quilt, his grandma Cassandra. How she taught him to catch crabs in Chesapeake Bay, how they scrabbled around in the trap when he hauled it, dripping water and seaweed, onto the dock.

How he learned to grab them just right so they don't pinch, then drop them into a pot of boiling water.

"My grandma taught me the names of all the constellations when I was so little I could hardly read," he says, his eyes still closed. "I coulda been a sailor. I could steer by the stars, that's how much I know about them."

"Would you ever want to go to the stars, Dad?"

"Naw," he says. "They're up too high. All's I want to do is look at them." He opens his eyes and points to the sky just over the horizon above the water. "Look over there. See that big 'W'? That's the constellation that's named after you: Cassie-opeia." He tells me I have to share it with the other person it's named after, Queen Cassiopeia, who was sent into the sky because she bragged about her beautiful daughter.

I look but all I see is black sky and a whole bunch of scattered stars. "Where's the 'W'?" I ask.

"Just follow the dots of stars," Dad says, but I still can't see the queen. I squint, trying to follow where his finger is pointing, but she's lost somewhere in the glitter. I stare and stare and all of a sudden there she is, stretched out across the sky.

"I see her, I see her!" I say to Dad. "She just popped out like magic."

"There's nothing magic about it," he says. "She's been there all along."

I tell Dad what this man on test-pattern TV said about stars. That there are stars way beyond the stars we can see. That they all began with one big bang. That all those stars could be suns to other worlds. And that one day our sun will get so big that it will swallow up the earth.

"Where did you hear that?" he asks.

"On test-pattern TV."

He gives me a look. "Aren't you getting a little old to be making stuff up?"

"I'm not making it up. I'm telling the truth."

"Remember Pookie?"

Oh, no, Pookie again. They never let me forget Pookie. "I was little then," I say. "I *know* I made Pookie up."

He's quiet a minute. Then he says, "What else do you see?"

I don't feel like telling him. I know he won't believe me.

"Nothing," I say.

He looks off across the water and doesn't talk anymore. I lie next to him, not touching now, and look up at Cassie-opeia. I think about what the man said on test-pattern TV. "Billions and billions of stars," he said. Billions and billions of stars.

L O R E N A

ON THURSDAY, BINKY arrives with a box in his bag. Purple-wrapped, pink-bowed, the box is from Naughty but Nice, a shop Lorena has passed but never had the nerve to enter. She peels back the purple tissue paper and stares at the little black wisps, transparent as smoke, that lie within. She lifts the bra, amazed at its lightness, its laciness, its complete lack of function.

She has never seen panties like these. Why, she could see right through them. And what was this? A garter belt? He wants her to wear stockings? These stockings? Black lace, the seams accentuated with little hearts? She never knew there was such a thing. And, he adds before she takes the box into the bathroom to try everything on, put on your high heels.

How does she look? She studies herself in the mirror. She's never dressed in lingerie like this. Does she look like a movie star? Like Mitzi Gaynor? All she can see of herself in the medicine-chest mirror is to the bottom of the bra. She jumps to get a better view but can't jump high enough, so she steps on the toilet lid and stretches herself over the sink to look in the mirror.

"What happened?" she hears Binky call as she crashes to the floor, taking the toothbrush holder with her. "I just tripped, it's nothing," she sings, wiggling her elbow to test it before languidly limping out.

Binky sits naked on the bed. His uniform is folded neatly over the chair. His mailman's cap sits at attention on top of his clothes, looking official. "You okay?" he asks.

She nods. Her elbow hurts. She's okay, but more important, does she *look* okay?

She must, for Binky pounces. He springs off the bed and, balancing on his sturdy legs, pulls her into his grip. She gasps as he crushes her against his body. She is Lana Turner; he is Robert Mitchum. He is Bogey; she is Bacall. She is . . . in pain.

"Aaaaa-a-a!" she wails, grabbing at her elbow.

"What's wrong?" He leaps back as if she were a leper.

"I hurt my elbow," she confesses. "In the bathroom."

"Bad?"

"I don't think it's broken."

"Good," he says, relieved. "Just relax. I'll help you forget it." And then he does, and does again, and they thrash about until the sheets are tied in knots. She revels in the power of wispy bras of black lace, of barely-there panties Binky slides down with his teeth, of sexy stockings that make her legs look so good wrapped around Binky's neck. "Ooooh," she hears herself moan, "Oooh, Wally."

"Wally?"

"I meant Binky."

"You said Wally." He backs off, pulls the sheet over himself.

She doesn't know what to say. She doesn't know how Wally popped up just at this moment, just when she was having such a good time with Binky. "I had been thinking about him, you know, being a talent scout and all."

"Now? You think about him now? Are you bored or something?"

"No!" And she means it. "That was the most . . . *incredible* sex
I've ever had. I guess I was thinking about the things I like the
most in this world and one is you and the other is dancing. And
somehow they all got mixed up and came out 'Wally.' "

"The most incredible sex you've ever had?" he asks, preening.
"Really?"

"Oh, yes," she breathes, and lays hands on his still-tender parts.
"The very best." And then it happens again, and this time it truly
is the most incredible sex she's ever had.

As Binky slides into a doze, Lorena traces a finger around his
ear, along his neck, then follows the path of the scar that wanders
over his shoulder and down his back. "Do you remember the
explosion?" she asks, lazily grazing the scar's lumpy Cream of
Wheat surface with the tip of one curved fingernail.

"What explosion?" he murmurs.

"In the war. When you got the scar."

"Wasn't an explosion."

"Was it a bullet?"

"Nah."

"A bayonet?"

"Nah."

"Well, what was it?"

"Barbed wire."

"Barbed wire?" She examines the scar closely. "How?"

"Crawled under it."

"Escaping the enemy?"

He chuckles. "Y'might say so."

"The Germans?" She shakes his shoulder. "Come on. Tell me."

"No Germans. Belgians."

"We were fighting the Belgians?" Lorena's forehead wrinkles
in puzzlement.

"Well, *I* was. Two of them, anyway."

"I don't get it."

Binky raises himself onto an elbow, eyes twinkling with mischievous memory. "I was escaping back *into* camp. Had this Belgian girl, had her in a haystack, and then her brothers took after me like they woulda killed me." He shakes his head. "They would have, too, if I hadn't gotten under that wire first."

Lorena backs away from him. "You told me you were wounded. In battle. The Ardennes."

"Well, it was near the Ardennes. And it was kinda a battle." He gets an aw-shucks look on his face. "I never really *saw* battle," he confesses. "But I *heard* it."

Lorena moves to the other side of the bed. "You lied to me."

He gives her a lopsided grin that both infuriates and charms her. "Naw. I didn't really lie. Just . . . stretched the truth."

"That's lying."

"Naw it's not. Lying is when you swear you're telling the truth. Did I swear? I did not."

Lorena doesn't answer. Binky continues.

"If you just mention something, that don't mean it's necessarily true, it just means you're mentioning it. But if you *swear* on something like God or your mother or like that, then that means it's really true." He looks contrite, gazes at her from beneath sorrowful eyebrows. "If I lied, it was only because I wanted to impress you."

"You wanted to impress me?" She is impressed.

"Well, you looked so pretty that day in the parking lot. And I felt like such a goofus when I realized it was you I had yelled at outside the trailer. So I guess I just wanted to make myself look good."

"Aw." Lorena feels bad for him now. "You looked good to me anyway."

"You look good to me now," he responds, moving his hand slowly up her leg. She is quite astonished at her response, which exceeds the avidity of just a short while ago. This time, whatever inhibitions she had held in reserve have vanished. As she and Binky complete their acrobatics, she realizes she's chalked up a personal record.

Three times, she tabulates, I've never done it three times in one day—in one *hour*—and then it dawns on her. She grabs at his watch. "Oh my God," she gasps. "It's almost four o'clock!"

Flinging her gray flannel robe around her, hastily stuffing bits of lingerie into its pockets, she steers Binky out the back door just as she hears Cassie fumbling with the key to the front-door lock.

Lorena scurries into the living room to greet her. "How was your dancing lesson?" she asks, heart pounding.

"Okay." Cassie doesn't look at Lorena.

"Good," says Lorena. She thrusts her hands deep into the pockets of her robe, clutches the wispy remnants of her three-times-in-one-hour with Binky. She's relieved when Cassie skips up the stairs to her room without uttering another word.

I'VE DONE IT again, Lorena thinks, stretching to see the hair disaster reflected in her rearview mirror as she drives home from Maybelle's. She had asked for a double dose of bleach for a more Mitzi look, but now she looks electrified. She hopes Binky doesn't hate it as much as she does.

She parks, then skulks hurriedly down the sidewalk hoping no one will see her. It's a long walk from the street, past the court, past all the other houses with their flaking white paint, to her house at the end. She fumbles in her purse for her keys, buried in a disintegrating wad of Kleenex from a sneezing session she endured at Maybelle's. It's a wonder Maybelle herself hasn't dissolved from all those chemicals, she thinks.

After the crisp breeze that swept the outdoors, the living room seems musty, dark even though it's early afternoon, thick with the burned odor from the Swanson's she left in the oven too long last night. The window shade, dull ocher in the gloom, is pulled all the way down, its frayed ring dangling far below the sill. It was yanked there by Pete before yesterday's dinner to shut out the distraction of kids playing kickball while he was trying to watch *Treasury Men in Action*.

She flips up the living-room shade. Sunshine spatters the orange velvet couch, the Naugahyde chairs, the boomerang-shaped coffee table cluttered with yesterday's paper. She reaches to pick up a chipped cup half-filled with cold coffee and three drowned Chesterfield butts.

Then she sees the drawings. They are everywhere, outlined with pencil on notebook paper, colored in with Crayolas. She picks up a drawing of a mutated yellow chicken: big pop eyes perched over a beak, impossibly long neck, ridiculous little wings with hands on the end. "Big Bird" it says in Cassie's crooked printing.

Here's another, a fat furry creature, bright blue with a cavernous no-lip mouth, holding an armload of what looks like cookies. And here's a strange green froglike being with a bright red tongue, snuggling up to a yellow-wigged pig-woman whose tarty makeup looks like Della's on a heavy date.

Lorena studies the drawings. They are, she must admit, pretty good. She knew Cassie liked to draw, she was always drawing something, Mickey Mouse, Cinderella, what she called her "fashion ladies." But these drawings, these cartoony people-animals, Lorena's never seen anything like them.

When did she do all this? These drawings weren't here when Cassie left for school this morning, before Lorena's fateful appointment with Maybelle. Maybe she came home sick. Lorena skips up the stairs to Cassie's room, looks in. The bed is empty. What is going on?

17

CAN'T BELIEVE I was so dumb, leaving my drawings around when I came home from school at lunchtime to watch test-pattern TV. I'd done it a few times before—check to see if Mom's car is parked, watch my show, eat what's in my lunch bag, go back to school. She never would have found out if I hadn't been so late that I ran out without thinking and left the drawings behind.

"What are these?" she says, waving them under my nose as soon as I walk in the door after school.

"Drawings," I say.

"When did you do them?"

"Today." I decide to lie just a little. "I felt sick at lunchtime, so I came home. Then I felt better and went back."

She frowns while she studies the drawings. "They're not bad," she says, and before I can even say thanks, she asks, "Did you copy them from something?"

"Off a TV show." I'm trapped.

"What TV show?"

"This puppet show. Cookie Monster. Miss Piggy."

"What puppet show?"

I can tell she knows what I'm going to say because her eyebrows collide and her mouth gets her puppet-mouth look, like it's on hinges. "A show on the test pattern," I mumble.

She covers her eyes with both hands and gives a dramatic sigh. "Oh Lordy. Lula lives."

"Aunt Lula's still alive?"

Mom just shakes her head and looks at me. "Lula made things up, too," she says. "Maybe Dad's right. Maybe making things up is just in your blood."

Well, they're both wrong. Aunt Lula's dead and there's nothing in my blood. The things that I see I could never make up.

BECAUSE OF THE drawings and the test-pattern thing, Mom's got all these rules now, like doing homework before TV, saying yes and no ma'am—stupid rules she just made up because she says Mama Hansen on the *Mama* show has rules, Mom's own mom had rules, and when you have rules everybody behaves like they're supposed to.

Her dumbest rule is that I can't ride my bike in the street. She had promised that when I turned eleven she'd let me ride everywhere like everybody else, but then she went back on her promise after she had this argument with Dad the other night during *Truth or Consequences*. Because of the no-TV-before-homework rule, I was doing boring multiplication problems at the dining-room table while they watched TV, but I could hear the whole fight.

"Would you tell the truth if they asked you something you didn't want anybody to know?" Mom asked Dad.

"It's a stupid show," Dad said.

"Well, suppose you could win a million dollars and get famous if you told something really embarrassing."

"All you can win on this stupid show is a toaster or something.

It would take a lot more than a toaster to make me tell something I'd be sorry for afterward. Especially if I had to do *that*."

I wanted to see what That was because I could hear the TV audience laughing, so I peeked around the corner. Some guy in a clown outfit was riding a big tricycle down the middle of a street while all the cars honked at him. That must have been his consequence for not telling the truth before the buzzer went off. I wouldn't do that for a toaster either.

"What would be the worst truth you could tell?" Mom asked.

Dad looked like he was going to say something but then he didn't, just stared at the TV set.

"Suppose they said they would stick bamboo under your fingernails like the Japs did in the war. Would you tell?" Mom asked.

"I got nothing to tell," Dad said. "Anything anybody wants to know about me, they already know it."

Mom watched, one finger tapping her chin, as the clown guy got off his tricycle and ran to the side of the road. Then she said, "Truth or consequences: Have you ever, you know, been with anybody else?"

"Whaddaya mean, *been* with?"

"You know. Been to *bed* with."

"Who are you, Bob Barker?" Dad asked, then turned and looked hard at Mom. "Why? Have you?"

"Of course not," Mom huffed. She looked away and crossed her arms and made a prissy face. "Besides, I asked you first."

"Boy," Dad said, moving away from her on the couch, "sometimes I think it was you got hit by that truck and knocked cuckoo, not Lula."

Mom got this aha look and asked, "Why are you changing the subject, talking about Lula?"

"You're crazy," he said, waving her off. "It's just that this guy in the clown outfit riding the tricycle reminded me that Lula got hit by a truck when she was riding her bike. Your mother said that that's when Lula started acting peculiar. So," he added with a snort, "what's *your* excuse?"

Mom made a little tent with her fingers and pressed them against her lips. "Omigod. I forgot she got hit on her bicycle. But she must've been crazy before that, crazy enough to ride a bicycle when she was old as thirty-three. Who rides a bicycle when they're thirty-three?"

"Don't matter how old you are if you land on your head."

"You think maybe that's why she was so weird, seeing things and all?"

"I'd say it contributed."

TODAY WHEN I ask Mom if I can ride my bike to the roller rink with some of the kids from the court, she says no.

"You *promised*," I say, and she says, "Don't whine." But I want to know why she broke her promise and she says, "Because you can get hit by a truck." Then I remember last night and how they were talking about truth and other people and Aunt Lula on her bike, and I say, "That is so unfair!"

"What's unfair?"

"That just because Aunt Lula got hit by a truck, you broke your promise."

"How did you know about Lula and the truck? Were you snooping instead of doing your homework?"

"You were talking loud."

"You were snooping." She makes her frowny face. "I'm not going to argue with you. No bike riding in the street. And that's final."

I hate her. But I love my bike. It's blue, a Schwinn, and it has a bell that has rusted a little but still dings. I fling my leg over its saddle, boy-style, and feel as if I could fly. I speed away from home with the wind flipping my hair in my face, all the houses and trees rushing by in a blur. I don't ride in the street because

I'm afraid she'll find out, but I do ride down to the beach, down the steep hill, a no-hands kamikaze run that makes me scream "Banzai!" like in war movies.

When I get down to the water, I sit in the damp crunchy sand and look over at Norfolk and wonder about stuff: Are Siamese twins always Siamese? How high would you have to go up in the sky before you couldn't see people anymore? When would be the best time to tell Mom that I quit dancing class?

When I get home, Mom gives me the third degree, hands on her hips. "Well? Where did you go? Tell me the truth, now."

"I went down to the beach." I feel good because it *is* the truth. It's not like that sneaky feeling I have when I come home after I've faked going to dancing. I don't know how much longer I can keep that up. All I know is I can't keep pretending, riding the bus and hiding out at Al's newsstand.

I'm okay at lying a little. I just can't keep lying big.

18

L O R E N A

LORENA IS DRESSING for Binky. She knows how he wants her to look by now after weeks of Thursday love: hot, hasty, clock-watching love. On Thursdays she waits, tense and edgy, for Cassie to leave for her dancing lesson. When she hears the door slam, Lorena whips into action.

She's become more adept at makeup. Swivels out her flat-topped tube of Red Flame. Draws on semisymmetrical cupid's-bow lips. Blots them, folds them in until all that's left is a thin slash of red, then out they pop, bright and shiny as a cinnamon heart. She smiles. She does like the way she looks.

She knows by now to greet Binky in her lingerie. She enjoys the ritual, sliding black stockings over freshly shaved legs, center-ing the seams exactly from heel to thigh. Bending over to shimmy her breasts into the lacy cups of the bra. Turning to admire the contrast of taut black panties arching above the smooth white cheeks of her butt. She loves the transformation these simple acts create. They make her feel like a showgirl.

She hears the doorbell, peeks out the window for a verifying glimpse of gray hat, opens the door just enough to let him in. She poses, flaunting the bits of black beneath her flannel robe, which she then lets fall in a heap at her feet.

Binky drops his mailbag with a thunk. He grabs both cheeks of Lorena's thinly clad bottom, pulls her to him, and gives her a long, breath-sucking kiss. He leans back to admire her. His gaze meanders leisurely over her lace-clad bosom, her skimpy see-through panties, her garter-clamped black stockings. It stops with an almost audible screech at her shoes.

"What are *those?*" he croaks, backpedaling. Instead of high heels, she's wearing a pair of big-bowed, shiny black tap shoes.

"Surprise!" She gives him a sly smile. With a hip-slinging pirouette and a crook of her finger, she clickety-clacks up the stairs. "Well?" she says, looking down at him. "You coming?"

"Uh. Yeah." He follows her, slowly undoing his tie. He looks worried.

"Now you just lie down and relax," Lorena purrs. She unbuttons Binky's shirt, unties his thick-soled oxfords, slides his double-pleated postman's pants over his black nylon socks. She places the hat at the foot of the bed. Stripped down to his Jockey shorts and socks, he props himself stiffly against the pillow on Lorena's side of the bed and watches her over the tops of his toes.

She carefully slides a lime-green record over the fat spindle of the 45 player by her bed. The record drops, the plastic arm reaches over, and the speaker wails the first note: "WOOOO WOOOO..."

"Ooooo," sighs Lorena with a provocative wiggle. Her right foot goes into palsy, tap-tap-tapping against the wood floor. Her left foot follows and she is into her routine, arms flailing, feet tapping, torso contorting in a thigh-jiggling frenzy. Binky looks dazed.

"Pardon me, boy..."—she mouths the words—"is that the Chattanooga choo choo?" She reaches for Binky's cap, pops it on her head, anchors it with a perky pat. Tapping nonstop, she twists her arms behind her back and unhooks her bra. ". . . Track twenty-nine, boy, you can gimme a shine . . ."

Binky, suddenly alert, sits up. She rips the bra off, flings it to Binky, who misses the catch as it flies by him and lands on the pleated lampshade, almost knocking it over. She turns her back to him—teasing, tapping, shock waves quivering the cheeks of her buttocks—then twirls forward again to cup her breasts and play peekaboo with her nipples.

Binky is now on his knees. "I never knew you were such a good dancer," he says, his voice breaking.

She gives him a cartoon wink as she sings along: ". . . You leave the Pennsylvania Station 'bout a quarter to four, read a magazine and then you're in Baltimore . . ." Now she's bumping, grinding, a snapping tapping whirlwind of syncopated rhythm. ". . . Dinner in the diner . . ." She throws in a few moves she's seen Cassie do, that backward-forward step, some up-in-the-air arm movements with a twist of the hips. ". . . Nothing could be finer . . ." Binky leans forward, grabs at her crotch, but she dips away, tapping madly, faster, faster . . .

"Mom?"

"Cassie!" Lorena freezes in midtap.

Cassie stands in the doorway, pale, unmoving. Looks at Binky, looks at Lorena. "What's going on?"

Lorena whips the cap off her head to cover her bare breasts. "Why are you home?"

"I quit my dancing lessons." Cassie is staring at Lorena now. "Who's that? What are you *doing*?" Her voice ripples around the edges, ruffling and stretching like a crepe-paper streamer.

Lorena edges toward her robe, hastily ties it around her, tosses the hat to Binky, who has slid off the edge of the bed and is sitting on the floor, pulling on his pants. All Lorena can see is the top of his pomaded hair and she gapes at it as if expecting words to balloon overhead like a comic strip, words that would excuse her, words that would somehow make what happened vanish, go away, never have happened at all.

But no words are coming from Binky. Just some grunts as he leans over to tie his shoes, and some indecipherable mutters. He stands, claps his hat on his head, and, shirt still unbuttoned over his pale chest, smiles feebly at Cassie as he edges by her in the doorway. "Gotta run," he says, and Lorena hears him bound down the stairs and out the door.

"Chat-tanooga choo choo, won't you choo-choo me ho-o-ooooome," wails the record before Lorena drags the player's arm across it in a teeth-chilling shriek.

She can't look at Cassie, so she stares at the record she's removed from the spindle. "I was just . . . um . . . practicing my routine," she says to the record. Shut up shut up, she says to herself, but she can't, she has to fill the silence in the room with words, lots of words, any words, it doesn't matter.

"I know it looks funny but that's my costume, maybe it's a little daring, I want to do something, you know, different, and I just wanted to get someone's opinion and he just happened to be here when I was trying out everything, so I thought . . ."

She looks at Cassie's still face.

". . . so I thought . . ." What did she think? She feels as if someone took a big eraser and wiped out her mind.

When Cassie turns without uttering one word and slams the door of her own room behind her, one thing surfaces in Lorena's brain like the floating question in a Magic 8 ball: Now what?

19

C A S S I E

I AM LYING on my bed, staring at my brown wall. It's like a movie screen. On it I see Mom, dancing. Her behind is shaking like Jell-O. She's naked, except for see-through underpants and stockings. And tap shoes. And a hat.

It's his hat. The mailman's. He's watching. His eyes go googly as Mom's titties bounce all around and he reaches out and tries to grab at her.

I feel like I'm going to throw up.

I close my eyes but I still see them, Mom and the mailman. Mom's mouth moving, talking to me. Shiny red lips, twisting. Lips, teeth, the pink tip of her tongue. Puppet mouth.

I hear her. Knocking. I can't move. I feel heavy, heavy. Lying on my side, staring at the wall, sunk in the bed like quicksand.

Knock, she goes. *Knock. Knock.*

"Cassie?"

The doorknob jiggles. I locked it. She could open it with a nail file but she doesn't.

"Cassie?"

I don't answer. I'm not here. Go away. I'm not here anymore.

I know about you, I feel like saying. You think I don't know these things. You think because you gave me that dumb book about menstruation, that's all I need to know. Well, I know more than that. I know all about sex.

I see lots of it on TV.

Not *your* TV. *My* TV.

Naked ladies. I see them. Men touch them, touch their titties, get on top of them. Do sex with them. Last week I saw that on test-pattern TV, saw the way it's done. I never saw that before.

Before, I saw people just talking about doing sex. Like those shows where leaders get the audience and people on the stage to yell at each other. I wonder if any of those people have a mother who did sex with the mailman.

"Cassie!" She hasn't gone away. "Cassie, I know you're in there."

I still don't say anything.

"We have to talk. It's not what you think."

Oh, yes it is.

DAD MAKES ME come down to dinner. When I won't open my door, he unlocks it with the nail file. "What's the matter with you?" he says. His face is pulled into a knot. When he gets angry, his neck turns red. Right now it's the color of a kickball.

"Wash your hands." He steers me into the bathroom, turns on the faucet with a yank, watches while I spin the sliver of Ivory between my palms until it foams with gray bubbles. Before I've even dried my hands, he's shoving me out the door, growling "Get yourself to the table."

He's mad at Mom, mad at me, mad at everybody. When he gets like that, I know something bad happened at work. I scuff downstairs, sit down, stare at my plate. I don't want to look at Mom but there she is across the table from me, looking scraggly.

All her lipstick is gone, face scrubbed white as my plate. Puffy eyes, pink and ugly. Ratty bathrobe, those dead-squirrel slippers I hate.

"No biscuits?" Dad says to Mom. "What's this?" He pokes at some stiff pink slabs dealt out on a platter. "Spam? For dinner?"

"I don't feel good," Mom says. She doesn't look at me. "I think I've got the flu."

"Great. Don't breathe on me." Dad stabs a piece of Spam with his fork, flings it on his plate. "I guess it would be too much to ask if you had any bread."

Mom gives him her beagle-dog look, shuffles into the kitchen, comes out with half a loaf of Wonder bread. "Here," she says, and flops it on the table.

"Mustard," Dad growls.

Back in she goes, comes out with the French's, clonks that on the table. "Anything else before I sit down?" she asks in a prissy voice. If I talked to her like that I'd get smacked.

Dad doesn't say anything. Forks the Spam onto a slice of bread, paints a streak of mustard across it, folds it like an envelope, and bites it. Chews, jaw pumping up and down, cheek bulging, prickly and stubbly. Swallows. I see his Adam's apple jump, imagine a pink jumble of Spam and bread going down his stomach tube like in my science book, wiggling down and down till it hits bottom. He stares at his plate, throws what's left of his sandwich on it.

"I got a good mind to quit," he says.

"Quit what?" Mom's eyes go big.

"Work."

"Oh." She takes a breath. "Why?"

"Foreman's got it in for me. Knows that I shoulda had his job, knows that if it wasn't for this gimp leg of mine I'd be his boss." He picks up the sandwich again, jams the meat back in with his finger before he takes another bite. "Know what he did?" Dad says, still chewing. I can see the soft white bread mushing in his mouth. "Called me an *asshole*!"

Mom's eyes flicker over at me for a second, like I never heard that word or anything, like I never hear it all the time on my test-pattern shows. "Watch your language," she mutters.

"Asshole. Right in front of everybody. Nobody calls me ass-hole," he says. "I like to punch him out right then and there."

"You hit him?" Mom says, eyes getting bigger.

"Nah," Dad says. "But I *coulda*." He folds another slab of Spam into bread, bites it in half. "Maybe I can get transferred, just get away from the guy." His eyes get droopy and his chewing slows down until it stops and he looks down at his plate. He looks like he might cry.

"What did you do? To make him mad?" Mom asks.

"Nothing!" Dad's head snaps up and he slams the table with his fist. "Not a goddamn thing." He shoves his chair away from the table and points his finger at Mom. "Why is everything always *my* fault?"

BAM goes the front door and Mom and I sit there staring at each other. She blinks and two fat drops race each other down her white-plate cheeks. Her nose is drippy, too, and I can't look at her anymore. I don't know what to say, so I don't say anything. I push myself away from the table and go into the living room. I flick on the TV. *The Lone Ranger* is on. I wish I was Tonto. I like saying "Kemo sabe." Kemo sabe, kemo sabe, kemo sabe.

What happens to other kids when their moms and dads fight? I must be the only one. I don't know anybody whose mom dances naked for somebody in her bedroom or whose dad is all the time mad about work. Part of me wants to tell Dad about Mom and what I saw, and the other part is scared he'll find out. The way he's been acting lately, he might do what they say on the news that guy, Dr. Sheppard, did: kill his wife and pretend somebody else did it.

If I try to remember when this Mom-and-Dad trouble began, it seems like it all started around the time we got the TV. That's when Mom began talking about how she could've been a dancer, how she could've been famous. That's when she started to prac-tice her stupid routine. About that same time, Dad was getting quieter, watched TV a lot. I thought he was mad at me but then I realized it wasn't just me, it was everybody: Mom, Della, people at work.

Before the TV, Dad and I used to play checkers after the dinner dishes were cleared off the kitchen table. While Mom did the dishes, we'd turn the radio up loud so we could hear over the noise she made banging pots and pans in the sink. Sprinkled between the clang of Mom's pots and the rumbly voice of the Great Gildersleeve were the splash of running water, the *tick-tick-tick* sound of Dad sucking on a licorice twist, the *click-clack* of checkers being moved around the board. It all made a kind of music. Steam from the sink settled like fog all around us and it seemed like we were floating on a soft and singing cloud.

Now I remember times like that and wish I could get them back. I didn't know it then, but that's when I must have been happy.

20

L O R E N A

T'S RAINING HARD, one of those early summer storms that boils up over the water and races inland. Gusts of soggy air rush through open windows that Lorena runs around slamming shut. The whole house feels damp, smells musky as a stray dog.

She's making biscuits. The dough feels saturated, leaden under her palms. She works in silence, the only sound the static of the rain. Her fingers absently work the malleable lump, kneading it over and over until it looks old and used and gray as the sky. She stares out the window as she works, seeing, not the sheets on the line snapping like sails unfurled in a storm, but Cassie. Cassie, her face blank and unyielding to Lorena's yammering excuse for what she and Binky were doing in the bedroom.

Cassie is at Molly's. She left early in the morning without saying good-bye and hasn't been back all day. Lorena had to run after her to ask where she was going. "Molly's," Cassie said, and that's all she said. Lorena supposes she'll have to call there to tell her to come home for dinner. She doesn't know if Cassie will.

Lorena has finished assembling the casserole for dinner, a Betty Crocker recipe she cut out of *Life* magazine: Dutch Pantry Pie. She had rifled her shelves to find something for dinner, something she could make without having to go to the A&P. She couldn't deal with the A&P right now. Too many memories. Thankfully, she had all the ingredients she needed for the Dutch Pantry Pie: left-over Spam from last night. Carnation evaporated milk. Velveeta cheese. A couple of potatoes. And Pete will have his damn biscuits.

Her mind races as she pummels the dough, skips right past too-painful thoughts of Cassie to Pete. What's wrong at work? What's wrong with him? And Binky. He hasn't called. Not that she expects him to call, or even wants him to call. But why hasn't he called?

The doorbell startles her. Somebody's at the door in this weather? She wipes a circle on the fogged-up window, peers out.

Max?

She opens the door, grabs it as a gust yanks it away. Max is dripping, hair curled in commas across his forehead. His mustache droops like an old mop. His paint-smeared dungarees and work shirt are soaked through and cling to his beefy body.

"Got caught in the rain," he says, shivering.

"I see." She doesn't know whether to invite him in, whether he'll shake off the water like a dog.

"I was walking over to talk to you about Cassie when it started to pour."

Cassie? "Come on in," she says.

"I'm soaked. Got a towel?"

She runs upstairs, returns with a couple of ratty beach towels. He stands on one, wraps the other around him. "I played hooky from work today so I could paint," he says between chattering teeth. "Cassie and Molly are at our house playing Monopoly."

Lorena nods.

"I overheard them talking," he says.

Oh, God.

"Normally I wouldn't pass on to you the harmless little conversations I overhear, but I think this is something you need to know about."

She can barely understand him. His teeth are clattering like castanets. "You'd better dry off," she says, hoping to delay this talk. "Go on up to the bathroom and take off those wet things. I'll give you a robe. Want coffee? Hot tea?"

"You got some Scotch?" He lumbers up the stairs, trailing a glistening wetness behind him like an overgrown snail. She can hear the suction of his wet sandals flapping on each step.

Robe. Robe. Her gray flannel robe would be too small for him. She rifles through the closet for the tartan plaid robe she gave Pete several birthdays ago. He never wears it. Does he still have it? She finds it crumpled on a hook in the back of the closet and hands it to Max through the bathroom door. He emerges, struggling to stretch the robe around his girth. Judging from its electrified appearance, his hair has been vigorously rubbed with the towel, wiry curls all whichaway, haloing his head.

"Much better," he sighs. She sees his wet clothes hung to dry over the shower-curtain rod.

She hands him a Welch's jelly glass half-full of Scotch. Pete doesn't drink Scotch. He'll never miss it. "This okay?"

"Perfect." He takes a noisy gulp. "Aaaah." He leans back into the couch, wiggles his bare furry toes. Lorena perches on the edge of a chair, one foot tapping nervously.

Max studies Howdy Doody's embossed face on the jelly glass, thrown into contrast against the amber fluid he swirls in a slow circle. Takes another swig. "Cassie has a wonderful imagination," he begins.

Lorena nods.

"Sometimes when she describes things she's made up, it's almost as if they're real." Max squints at Howdy's face, doesn't look at Lorena. "Like those shows she says she sees on the test pattern."

"Oh, those." She rolls her eyes.

"You don't think she really sees them."

"Do you?" She gives him an incredulous look.

"Remember the things I told you she saw—that Ronald Reagan was the president and that she knew about the new integration law before it happened—those things that made me wonder?"

"Not me. They didn't make me wonder." She doesn't mention wondering whether Cassie's delusions were related to Lula's craziness.

Max takes another sip of Scotch. "She told me something that made my hair stand up like a cat with its tail in a socket, something about an artist I met years ago. He was, you might say, strange. Strange-looking, strange acting, such a meshuggener that I never forgot his name. Warhol. Andy Warhol."

Lorena shrugs. "Never heard of him."

"Well, Cassie said she saw on her test-pattern show that some woman shot him in the stomach. She remembered his name because of what happened to him: War. Hole. I don't know where else she would have heard of him. Nobody even knows the guy. I wasn't impressed with his work, it was mostly ads—shoes and things. But, according to Cassie, he's famous. *Really* famous. The thing is, Cassie is the only person who seems to know this."

"Yeah," Lorena says with a slow nod. "Cassie's always pretending to know stuff no one else knows. I think she reads too much."

"Well," says Max after a contemplative moment. He closes the robe over dough-lump knees. "That's not what I came here to talk about." He clears his throat. "Now, we know Cassie does tend to make things up."

"Um-hmm."

"This morning I overheard her tell Molly something so . . . bizarre, that I think you might need to talk to her about it."

"Bizarre?" Lorena's mouth feels dry. She could use a swig of Scotch herself.

"I think that might describe it." Max studies Howdy a bit more. "I won't trouble you with the details, but Cassie's tale involved you, your mailman, black stockings, and a tap-dance routine."

"Ha, ha. That Cassie." Her grin feels taped on.

"I know. It's embarrassing for me to tell you about this, but I thought you might want to know. After all, it's not a story you'd want her to tell the world."

Lorena's body goes limp as a noodle. "Nope," is all she can say.

"Well, you know kids," Max continues with an uncomfortable chuckle. "They like to impress their friends in funny ways." He reaches over and pats Lorena on the arm. "Don't take it like that, now. It's nothing that a little mother-daughter chat won't take care of."

She snaps her head up at the rattle of a key in the lock. The door flies open with a blast of wind and rain and Pete is standing there, a stunned look on his face.

"You're home early," Lorena blurts.

Pete is soaked through. He looks like he's been held underwater. Hair plastered down, work shirt sagging with wetness, pants flapping heavily against his legs. His metal-toed boots squish as he stalks inside and points his finger at Max. "What is *he* doing here?" Then, "Is that my bathrobe?"

Max leaps to his feet, clutches the robe against his bareness. Holds a palm out, pacifying. "Got caught in this rain on my way here. Just wanted to stop by to talk to Lorena about Cassie." He manages a chuckle. "Looked like you by the time I got here, dripping like a faucet. Lorena let me dry off."

"Hah!" spats Pete. He slams his lunch bucket against the wall, then lunges at Max, fists clenched and trembling. "Caught you!" he yells as Max backpedals, trips over a chair, then plops ingloriously on his ample bottom. His legs fly into the air, exposing frayed white underwear which he had modestly left on despite its sogginess.

"Stop!" Lorena screams. She is terrified, not just that Pete will pummel Max, but that Max will defend his presence by revealing Cassie's story. *"Stop,"* she screams again, as much to Max as to Pete. She wedges herself between them, enabling Max to gather himself, scramble up the stairs, and lock himself in the bathroom.

"I knew it." Pete throws himself on the couch. Spies the jelly glass, picks it up, sniffs it. "Scotch! My good White Horse scotch! Drinking my liquor! In my bathrobe! With my wife! In my house!" He leaps up off the couch, leaves a large wet oval on the velvet cushion. "I knew you and that . . . that *Commie* were up to something." He heads for the stairs but Lorena blocks his way.

"Leave Max alone," she pleads. "It's not the way it looks." She can't tell him anything more, not without telling him too much, so she stretches Max's story. "He wanted to talk about Cassie, about those things she says she sees on TV. And he got wet, walking here in the rain, so I told him to dry off and I gave him a robe and some Scotch to get warm." That part was true, and its truth gives her the righteousness to go on the offense. "And what are you doing home so early? Don't tell me you did something stupid like quit!"

Pete's eyes narrow and focus on Lorena for the first time. His rage subsides, slides into contempt. "No. Not yet. I just left. Walked out." He runs square fingers through his thick black hair, tears off his shirt without bothering with the buttons, stands there with his pants riding low on his hips, bare skin glistening, slick with rain. Lorena gets a flash: Clark Gable.

Why, Pete looks like—like Clark *Gable,* all wet like that. Lorena is confused, flushed with heat. It's the same feeling that overwhelmed her the first time she met him, when she was working at the shipyard and he walked in—that same dissolving sensation between her belly button and her knees. Only now it's compounded by this magnificent fury. She's never seen him like this, never seen so many layers of anger in him before, never seen his jealousy acted out this way. His moods have never manifested themselves in violence or passion. This is . . . well, *romantic,* this sudden jealous rage.

"What happened?" She has an urge to touch him, a compulsion she quells like the impulse to touch a coiled snake, sleek, dangerous. He seems to sense this need, turns to face her, slips his hands beneath the waistband of his pants. She can almost feel the tender skin he's touching with his fingers.

"What do you care?" he says with a sneer. "You don't have to go to work. You don't have to climb all over that gantry in the rain, wondering if this time your leg's going to give out under you and you'll wind up an inkblot on the cement ten stories below. You don't have to take abuse from some asshole who has the job you should have had."

"Well, why don't you go to his boss—"

"All's you got to do all day is nothing but sit around, go to the movies with that tarty Della, sneak around behind my back with that damn Commie." Having reminded himself of Max, he strides up the stairs two at a time and bangs on the bathroom door. "Come on outta there, you Commie bastard," he yells, beating a tattoo on the door until Max, fully dressed in his wet clothes, opens it and steps out with as much dignity as he can muster.

"I realize what this looks like," Max says, "but you're wrong. I'm not going to stand here and apologize for something I haven't done." Sweeping his big hand like a paw to clear his way, he marches down the stairs and out into the rain.

Pete glares at Lorena after he hears the door shut. "And I'm supposed to believe that?"

Scarlett O'Hara. That, Lorena thinks, is who she could be right at this moment, a moment of sudden guilt and sorrowful repentance. Although Pete's jealousy is aimed in the wrong direction, his wrath has given her pause, made her fearful of the consequences if her true deception is ever discovered.

For if Binky has truly ridden off into the sunset, all she's got is

Pete. And if he abandons her, too, whatever will she do? She pictures him cocking a Clark Gable eyebrow. "Frankly, my dear," he will say before turning his back on her forever, "I don't give a damn."

She shivers with the drama of it all. Her life has taken such strange twists and turns. It's just like in the movies.

TODAY WHEN I'M playing at Molly's, Mr. Finkelstein goes out, doesn't say where, just says For a walk. It starts raining like crazy but he doesn't come home for a long time until we hear him slam the door and he's inside, all dripping wet and mad about something. And when Mom calls for me to come home to dinner, he makes me go even though I tell him I don't want to.

As I'm walking out the door, Mr. Finkelstein looks at me kind of strange and asks, "How do you know what's real and what's not?"

"If it's real, it's on the outside," I say, "and if it's not, it's in my head."

"Where are the shows you see on the test pattern?"

"Outside."

"Like my paintings?"

I have to think about that. "No," I decide. "Your paintings

start inside your head and then you bring them out. The shows I see are already there."

And then he nods. He knows what I mean.

Molly doesn't pay much attention when her dad and I talk. She still doesn't believe I see shows on the test pattern but she did pay attention this morning when I told her about Mom and the mailman. I had to tell somebody. It was like this great big balloon blowing up inside of me, and I felt like I was going to explode if I couldn't talk about it.

Molly said that they were probably doing sex. I told her about the dancing part, that maybe Mom really was just showing the mailman her routine because she's always practicing like she's going to go on TV or something. But Molly said I was crazy, of course they were doing sex if she was wearing those see-through pants and no top.

I don't even want to think about it. But I do, I think about what it would have been like to actually see them do It. I don't even know how that works, him inside her, all that. Maybe they haven't done It yet, maybe it'll never happen. Maybe she really was dancing.

MOM AND DAD don't say one word at dinner, don't even look at each other. Mom scoops out this pie thing she made, all pasty with leftover Spam lumps in it, and plops it on Dad's plate. He hardly eats it, just moves it around with his fork. The biscuits are flat and hard as checkers.

Mom is crying in the bathroom after dinner and Dad is outside looking at the stars. When he comes in after I've gone to bed, they argue in their bedroom where they think I can't hear but I do, lying in my bed, pretending to be asleep. At first I think they're fighting because of the mailman but that's not it. They're arguing about Mr. Finkelstein.

What is there to fight about? I like Mr. Finkelstein. Sometimes he plays Monopoly and Sorry with Molly and me. He always loses, maybe because he's so busy talking. He tells stories about artists that died a long time ago like Vango who was poor and nobody appreciated him so he cut off his ear and now he's dead and doesn't even know he's famous.

Mr. Finkelstein listens to my stories, too, the ones I see on test-pattern TV. He's the only person who believes me even though when I tried to turn on my show for him the other day, it was like when I tried to show Molly. He couldn't see anything either.

But he doesn't think I make it all up like Mom and Dad do. Mr. Finkelstein asks me questions and wants to know what I think about things. Nobody else really cares what I think. Sometimes when I tell him stuff, he purses up his very red lips, smooths down his beard with his thumb, nods his head, and goes, "Hmmmm," like he understands.

He wants to know more about that famous artist that got shot but not killed, Andy Warhol. What do his paintings look like? he wants to know. I tell him about the paintings they showed on test-pattern TV, grocery-store things like Campbell's soup and Brillo. And what does *he* look like? asks Mr. Finkelstein. I said he's funny-looking, real white skin and glasses. Mr. Finkelstein nods his head and says, "So he's really famous, eh? Who would have guessed it?"

And he doesn't say I made it up when I tell him about the polio vaccination that you can eat. He says, "Well, I read about this new vaccine that was just developed, but it's a shot, not a snack."

"No, no," I say. "They put it on a sugar cube, and you just suck on it."

He gives me a look, pets his beard, and smiles. "Whatever you say," he says, but I'm not sure he believes me about that.

I don't care whether it's a shot or a sugar cube. I just want that vaccination so I don't wind up like Edgar, who lives over in the next court. He got polio and he's in an iron lung that breathes for him. All day long, he just lies there in this big metal tube. When Mom and I go to visit him all I can see is his little shriveled monkey face in the mirror overhead.

"See what happens when you swim in the water?" Mom says when we leave. "Now Edgar will always have to look at the world upside down and backward."

That's how I feel, like the world has turned upside down and backward. Mom and the mailman, Dad and work, the stuff on test-pattern TV—all whirling around me like the cyclone that picked up Dorothy's house and took her to Oz. In the end she woke up and everything was the way it used to be. I wish that would happen to me.

WITH MOM AND Dad fighting like they are, it's scary to be around them. It makes me think about this show I just saw on the test pattern, a courtroom show where this colored guy killed his wife and another man only he says he didn't do it. She was a white lady so I don't know if they were really married or not because I don't think that's allowed, but the lawyers said that sometimes he would beat her up so that meant he killed her.

Dad's never hit Mom but at dinner tonight he looked at her like he could. She looked right back at him so mean that it gave me goose bumps. For a minute, the way they looked at each other was like on some of my TV shows, where people don't just get mad, they get mad and then they shoot each other. On test-pattern TV, everybody has a gun.

Dad has a BB gun in the closet. He uses it to shoot tin cans down on the beach. Sometimes he lets me go with him to watch, shows me how to load the BBs and pour them into the chamber, but he never lets me shoot. He's good. Hits the cans almost every time, knocks them right off the fence.

You can kill people without a gun, like the guy who killed his wife. They said he did it with a knife. On TV shows like *Dragnet,* people are killed by all kinds of stuff—guns, knives, poison. Sometimes they're drowned or strangled or burned, but shooting seems to be the most popular.

There's more and more shooting on test-pattern TV lately, more and more blood. I liked it better when there were just fun shows, or weird stuff that made me wonder about things I don't know about. All this shooting is giving me bad dreams, dreams about Mom and Dad like the one I had last night:

Mom is dancing in nothing but those black panties and stockings and the mailman's hat, but she's dancing for Dad. He's in the bed, pointing his BB gun at her and making her dance, faster, faster, like in a cowboy movie where the bad guy shoots at the feet of the good guy and says, "Dance, you varmint." I don't know what a varmint is, but in my dream, that's what Dad says to Mom: "Dance, you varmint."

Today I'm watching the test pattern and I see something so spooky I forget how mad I am at Mom. "Hey, Mom," I yell, "remember the pretty lady that we saw get married last year in that fancy wedding?"

"What fancy wedding?" she calls from the kitchen.

"The one we saw on TV at Della's. Remember? She looked like a movie star and he was a senator and you said if you could've had a wedding gown when you got married, you'd have wanted one just like hers?"

"Yeah? So?"

"Well, her husband got killed! *Look.* She's got blood all over." Mom comes running in from the kitchen. "Now they're talking about how her husband's the president," I say, and then all of a sudden I realize, Boy, am I stupid. It must be a play, like on *Studio One.* President *Eisenhower* is the president.

Mom stares at the TV set and her face gets all red like somebody poured ketchup into it. "Are you watching the test pattern again?"

"It's just a play about this president who got shot."

"Nobody got shot. I don't know what I'm going to do with you, scaring me like that with the things you make up."

I scare *her*? What a joke.

22

L O R E N A

AYBE IF SHE makes a coffee cake. Isn't that what Mama Hansen did on the *Mama* show last night when all the Hansen kids were bickering? Made a coffee cake. Its cinnamon fragrance lured them into the cozy kitchen, one by one, until they were all chattering together around the Hansen table, their differences forgotten as they shared the still-warm cake. Lorena had watched Mama work her magic, and decides to pull the same trick.

Lorena rustles through the pantry shelves looking for ingredients. Flour, got that. Sugar. Eggs? Yep. Pete slammed out of the house this morning without breakfast, so there are enough eggs. Cinnamon, where's the cinnamon? It won't be coffee cake without cinnamon. She knocks over the spice rack in her growing frustration.

She'll make it all better with coffee cake, just like Mama Hansen did. Pete will realize she wants him back when he gets a whiff of her cinnamon kitchen, a taste of her crumbly cake. And Cassie will not only know the Binky thing is over, maybe, like magic, she'll never remember it happened.

Lorena wishes it never happened. She tries not to think about it but can't stop thinking about it, wonders Why hasn't Binky called? He could've called just to say I know it's over but I just wanted to tell you how much it meant to me. That would have been the gentlemanly thing to do.

She knows he's out there; he's made two deliveries since Thursday. She hears the mail spitting through the slot, so she knows he's on the other side of the door, shoving those letters through. Maybe she should call and say Hey. Just stay in touch, no reason they can't be friends. No reason she still can't meet Cousin Wally the talent scout.

She has to meet him. The possibility of that never happening makes her nostrils pop in fear. Somehow she has to *make* it happen. Binky is her last chance, her only chance. Binky . . . No, stop it, that's over. But maybe . . . damn. If only Cassie hadn't come home when she did . . .

Lorena doesn't answer the phone at first, doesn't hear it actually, is too far inside her head to hear anything. But the phone rings and rings until it jars her out of her reverie and she runs to answer it.

"Miz Palmer?" says an unfamiliar voice. "This is Dwayne, Pete's foreman. I got some bad news."

Lorena feels her innards drop through the soles of her feet. "What?" she whispers.

"Seems like Pete fell and broke hisself up a bit."

"Broke? What broke?"

"Oh, a leg. And a arm. Cracked his head a little, too."

"Oh God. Oh God. Is he okay?"

"Well, now, I don't know if okay is the word, seein' as how he's pretty smashed up and all. But," he adds cheerily, "he ain't dead."

"Where is he?"

"Ambylance took him over to Buxton Hospital."

Lorena's knees feel like they're held together with raw egg white. She sits down on the floor next to the phone. "What happened?"

"Don't rightly know, but to tell you the truth, he ain't been hisself lately. Seems like he's just plain pissed off at the world—excuse me, ma'am—or somethin' that's made him pretty careless. Had to talk to him a bit about that a few times already. But today he was just raving mad when he came to work, so when they told me he tripped and took a dive off the gantry I wadn't too surprised."

"Oh God." She hangs up the phone, puts her head down on her knees. Why would this happen now, just when she was repenting the Binky thing, just when Pete was looking good to her again? Was it because she was thinking about Wally right then? Is this some kind of punishment? Maybe this was a sign, a crossroad, a test.

She feels flooded with sudden saintliness. Yes! That's it. It's a test of her good intentions, a test she could pass by sacrificing her own dreams and ambition. She would renounce her talent, abstain from dancing, become the ideal wife and mother. Mama Hansen, the warm, dependable mother of all mothers, would become her model of domesticity.

LORENA'S BROUGHT BISCUITS to Pete in the hospital but he can't eat them. It scares her the way he looks, flat on his back, head swathed in bandages, left arm in a cast, left leg hanging in a sling from wires attached overhead.

She attempts cheerfulness. "Biscuits!" she chirps as she enters the room, Cassie following fearfully behind. He doesn't answer. His right eye, the one not covered by a bandage, blinks like an owl's, slow and wary.

The room is still and hot. A faint breeze hovers around the wide-open window, its sash propped up with a stick, but goes no farther. The sheets on Pete's bed are damp and rumpled. He looks like an oversized child in the gray-striped hospital gown tied high up on his neck. Lorena fusses with the sheets, arranges them awkwardly around his raised leg in its cast.

"Better?" she coos.

His good eye narrows, its blue glittering iridescently beneath the lid like an insect hiding from a predator. "Whad do you care?" he says, the words slurring from whatever drug they pumped into him.

She doesn't know what to say. Now, she figures, is not the time to get defensive, especially with Cassie glaring at her from the end of Pete's bed, caressing his foot that protrudes from the rumple of sheets.

"Hey, Dad," Cassie says, "the lookout toe is looking out."

His mouth twists into an attempted smile. He closes his eye.

"Well," Lorena says. "Well. Guess I'll just put these biscuits right over here until you feel like a little snack. Okay?"

He doesn't answer.

"Well." She plunks the biscuits in their brown paper bag on the night table. Her hair is plastered to her neck and there's a faint line of moisture above the painstakingly drawn cupid's bow of her lips. She has dressed carefully for this visit, light summer print dress, spectator pumps that Della says look smart. She wants to appear responsible. She wants Pete to trust her again.

Cassie stares at the toes peering out of the cast swinging overhead. "All your toes are okay, right, Dad?"

Pete nods, eye still closed. "Toes're okay. Rest of me's not." He shifts a little, grimaces, gives a painful groan. "Woulda been better if I got killed."

Cassie's stricken look is mirrored by Lorena. "No, no," Lorena protests. "You'll be home before you know it, good as new. It'll be like nothing ever happened. I'll take good care of you."

LORENA VISITS THE hospital every day, determinedly cheerful, brings baskets filled with biscuits, bologna sandwiches, Little

Debbie Cakes. She even smuggles in some Ballantine as a peace offering.

It's a long two weeks, being home alone with Cassie. School dwindles down to its last, lazy days and then ends. Cassie leaves the house early and returns late, stays often as not for dinner at Molly's. Both Cassie and Lorena avoid speaking of the Mailman Incident, although Cassie discovers she can alarm Lorena with the pointed use of certain words: Stamp. Envelope. Mail. Post office. She manages to invoke all of those words in one sentence by polishing off an entire jar of Ovaltine in two days in order to send off for a Captain Midnight Decoder Ring, thereby sending Lorena into a paroxysm of guilt by word association.

She jumps each time she hears the door slot slap open, spew mail on the floor, then snap shut again. She pictures Binky on the other side. She runs to the window to catch him but he's too quick, gone by the time she hears the mail come through. She knows Cassie hears it, too, so she tries to be nonchalant. Thumbs through the mail, leafs through *The Saturday Evening Post,* studies each page while Cassie studies her.

Lorena senses that Cassie is up at night watching the test pattern, but there are more important things to worry about now. So what if Cassie's like Lula? Lula never hurt anybody, lived a normal life, just had those little spells. Maybe people laughed at her, but it didn't bother Lula. She and Rudy were happy, married a long time, one died right after the other, couldn't live without each other. Goes to show, you can be crazy and happy, too.

Now Pete is home. He hobbles on crutches and delicately lowers himself onto the couch Lorena has made up into a bed in the living room. This is where he'll stay until he's able to get up the stairs. They can start all over, like nothing ever happened. She'll nurse him, she will, and he'll be his old self again. No. Not his old self. He'll be better. She'll make him better. Then she will be better, too.

To help him pass the time when there's nothing on TV, Lorena buys Pete a Revell hobby kit of the battleship *Missouri*. When she hands him the box, he sneers—"I build *real* ships, not models"— and the box sits by his bed for days. Well, there's $1.98 down the drain, Lorena thinks, until one morning she comes downstairs to find Pete painfully gluing tiny turrets and minuscule guns to the gray plastic hull of the model.

Pete concentrates, squinting as his good hand ekes a teardrop of glue from the tube onto the base of a delicate cannon or anchor, then, steadied by fingers that peek out from the cast on his injured arm, plants it precisely in place. The once-benign-looking ship grows into a prickly porcupine bristling with weapons aimed at an imaginary foe. When the battleship is complete, Pete places it next to his bed, where the light from the elephant lamp illuminates it like a hard-won trophy.

MMMM MMM GOOD. Mmmm mmm good. That's what Campbell's soup is, mmmm mmm good. Lorena hums to herself as she prepares Pete's lunch: chicken noodle soup. She heard it makes sick people well. She turns the key on the can opener. The Campbell Kids rotate slowly; the metal lid detaches jaggedly from the red-and-white can. She pours the golden goop into the white enamel pot, adds a can of water, ignites the gas flame with a *whup*, watches the pale noodles chase each other as she stirs the bubbly boiling soup.

She sets the tray up proper: flowered dish for the biscuits, paper napkin, big spoon, bottle of Nehi orange. She ladles piping-hot soup into a big bowl, then carefully balances the tray as she glides into the living room. "Mmmm mmm good," she sings as she sets the tray on the TV table next to Pete's bed.

"What's that?" He makes a face.

"Lunch."

"I know. But what's *that*?"

"Chicken soup."

"Soup? It must be a hundred degrees in here. Are you crazy?"

She isn't going to let him get to her. She pushes her mouth up into a simper. "Oh, come on. I'll feed you."

"I can feed myself." He grabs at the bowl.

"No, no, it's easier if I do it." She perches on the side of his bed, cradles the steaming soup bowl in one hand beneath his chin, scoops out a spoonful. "Yummy yummy for the tummy," she says, holding it to his mouth. Pete presses his lips together like a stubborn kid.

"Oh, come on," she snaps as the soup dribbles from the spoon down his chin. She mops at it with the napkin, tries again, forces a smile. "Open wide."

He gives in, opens wide. "AAAA! HOT!" he yowls, spraying her with a mouthful of noodles.

"Now look what you did." She dabs at her dress with the napkin, plucks a squirming noodle from the sheet. Count to ten. Start again. "I'll blow on it first." She dips the spoon back into the bowl, daintily puffs on its surface.

"I don't want any—" he begins, edging away from her.

SLAP. The mail slot opens and *kshwssss* regurgitates an avalanche of letters before smacking shut. Startled by the sound and a sudden vision of Binky on the other side of the door, Lorena leaps from her chair, catapulting the bowl of soup from her hands.

"AIEEEE!" Pete screams as scalding chicken soup rains down on him like a monsoon from hell. "Are you trying to kill me?"

Cassie stampedes down the stairs from her room. "What happened? What happened?"

"Ice. I'll get ice." Lorena dashes into the kitchen and wrestles cubes from the ice tray into a bowl. She almost trips over Cassie, who is blocking her way back into the living room.

"No!" Cassie yells. "Keep away from him. If you don't, I'll . . . I'll call the police."

Lorena shoves her way past Cassie. Ignoring Pete's protests, she rubs ice cubes over his burned face and arm, mashing noodles beneath the rapidly melting cubes in her frenzy.

"Look what you did!" Pete pokes at the cast, which has turned to mush where the soup soaked in. The sheets are soggy with soup, sloppy with noodles, several of which are wiggling through Pete's curly black hair. The room smells like chicken.

Cassie watches the cleanup from the stairs, pressing her forehead against the banister railing until two vertical lines are imprinted on the skin. Lorena glances furtively at her as she helps Pete to a chair and changes the sheet on his bed. She doesn't speak. Neither does Pete, aside from an occasional moan when he shifts his weight in the chair.

He is shiny with the butter Lorena smears onto the burned areas, basting him like a turkey. His face gleams in the afternoon sunlight. Now and then he nods when Cassie asks at intervals, "You okay, Dad?" He doesn't look at Lorena as she wipes up noodles from the rug on her hands and knees.

The cleanup is complete. Pete is propped up on the couch, glaring at *The Brighter Day,* which Lorena has turned on despite his protests. She sticks a straw into a Ballantine and hands it to him, then clumps upstairs to fling herself on the bed.

Suddenly overcome by an image of herself and Binky lying on this very spot in happier days—limbs entwined, bra unsnapped, stockings degartered and unrolled—Lorena breaks into sobs she muffles with her pillow. She tries to conjure up the comforting figure of Mama Hansen, but all she gets is a naked, hat-free Binky. Exhausted by the effort to think good thoughts, she gives in and allows Binky to dominate her fantasy. At its heaving, breathless conclusion, she falls into a deep and dreamless sleep. All this penance is wearing her out.

23

MOM TRIED TO kill Dad. Death by soup. It's like on test-pattern TV where people kill their husbands or wives so they can do sex with somebody else. I asked Molly if maybe I should warn Dad or tell the police even if it meant telling on my own mother. But Mr. Finkelstein heard me and said, "No, don't do that. Accidents happen. If you say something, it'll just upset your mom and dad." I bet anything Mr. Finkelstein would feel different if I told him about the mailman thing. I bet he would help me rescue Dad.

Maybe Mr. Finkelstein is right. Maybe Dad doesn't need saving, maybe it was just an accident. Still, I can't help myself, I have this weird feeling like something bad's going to happen to him unless I do something. And then it would all be my fault.

Sometimes I dream that I'm flying. Faster than a speeding bullet, more powerful than a locomotive, able to leap tall buildings in a single bound. People see me and say, "Look—up in the sky!

It's a bird, it's a plane, it's *Cassie Palmer*." In my dream I have a cape and I fly around and rescue people.

I don't think you really need a cape to do that because Wonder Woman doesn't have one, but she does have those big cuffs on her arms that bounce bullets off. I guess you have to wear something unusual like a cape or cuffs if you want to be a hero, or else you just look like anybody else. If you're not dressed right, people might not let you save them.

DAD'S LYING ON his bed in the living room, so we watch TV until he falls asleep. Usually that doesn't happen until *What's My Line* or *Your Hit Parade,* but tonight right in the middle of *Our Miss Brooks,* one of my favorite, favorite shows, I hear Dad snore.

"Bedtime," Mom announces.

"Why? It's *summer*." I hear the kids outside playing hide-and-seek in the court, Ginny Sue squealing like she does when she gets caught. "Well, can I go out and play?"

Mom looks down at her hands, studies them with this worried look like she just grew extra fingers. "I thought this might be a good time for a little mother-daughter chat."

Uh-oh.

"Why don't you go upstairs and put on your jammies," she says. *Jammies?* She hasn't said "jammies" since I was six. "And then," she adds, "we can get all cozy and talk."

Oh boy. I can't wait. Mom's idea of a cozy talk is like the time she handed me the book on menstruation, a box of Junior Kotex and what she called a sanitary belt, and said if I had any questions, just ask her. So I did. I held up the belt and asked, "How does this work?" and she said, "I'll explain when you need it." If it wasn't for Molly, I'd still be waiting for an answer.

So I go upstairs and put on my pajamas and brush my teeth and when I come out of the bathroom there's Mom, sitting on the edge of my bed, studying those extra fingers again.

She gives a little cough, like she's going to give a speech. And then she does: "I just want you to know that things will be different from now on." She doesn't look at me, starts picking at a hangnail. "Sometimes people make mistakes. But that doesn't mean they're bad people. Or that they're not sorry about what they did."

I don't say anything. She goes on: "So what you have to do, when that happens, is kind of . . . forget the bad things and remember the good things. Forgive and forget. That's what you have to do." And then she looks at me, her eyes all fluttery and damp.

Why doesn't she just say it? Say, "I was doing sex with the mailman and you caught me and now I'm scared you're going to tell." I almost blurt that out, but then I think, What if she really means it? Maybe she's not just faking. Maybe she really is sorry. Maybe all her taking care of Dad is for real and we can just go back to being a regular family. I almost forget what that was like, being regular, not thinking about stuff like mailmen and hospitals, just being like we were before, Mom and me talking without crying, and Dad when he used to laugh.

So what I say is, "Well-l-l, okay. Long as you don't try to hurt Dad again."

"What?" she squeaks.

"Yeah. Don't burn him with soup. Or think about other ways to get rid of him."

"Where did you get *that* from?" She's standing up now, the old Mom again, frazzled as ever. "What gets into your head? I swear, you *are* just as crazy as Lula." And she stomps back downstairs.

I'm as crazy as Lula? How crazy is that? I don't remember Aunt Lula, all I know is the stories about her, how she made up things, saw things that weren't really there.

Well, I'm *not* like Lula. I know the things I see are real.

But then I wonder: Did Lula think so, too?

*   *   *

I WAKE UP with the moon in my face. It's full and fat outside my window and lights up the whole outdoors. Long shadows stretch like goblin fingers over grass as white and silent as snow. It's late, so late that the crickets have stopped singing.

Mom's asleep. Her door is closed. There's no light underneath, so I know she's not up. I slide off my bed and feel the cool wood floor under my feet as I tiptoe down the stairs, cringing at each creak.

Dad is snoring away on his living-room bed. I turn on the test pattern but it doesn't wake him up like I hope it will. If he wakes up, I'll make him watch till he sees the shows I tried to tell him about. Then he'll know that I'm not crazy like Lula.

The test pattern is sharp and crisp in black-and-white, starts to spin like a pinwheel, and then, like always, it fades. The lines blur, it gets all fuzzy, and I get that tingly pins-and-needles feeling. I tried to explain the feeling once to Mr. Finkelstein but I couldn't describe it. It's like I know something is about to happen, something that I never saw before.

Tonight what comes on is a foot. A foot in a boot, a fat, funny-looking boot stepping on ground that's covered in powder. Then the man whose boot it is says, "That's one small step for man," only his steps aren't little, they're boingy giant steps, like he's jumping on a trampoline. He's dressed like a spaceman with a big bubble helmet, just like another man who climbs out the door of their rocket ship. They both boing around in this desert-looking place, then they stick a flag in it.

I've seen lots of rocket ships on test-pattern TV. They're much better than that dinky Polaris on *Tom Corbett, Space Cadet* on regular TV. The best is this neat rocket ship called the *Enterprise*, which has girl space cadets, too. One of the crew is from another planet. You can tell because he's got pointy ears which the regular guys on the ship don't even seem to notice.

I wanted to be a space cadet until I saw this rocket that took off like the others but then it made a big puffy Y in the sky and crashed. That's when I changed my mind about wanting to travel to the stars.

But these guys that I'm looking at are really up there somewhere, boinging around, looking at the constellations up close. I know Dad would like this because he knows so much about the stars.

"Whazzat?" It's Dad. His voice is all slurry because he just woke up. He looks at me like he's not sure I'm really here.

"Look, Dad," I say, pointing to the guys who are still boinging around. "Spacemen. Just like Tom Corbett, only better, realer."

"Wha?" He leans on his good elbow, squints at the TV.

"Spacemen, Dad. Up in the stars!"

"Turn that thing off," he grumbles, flopping back on his pillow. "Wakin' me up with that damn test pattern, that's all I need."

"You never believe anything I say." I'm so mad. So mad I add, "I bet you wouldn't believe me if I told you why Mom tried to kill you."

"You've been watching too much TV."

"But, Dad . . ."

He gets all red, reaches down, and throws his bedroom slipper at the TV screen. "*Turn it off.* And get your butt up to bed!"

I snap off the TV and go upstairs. I wish I had Molly's parents. They listen to her. I even heard Mrs. Finkelstein tell Molly she loved her. When I told Molly nobody ever told me that, she said, Well, you know they love you because that's what parents do. I said that *being* loved isn't the same as *feeling* loved, but I don't think she understood.

I get in bed and study the ceiling. It looks like the powdery ground the spaceman's boot stepped on. If I look real hard, I can even see footprints.

24

L O R E N A

PETE IS SITTING up, parked under a TV tray in the stifling living room. A fan whines fretfully as it swivels in a corner. Summer explodes in bright sunshine outside, but inside it's clammy and dark. Pete has refused to go outdoors since a neighbor innocently asked him how he happened to fall. His entertainment is limited to radio, television, and meals, the most recent of which Lorena is placing before him.

"What's this?" He pokes a finger into the intestinal entanglement slithering over the sides of a soup bowl.

"Chef Boyardee." Lorena is all smiles as she tucks a paper napkin under his chin.

"Looks like guts." He rips the napkin away, balls it up. "I like sandwiches for lunch. You know that." His chin is rumpled in a pout.

Lorena bites her lip, holds her breath. Waits for him to mention chicken noodle soup. He doesn't, so she ventures, "I thought we'd try something different." She offers him a hesitant smile.

She doesn't want to spoil her mood. She just got back from Maybelle's and her new hairdo has given her a new outlook. The sedate style reflects her desire to emulate the serene maturity of Mama Hansen. Lorena willingly credits Maybelle for her transformation.

"Hon," Maybelle had said as she snipped away the last wilted spiral of the poodle cut until all that was left was a skull-hugging cap of hair the color of Ovaltine, "I unnerstand how you feel, with your hubby home alla the time now. You gotta get practical. What with emptying pee bottles and all, you don't wanna have to fuss with your hair." She flattened Lorena's bangs in a C-shape that stuck to her forehead, then whipped off the plastic cape, scattering clipped wisps of curls across the green linoleum floor. "Now," she pronounced, "you look serious."

Good-bye Mitzi Gaynor. Hello Margaret Truman.

But Pete hasn't noticed her new hairdo. His focus is on lunch. "I'm dripping with sweat and she's feeding me spaghetti," he mutters as he prods the congealed clump of noodles with his fork. "Don't you have any bologna?" he calls out to Lorena, who is already on the kitchen phone, dialing up Della to report on her new haircut.

"I threw it out," she calls back. "It was turning blue. Oh, hi, Della," she says into the phone. "It's the new Me."

"Blue?" he yells. "Why do we have blue bologna?"

"Wait a sec," she says to Della. She puts her hand over the mouthpiece, yells to Pete, "We don't. I threw it out." Back to Della. "It's real chic, very . . . serious. You know. Like Mama Hansen."

"GET. ME. SOME. REAL. FOOD!" Pete bellows.

Lorena puts a hand over her outside ear so she can hear Della. "*Roman Holiday*? I'm dying to see it, sure, I can get away. Cassie can watch Pete for a couple of hours. I'm not in prison, for God's sake. Although"—her voice recedes to a whisper—"it sure feels like it sometimes."

"Lorena!"

"Be right there, sweetheart," she warbles. To Della, "See what I mean? But this, too, shall—"

"*Goddammit,*" she hears, followed by a crash.

"Callyaback." She throws the phone back on its hook, runs into the living room.

A wriggling glob of spaghetti is stuck to the wall over the TV. Shards of tomato-speckled bowl are scattered beneath it like blood offerings. Pete's face is as twisted as a wrung-out rag, his throwing arm, still bandaged from the soup burn, extended in a follow-through. "I said," he says, his voice low and threatening, "to get me some real food."

"Look what you did!"

"If you'd get offa the phone with that dingbat and fix me a decent lunch, you wouldn'ta made me do that."

"*I* made *you?*"

"Yeah. You're making me goddamn nuts."

"I'm making *you* nuts? You're making *me* nuts." Lorena flaps her arms up and down like a bird with clipped wings. "I fix you bacon and eggs. You complain the eggs are scrambled not fried. I turn the TV on and you want it off. I turn it off and you want it on. The room's too hot. Your sponge bath is too cold. Nothing I do makes you happy." Her voice breaks into a sob. "I even cut my hair for you."

"Is that what happened to your head?"

"What do you mean?"

"I thought it just got smaller."

Lorena stares at Pete for a mute moment, then, "Cassie!" she calls upstairs until Cassie's pale face peers down at them.

"What?"

"I'm going to the movies. Watch your dad until I get back." Lorena stomps up the steps, turning before she reaches the top. "Oh. And please clean up the mess he made. Because I won't."

When Lorena marches downstairs several minutes later, Cassie is on her hands and knees, picking up the pieces while Pete watches, looking contrite. Lorena notes with satisfaction that this is how Mama Hansen would have handled such a situation, and she smooths down her new brown bangs as she closes the door behind her.

"I LIKE IT. It makes you look like Audrey Hepburn."

"Yeah?" Lorena turns her head from side to side, studying her reflection in the ladies'-room mirror of the Paramount. "I have to get used to brown again." She wets the bangs and forces them back into the comma curve over her forehead, but they flip up stiffly, stubborn as a coxcomb. "Pete says it makes me look like I have a little head."

"Pete. Pete. You've turned into a doormat for Pete." Della pulls a big brush through her brash tangle of curls, reaches under her sweater to shake her breasts back into their Playtex cones. "Farley treated me like I was his personal slave, always 'do this, do that' until one day I said 'Farley, I was not put on this earth to clip your toenails.' Stopped *that* right then and there."

Lorena gives her lips, worn bare from the continuous ingestion of buttered popcorn during the movie, a quick swipe of lipstick. "Well, what can I do? He needs me, now that he's on crutches and all. I think when he understands how much I'm trying to make things better, he'll come around." Lorena gives her bangs one more futile pressing with the palm of her hand, sighs when they levitate, turns her back on her reflection. "All I want is for things to go back to . . . well . . . the way they were before Binky."

"Really?" Della raises a penciled eyebrow.

"Binky was a mistake," Lorena answers, even though life before Binky seems in retrospect drab and gray, empty pages in her mental scrapbook. "Seems like everything I do is a mistake lately. Spilling hot soup on Pete, losing out to that blonde in the audition, that business with Max in Pete's bathrobe."

"You're like Lucy," Della agrees. "Everything you plan goes haywire."

"Yeah. Except when it happens to Lucy, it's funny. I don't feel funny. I feel like a Lucy gone bad." Lorena lifts her chin, sets her mouth into a line of resolve. "Things will be different from now on. I'm a changed woman."

"Well," Della says, "I got to tell you something. I'm glad to hear that. Because of Cassie." She hesitates. "I been thinking a lot about Cassie since, you know, the Binky thing. Worrying about her, you know? 'Cause she's kinda, like, the kid I'll never have. So when you told me about Cassie catching you and Binky, I thought, How could Lorena be so—I guess the word is—dumb? To do it in your *house*. But you seemed so upset about it that I didn't say anything."

Lorena looks stricken. "I thought she was at her dance lesson." Which reminds her. "I haven't even practiced my routine once since Pete's accident. Here I am, putting off my career so I can do what's right, take care of my family and all." Her face sags in mournful acceptance.

"Well," Della says with a shrug, "it's all water under the bridge now. Nothing you can do but what you're doing."

"Then Cassie goes and accuses me of something just so awful I can barely say the words." Lorena puts her hand over her mouth in a tragic gesture before she does say the words: "She thinks I tried to kill Pete. The soup thing was an accident, for God's sake. I heard the mail slap through the slot and—well, it just makes me jump a foot every time that happens. Does she think I burned him on purpose? Where does she get these crazy ideas? I tell you, I'm worried about her."

"I got to give you credit. You're doing your best."

"All's I want now is to be a good wife." Lorena gives her mirrored image a last forlorn glance and jerks back, startled. For just a moment, she saw, not herself, but her mother gazing back at her, speaking the words she had heard so often as a girl: "You want a husband? You better learn to be a wife."

Well, she *had* learned all the wifely things. How to poke out an eye of a potato with one flick of the knife. How to pluck every last pinfeather from a just-killed chicken. How to make a bed with hospital corners, tucked so tight that your feet beneath the sheet felt as bound as a Chinese woman's.

She learned to scrub the ring around a collar. Dust the tops of moldings. Save string, iron around buttons, crochet doilies for chairs. And it worked. She snagged Pete. So then she mastered picking up socks and rolling out biscuits and how to make the best fried chicken in town.

That's *it,* Lorena thinks, fluttering her fingers in farewell to Della as they part ways at the Paramount. Fried chicken! She pictures herself serving it to her family gathered like the Hansens around a real table, not perched at TV trays. In her fantasy, Lorena, wearing a lace-edged apron, smiles prettily as Cassie and Pete beam with forgiveness at the sight of chicken so light and crispy it almost floats above the platter. Inspired, Lorena heads for the A&P.

She sails past the frozen food without a glance, then docks herself in front of the refrigerated glass case of the meat department. She gazes lovingly at a row of butter-colored chickens, their shapely drumsticks symmetrically poised in a June Taylor–like cancan. Admiring their perfect choreography, she hails the butcher like a long-lost friend.

"Long time no see," he says, drawing a slim curved knife against the sharpener with infinite precision.

"I'm back," she says brightly. "Can you cut me up a fryer?"

"With the greatest pleasure." His pallid, lavender-veined hand crawls into the glass case and fondles the contours of each bird in turn. His fingers close over a particularly plump specimen. He separates it from the chorus line in one swoop, then displays it between his palms for Lorena's inspection.

"Beautiful," she breathes. With minimal swordplay, the butcher deftly partitions the poultry. Tucking in a couple of extra livers, he snugly wraps all the parts in a crackling sheet of paper. "Come back soon," he croons as he presents the package to Lorena.

When Lorena gets home Pete is asleep, slumped over in his chair. Cassie is watching the test pattern. Folded on the floor in front of the TV, her chin resting on her knees, she barely looks up. Lorena opens the door, stares blindly ahead, and, blinking, takes in the scene as her eyes become accustomed to the dark.

Pete is snoring softly, his legs splayed apart on the footrest. His casted arm and leg flop heavily to one side and his hair spirals in damp whorls across his forehead. "How long has he been sleeping?" Lorena asks Cassie, who pretends that she doesn't hear her. "What are you watching?" she persists, not really expecting an answer.

"Nothing you'd like," Cassie answers, surprising her.

Lorena is wary. "You want to tell me about it?"

"It's a cartoon."

"Cartoon," Lorena repeats. She squints at the screen. Maybe if you look at it a certain way, you can see something besides the black-and-white circle, the geometric cross-hatching of lines, the mysterious numbers and letters of the test pattern. "What kind of cartoon?"

"About a family. The mother has blue hair."

"Blue? Where do you see blue?"

"Bart is one of the kids," she says, ignoring Lorena. "I like him the best. His sister's okay, but he's funnier."

"Oh." Lorena doesn't know what else to say.

"YOU KNOW I hate fruit in my Jell-O." Cassie spits a grape into the growing pile of fruit cocktail she's discarded into her dish. "Especially grapes. It's like eating eyeballs."

Dinner, silently served and eaten in front of the TV, is over in a fraction of the time it took for Lorena to prepare and fry the chicken; roll out, cut, and bake the biscuits; mash the potatoes, snap the beans, make the Jell-O.

"The Honeymooners" sketch is on *The Jackie Gleason Show*.

Lorena focuses on Ralph and Alice's final clinch as Ralph con-
cedes, as he does every week after being forgiven by Alice for
screwing up, "Baby, you're the greatest."

Just once, Lorena thinks, I'd like to hear that: "Baby, you're
the greatest." Ralph Kramden's bus driver's uniform reminds her
of Binky's postman's uniform. She shoots a furtive glance over at
Pete, but he is concentrating on the TV, which bathes him in blue-
gray splashes of light. The shade is up and the window, raised to
allow a feeble breeze to wander over the windowsill, frames a
raucous game of kick-the-can taking place in the limpid twilight
of the court outside. For once, Pete isn't complaining about the
noise.

"Oh, yuk. I hate cherries." Cassie noisily spits a bright red
chunk into her dish. "Why can't you make just plain old strawberry Jell-O without all this stuff in it?"

"Because I like it that way." Pete's voice, gruff yet hesitant,
startles both Cassie and Lorena. They swivel their heads away
from the clinching Kramdens to stare at Pete. He jacks himself up
with his good arm and looks over at Cassie. "You don't like the
Jell-O, don't eat it. I'm tired of your moaning and groaning."

Cassie's eyes grow big with tears. "But—"

"Go outside and play," he interrupts, even though it's getting
dark. She leaves the dish on the floor where she was sitting, jumps
up, and bangs the screen door behind her as she runs outside,
wiping her eyes on the sleeves of her shirt.

Lorena doesn't know what's coming next, so she clutches her
empty Jell-O dish in her lap and waits, stiffly poised. She stares
at the TV screen, now alive with singing gas-station attendants.

Pete clears his throat, once, twice. "Pretty good chicken," he
says.

"Thank you," she says.

"Nice beans."

She nods.

"Biscuits. Big and puffy."

She waits.

That's it. It was a painful apology, but there it was. All her efforts, all her suffering, all her sacrifice had succeeded. They had made up.

That done, they turn their attention to *Your Show of Shows.* Pete snorts, his version of a laugh, as Sid Caesar and Imogene Coca as the Hickenloopers entangle themselves once again in domestic confusion. Lorena forces a lethargic grin, more in reaction to Pete's new good humor than because she finds the skit funny, for she sees herself and Pete in the loopily mismatched Hickenloopers.

What is the matter with her? Isn't this cozy hearthside scene—she and Pete and the TV set—exactly what she says she wants? Shouldn't she be celebrating? Why does she feel that this sweet domestic confection she worked so hard to create is as hollow as the hole in a doughnut?

A sudden swirl of dancers spins onto the screen, kicking high in a lavish production number. Their energy pops Lorena out of her seat as if she's been zapped by lightning. The throbbing rhythm pulsates through her veins, awakens her from her stupor. Like Frankenstein's monster, she comes to life. Ten fingers tappety-tap on the cushions of the sofa. Ten toes test the confines of her shoes. The compulsion is beyond her control, writhing like an incubus whose only escape is through her fingers and toes.

She's gotta dance. Gotta dance. *Gotta dance!*

25

C A S S I E

THE THING I like about Bart Simpson is that he's real even though he's a cartoon, which you don't see much on regular TV. Mostly there are goody-goody puppets like Rootie Kazootie or Gala Poochie Pup or Kukla, Fran, and Ollie. What makes Bart real is that he's always in trouble. What's not real is his family seems to be normal.

Sometimes Mom and Dad act nearly normal and talk to each other like regular people. Dad even said he was sorry he got mad about the Jell-O thing the other night. I can't remember when he's ever said he was sorry to me. And Mom's cooking again, real food, not TV food. It's almost like nothing ever happened, as if the past couple of months were just a bad dream.

Tonight we're watching Dean Martin and Jerry Lewis and it's like it was Before, Mom and Dad and me watching together with nobody mad. I can do a great Jerry Lewis, Molly says so. She even called her dad to watch me the other day, so I crossed my eyes and bent my ankles in so I could walk funny like Jerry does, and said "Hey, De-e-ean!" through my nose. Mr. Finkelstein laughed his big beardy laugh and told me I should go on TV. But tonight when I try to show Mom and Dad my imitation, they just tell me to sit down.

"Well, Mr. Finkelstein thought my Jerry imitation was great," I say.

Mom doesn't say anything. Dad says, "Keep away from that Commie." And then they don't talk for a while but I can tell that what I said made them mad. I don't know why, but they still don't like Mr. Finkelstein.

Now I'm sorry I mentioned his name because when I did, Dad moved away from Mom. Now he's scrunched into his corner of the couch and Mom is staring straight ahead, her eyes white and shining from the reflection of the TV. I feel like it's all my fault they're mad again. I wish I could take those words "Mr. Finkelstein" back, but I guess this normal time with Mom and Dad wouldn't have lasted anyway. It's not like it was so great to begin with.

Great would be like *The Life of Riley*. I wish Dad was like Riley. Instead of getting mad over every little thing, he'd just say, "What a revoltin' development *this* is," and we'd laugh and it would be over. But that would be too normal, and nothing's ever normal around here.

IT'S TIME FOR *Your Hit Parade,* which I never miss since I got Snooky Lanson's autograph. I feel like Snooky is my secret pal. Even though he's gray and black and white on the screen, I know his skin is patchy and pink, he has hair like hay and eyes as blue as stationery. "To Cassie. Best regards, Snooky Lanson," he wrote on my napkin. I look over at it in its frame and wish again that Mom had had a pen that day instead of a pencil.

Mom and Dad are watching, too. Snooky is singing the number-three song, "Hey There." Mom says she wonders if that lady in the big hat we saw with him was his wife or his girlfriend and Dad says They all have girlfriends. After that, Mom and Dad don't say anything. "Hey, there," Snooky sings, "You with the stars in your eyes." Mom sings along with him, real soft.

The big dance number for "Sh-Boom" comes on. Mom leans forward in her chair and studies every move the dancers are making like she's going to take a test on it. When it's over and the commercial comes on, she goes upstairs, I guess to the bathroom, but she's still upstairs when the show starts again.

Then, right in the middle of Gisele MacKenzie singing "Little Things Mean a Lot," I hear on the ceiling above us where Mom and Dad's bedroom is: *Tappety. Tappety. Tap tap tap.*

Then I hear ". . . shovel all the coal in, gotta keep it rollin' . . ." *oh no,* ". . . woo woo Chattanooga, there you are."

"I hate that," I wail, and put my hands over my ears.

"I thought she quit that dance-routine stuff," says Dad. He stares at the ceiling, his bottom lip twisting around like he's really annoyed.

But I'm not just annoyed. I really *hate* it and I can't tell Dad why, not just because he won't believe me, but because I've been thinking about all the bad things that could happen if he *did* believe me, scary things like I see on the test pattern. And then I think, if those things ever happened, it really would all be my fault for telling. I turn the volume up real loud to make Gisele MacKenzie louder than Mom's tapping to that awful song but I hear it anyway, Chattanooga choo choo, *tappety tappety* on the ceiling over our heads, reminding me of the mailman and that terrible day that's stuck in my brain like a scary TV show.

SUMMER BAKES THE morning like a biscuit, warm and buttery with sunshine. Molly straddles her bike on the sidewalk in front of my porch. "Let's have a picnic in the woods," she says. I see a crumpled brown paper bag in her bike's basket. I smell corned beef and pickles.

"I can't," I say. "It's too far."

"Too far? It's ten minutes from here. Big fat deal."

"I can't ride in the street. I'm not allowed."

"You're eleven now. What do they think you are, a big baby?"

Yeah. What do they think I am? I glance behind me at Dad dozing off on the couch, shush Molly with a finger to my lips. "Wait a sec," I whisper, and go into the kitchen to quick slap together a peanut-butter sandwich and tuck it under my shirt. I holler upstairs, "I'm going out."

"Where?" Mom peers down at me from the top of the stairs, pink shower cap on her head, towel wrapped around her.

"Out."

"What are you going to do?"

"Ridemybike," I mumble.

"Where?"

"Just around."

"Well," she says, giving me her frowny face. "Okay. Long as you don't ride in the street."

I'M RIDING IN the street. Packed gravel sprays beneath my wheels. I feel Mom's eyes on my back even though I'm blocks away by now. She's here. She's sitting on my shoulder, riding in my basket. She has spies. Their eyes follow me as I pedal fast. They phone her as I pass their houses. They report, "Now she's riding down Ferguson Avenue. Now she's turning onto Sixteenth Street. She's *riding in the street.*"

Molly pedals next to me, talking about boys like this is just another day. I can't talk. I'm too busy looking. Is that Della's car in front of us? I just know that's Della looking at me through her rearview mirror, hurrying home to call Mom and tell her I'm riding in the street.

"Hey, we're here, and you're still alive," Molly says, smart-alecky. We're in the woods not far from our house. It's cool and green with trees all around us that whisper and shush like secrets told in the dark. We drop our bikes, sink down on our butts in the damp grass. I reach in my shirt for my sandwich, now glued to my stomach with sweat and peanut butter. I peel it off, munch it, look around for spies.

"This is great," says Molly. She clamps her bunny teeth over her sandwich, corned beef on rye with the crusts cut off. "I love summer vacation, sitting around, going to the pool, looking at boys." She tells me how Harold kissed her in the cloakroom on the last day of school, how she could feel his braces through her lips, how she peeked and saw him peeking and how his eyes looked big and crossed like an owl's.

I'm lying on my back on the ground listening to the buzzing noises in the grass, feeling sleepy, thinking No one's ever kissed me, not on purpose, unless you count Spin the Bottle where if you got lucky you got to kiss somebody like Harold but no, when it was my turn the bottle spun right at Percy Perkins with a big white pimple on his chin . . .

Yikes. What time is it? I jump up, brush off the grass, give Molly a nudge. "I gotta go."

Molly stares at me. "We just got here."

"My mom's going to kill me if she finds out I rode this far. Come on." I pull my bike up and brush off bits of grass.

"Why?" asks Molly, leaning back. "*I* don't have to be anywhere."

"Well, thanks a lot," I yell as I jump on my bike and pedal away. Up the street that leads from the woods, down Sixteenth Street, up Ferguson Avenue. My neck aches from swiveling back, down, around, looking for spies. Mom is heavy on my handlebars, she weighs down my shoulders, she crouches in my basket. I pedal faster, faster, faster.

A sudden spray of gravel peppers my legs as something big and fast whizzes by me. A car! It's a car! She was right! I lose control of the handlebars and the bike wobbles and rears up like a horse and I hear a crash and I'm flat on the street. The car travels on in the distance, a tiny green speck that turns the corner and is gone. It didn't hit me; it didn't even know that it had sent me off in a spin. I sprawl beneath my bike.

Nothing is broken because I can wiggle my elbow and my knee, although they're all scruffed and scraped. There is blood. There are pieces of gravel in my skin. I pick them out carefully. And then I check my bike.

Its shiny blue paint is chipped and scarred. One fender is bashed. Both wheels are bent. Its handlebars reach out like they're calling for help, and I know that I have killed it. Crying, more for my bike than myself, I limp toward home, dragging my wounded bike with me, hoping I can sneak inside without Mom seeing me.

Oh, no. There she is, outside, all dressed up on her way somewhere.

"What happened to you?" she asks.

"I fell."

"Are you okay?" She looks worried, leans over and examines my elbow. I grab it back.

"I'm fine," I lie, standing in front of my bike so she can't see that it's all bent up. "I just fell. Why do you make such a big deal out of everything?"

But it is a big deal. I'm all banged up and my bike is dead. If I weren't scared she'd find out I rode my bike in the street, what I really would want is for Mom to make everything better like she'd do when I was little, to say "poor baby," to carry me inside, clean me off, and kiss away my hurts. She'd put me in my soft granny gown, give me cocoa in my bunny mug, and read me my favorite part from *The Wizard of Oz*—the part where everybody falls asleep in the field of poppies—until I fell asleep.

But instead she throws her hands up in the air and says, "Okay, okay, so it's no big deal." She turns and walks fast up the sidewalk, muttering, "This is all I need when I'm late for Maybelle's funeral."

I hold my elbow and watch her go. Sometimes I wish I was still little.

26

LORENA

YOU KNOW SHE would have hated the way they did her hair—just *hated* it," Della says, checking her mascara in the rearview mirror as she edges the Nash into the procession from the Bide-a-Wee Funeral Home to the cemetery. The squat green car bolts as she shifts into second, cutting off the family of the deceased and almost ramming the hearse. Lorena catches a glimpse of Maybelle's gardenia-smothered coffin, pictures Maybelle's sturdy little body lying within, tiny hands folded in repose over her bosom.

"Spit curls," Lorena agrees. "The woman never wore a spit curl in her life and her forehead was just crawling with those things."

"And that dress—all those frilly ruffles." Della shakes her head. "I tell you, orange is not her color. Jeez Louise, if she had known how she would look at her last social appearance, why, I think she'd still be alive today, she'd be so mortified."

Lorena thinks that if death could be defied by simple mortification, she might live to be a hundred, but all she says is, "She

looked like Carmen Miranda, for God's sake. Give her a couple
of bananas and a pineapple and she would have rhumba'd right
out of that coffin." The Nash lurches as Della downshifts to avoid
hitting the hearse as it approaches the cemetery gate.

Multihued heads gather about the gravesite, some freshly
permed and colored, others obviously overdue for Maybelle's
services, which, due to her demise, will no longer be available.
The faces beneath the hairdos are deeply grieved, for Maybelle
was considered The Best Around, and the mourners mourn not
only for the sudden and tragic loss of Maybelle but for the future
of their coiffures.

Lorena is no exception, and she is beset with anxiety. What
will she do without Maybelle? Maybelle was the Freud of beau-
ticians, her pink plastic chair a couch for sharing secrets and spinning dreams. Each experiment with color and style that Maybelle
encouraged was a reflection of Lorena's inner life. Her hair would
never be so deeply understood.

And Maybelle was an inspiration. She was independent, bold,
opinionated. Lorena pictures Maybelle, chunky arms crossed over
her partridge bosom as she admonished in a voice as sharp as the
tips of her scissors: "Get outta the kitchen, you dumbbells, y'all
got better things to do in life. I got my byooty parler, I got my
own business, what do I need a man to tell me what to do?"

She had dreams of her own, Maybelle did. She shared them
with Lorena as she snipped and curled and colored. She planned
to move to a bigger, newer place, a place with mirrors all around
and chairs that not only spun but went up and down. She'd hire
somebody else to help her. Maybe she'd even have a Coke machine. Yes, Maybelle had dreams.

But Maybelle never dreamed that all her dreams would vanish
on her day off, a sunny Monday in July. How could she know
that she would cross paths with a pickup truck loaded with chickens on the way to market just as she was headed to Nachman's
Big Summer Sale? How could she guess fate would decree that
she would pull into the intersection of Jefferson and Mercury at

exactly ten thirty-seven, the very moment that the farmer driving the chicken truck lost his brakes? Who could predict that her life would end in a bloody flurry of feathers and exploded chicken parts?

And who can say that an equally dismal destiny doesn't await Lorena herself, cutting short *her* dreams? Lorena gasps audibly at the thought.

Dreams can disappear—poof, just like that. Where do those dreams go? Are they floating out there with no place to land—songs not sung, dances not danced, all those dreams that will never come true?

She sobs with such despair as Maybelle's casket is lowered into its grave that the family suspends their grieving to stare at her. Della, supporting Lorena as they weave between tombstones back to the Nash, says, "After that last haircut, I didn't even think you liked her that much."

But it is not so much for Maybelle that Lorena weeps. It is for herself. For lost dreams, repressed ambitions, for time rolling on without her. For her depressing past, her dismal present, and the possibility, like Maybelle, of a future slapped down by the hand of fate. For sad things that happen. For promises never kept.

For talent, forever undiscovered.

"NONONONONO!" MISS FRITZI is holding her head, ululating her disapproval of the elbow-swinging, hip-twisting variation on the Double Time Step Lorena is attempting. "What are you doing?"

Lorena stops, puts her hands on her hips, and regards Miss Fritzi with a weary air. Maybe it's not such a good idea, taking these private lessons to perfect her routine. Apparently Miss Fritzi is stuck in those Rockette numbers and doesn't appreciate innovation.

From the beginning, Miss Fritzi wanted her to change her routine from "Chattanooga Choo Choo" to something, she said, "fresher," maybe something from a movie like *Singing in the Rain*. Well, fine for Miss Fritzi, but Lorena's been working too long and hard on "Chattanooga" and besides, she's made it her own, what with all the tricky new steps she had learned from watching Cassie.

"Where'd you get *that* from?" Miss Fritzi had chirped in alarm the first time Lorena attempted the looking-like-you're-going-forward-when-you're-going-backward step.

"My kid made it up," Lorena said.

"Figures," said Miss Fritzi, rolling her eyes in obvious recollection of Cassie's brief but memorable bout of dance lessons.

Now, three lessons later, Lorena feels that her routine is eroding, rather than improving, under Miss Fritzi's tutelage. She blames Della, who had suggested that if she were serious about her career, she needed not just practice but private lessons.

So on Tuesday mornings Lorena dons baggy shorts and an old blouse, stuffs her tap shoes into a paper bag, and drives down to Miss Fritzi's studio, where it's just she and Miss Fritzi and Miss Fritzi's cat, a habitual barfer who blithely and regularly disgorges the remains of recently devoured mice onto the piano.

"Naughty Puff, naughty Puff, bad bad kitty," twitters Miss Fritzi as familiar hacking noises emanate from the dusty spinet in the corner. She abruptly interrupts Lorena's lesson to mop up the bony stewlike mess, leaving Lorena to wonder, Why am I spending two dollars for this? Clearly Miss Fritzi does not appreciate her unique talent, her ability to improvise, her primitive energy.

Lessons, Lorena decides as she watches Miss Fritzi scrape the last of the remains into the trash can, are beneath her. Talent like hers deserves freedom of expression without some faded ex-Rockette stifling her originality, trying to turn her into just another amateur who thinks getting some old Community Theater role in *Guys and Dolls* would be hot stuff. When you're blessed with the makings of stardom, tedious lessons interrupted by a barfing cat are just a waste of time and two bucks. She's better off practicing by herself.

*   *   *

YES, YES. SHE feels it clicking, each movement fitting into the next like a piece of a puzzle, and a one-and-a-two and a-*Chattanooga choo choo, won't you carry me ho-o-ome,* arms way up and *splat* she's into her split. Lorena lies motionless after her finale, splayed out on the bedroom floor, sweating, panting, exhausted yet exultant. Practiced all afternoon, fine-tuned her routine so the new steps blend into the old, choreography smooth and precise as any June Taylor number. It's second nature to her now, she doesn't have to think about it, her body works like a well-oiled engine, like . . . a Chattanooga choo choo.

Yes. She's ready, she's sure of it now. Ready for her audition with Wally.

She unties her tap shoes, places them side by side in their special place in her closet, then slips on her furry slippers.

Pete looks up from the couch, gives her a wicked glance as she pads down the stairs to the living room. "What a racket," he complains. "People kill for less than that."

Cassie looks up sharply from coloring some drawings she's made of Bart and Sally and their blue-haired mother. "That's not funny, Dad."

"Neither is listening to a herd of buffalo upstairs when I'm trying to relax, watch a little TV." He returns Lorena's aloof glance with a frown. "I thought things were going to return to normal around here. Guess I was wrong, huh?" No answer. "Still think you're going on *Talent Scouts*? Still think you're going to be discovered?" Still no answer. Then, frustrated, "I bet you've still got that stupid costume stuck away somewhere."

Cassie doesn't say anything, just bends her head over her drawing and colors, hard, until the crayon breaks.

Lorena busies herself in the kitchen, clanging pots, slamming the Frigidaire, moving her lips as she consoles herself. She tries, doesn't she? Tries to keep everything the way it's supposed to be, cooks dinner every night, hasn't opened a Swanson's for weeks but has he noticed? No. Just takes it all for granted. Hasn't complimented her once since the fried chicken night.

Bam. Bam. She whomps the biscuit cutter with such fury that it leaves circles in the wooden board beneath. She picks up the circles, slaps them hard onto the pan, *whap whap whap,* so hard they flatten out like pancakes. Throws the whole pan into the oven with a clatter, glares at the closed oven door.

Here she is, trying her hardest to be a good wife, a good mother, and what does she get? Pete's complaints, Cassie's sullen stares. What's wrong with expressing herself? What's wrong with having dreams? Look what happened to Maybelle.

She wishes Pete would get off his butt and get back to work. He's better now, isn't he? He's not even complaining about how lousy he feels anymore. She doesn't understand what Pete's talking about, that his foreman is stalling about getting him back on the job, that he says Pete's got to be evaluated first, whatever that means. Enough of his moping around. He better make himself useful.

"I THINK THE lady that got burned all over oughta win," Cassie says around a mouthful of Cracker Jacks.

"No, she's just going to be scarred up but at least she's got two legs," Molly says, spinning the plastic top prize from the Cracker Jack box. "That old guy there, he's only got one leg and they fired him and he's got nine kids."

"Well," counters Cassie, "she's burned *and* hunchbacked, so who's ever going to marry her?"

Molly and Cassie are sprawled on the living-room floor watching *Strike It Rich.* Molly is spending the night because Cassie begged and pleaded until Lorena gave in, so now they are all gathered in the living room debating the quality of degradation each of the contestants has exhibited in order to win money.

"Look, look, the burned lady got a call on the Heart Line," Cassie says. Warren Hull, the host, is assisting the woman, who is having a problem getting a good grip on the Heart Line phone. On the other end is a generous benefactor who offers her one hundred dollars cash plus a year's supply of his product, Slippery Sam's Salve, guaranteed to soften skin or your money back. The Burned Lady's scarred face contorts in gratitude as Warren Hull leads the audience in frenetic applause.

But the one-legged father of nine is still in the game. His pinned-up pants leg swings and sways as he gamely hobbles up on one crutch to relate his woeful tale, but not until his tiny, tidy wife appears with all nine children in tow does the applause match that of the Burned Lady's.

"I understand," Warren Hull oozes as he wraps a protective arm around the wife, "that in addition to raising all these wonderful children, you play the piano at a Steak 'n Shake several nights a week in order to pay the bills."

The tidy wife nods her head shyly, yes, she does do that. "Well," says Warren Hull as a piano is rolled out onto the stage, "how about a little song for the folks out there in TV land?"

Tidy Wife sits primly on the edge of the piano bench. After a prayerful pause, she raises her hands, throws her head back, and launches into a rousing rendition of "Alexander's Ragtime Band," her pixie-cropped hair flying as she pounds the keys. Incited by Warren Hull's question, "Isn't she great, folks?" the audience's applause swells and breaks into a roar that subsides only after Tidy Wife has taken several bows.

Lorena leans forward, envy enveloping her at the reaction evoked by the unilegster's wife. The Heart Line is ringing off its hook, and before the oldest child finishes relating how he had to quit school to work in the sweatshop, the family has raked in five hundred dollars' worth of donations.

Why, thinks Lorena, *I* could do that.

Pete has dozed off but she gives his shoulder a shake. "Pete, Pete. Watch this. Look, they're giving them *money*. We could go on *Strike It Rich,* what with your accident and all." She doesn't add that it could be her big break as well.

Pete blinks, stares at the screen, shakes his head. "Are you crazy?" he says. "We have money from my disability payments. We don't need charity."

"It's not charity," Lorena protests. "It's show business. We could be on TV!"

"I don't want to be on TV. I don't need to beg." He pauses. "I'm going back to work."

"Back to work?" she says. "So soon?" His announcement, which would have brought her pure delight just a few short minutes ago, is now cause for dismay. Until she saw the audience response to the tidy wife's piano proficiency, it had never occurred to Lorena that the very disability that kept Pete home, driving her crazy, could be her passport to fame and fortune. "Maybe we could go on *Strike It Rich* first," she insists.

"I'm not going on any TV show. I gotta get back to work, that's all there is to it. I talked to the foreman. He says maybe I can work inside the welding shop. Says I'm not ready to work outside, up high, at least not yet. But he'll think about letting me come back, long's I don't endanger myself again. Not that I'm a danger or anything," he corrects himself. "I'm good as anybody out there."

"Yeah, Dad," Cassie pipes up, then turns to Molly. "He's the best. He's not scared of anything."

Lorena can't argue. If Pete won't go on *Strike It Rich*, then the sooner he goes back to work, the better. He's making her nuts at home.

C A S S I E

T'S WINDY HERE on the platform. My skirt bells out all around me and I wonder if it could lift me like a parachute and carry me over the shipyard. How would it be to float above all the cranes and derricks and ships in their docks? I bet they'd look tiny as toys from up there, instead of tall as buildings, like they do from here. I've never been as high as a cloud.

From the platform we can look up at the U.S.S. *Forrestal*. It's an aircraft carrier, and Dad says when it's finished it'll be the biggest warship ever built in the whole United States, over a thousand feet long and two hundred and fifty feet wide. Dad knows all this because he was working on it when he fell, and he shows me just where that happened, points way way up, and then moves his finger down to this big deck sticking out from the side of the ship.

He says it's a good thing the deck was there or he would have splatted all over the building dock. "I looked down," he says.

"Can't look down, gotta look straight ahead, not let your mind wander even for a second. Can't let all the little worries of life get in your way when you're working for your country." Dad stands up straighter when he talks about our country, the "U S of A" he calls it. He says he couldn't serve in the army but what he does is even more important, welding together battleships strong enough to meet the enemy.

Trouble is, there's no enemy. At least not one we're actually fighting with guns and planes and stuff. "Now that there's no real war going on, they're building sissy ships," he says, pointing to a ship in another dock. "Like that one. Ocean liner. Passenger ships, sissy ships, floating hotels for rich people. Have to, I guess, or they'd be laying off people right and left. But what happens when the Commies try to take over? We gonna fight the Reds with that?" he says, waving the ocean liner away like it was a mosquito.

"Now this here is a ship to make you proud," he says about the *Forrestal*. "Jet planes are going to land, right on the ship itself, right there on the flight deck. Four acres, it's going to be. Do you know how big four acres is?"

I don't. I just know it's so big that even Dad is amazed because he's looking up at the *Forrestal* like it landed from outer space. He hasn't seen it since his accident and, he says, he can hardly recognize it now, it's changed so much. He says in a voice real soft and low, "It's like somebody had a party and I wasn't invited."

Dad's starting back to work next week but today he said he wanted to see the shipyard, just check it out before he went back. I've never been here, not inside the yard anyway, so I begged him to take me with him. Mom said, "Good idea," so here I am.

It's a bigger place than I thought it was, just from the times I've gone by it on the bus, going downtown. It's a whole city, a city of steel, stretching around us as far as I can see. Flashes of sunlight bounce off metal like stars thrown from the sky. I smell metal everywhere, feel it in the back of my throat, behind my nose, taste it like I'm swallowing iron and breathing rust. The sound of metal is all around us—banging, whistling, shrieking, clanging—until I wonder if it's inside or outside my head.

I'm ready to go home but it's just the beginning for Dad. He leads me through a passageway where we're stopped by a guard but it's somebody Dad knows so he lets us go up some stairs. We climb and climb until we're on a walkway high up on the *Forrestal*. Down below us are guys in hard hats, working, scurrying around. Dad stops, squints at them. "That guy," he says, pointing to one of them who's separate from the others, "is who's keeping me from my real job."

I can't see what the guy looks like, just the top of his hard hat, round and green like a big olive. Dad stares at him. He says, not to me but to the big space between us and the guys so tiny below, "This is where I belong. This is where my daddy and my grandaddy worked, outside with the wind and rain and sun on their backs. This is all I know."

"But, Dad," I say, worried because he looks so sad, "you know all about the constellations. You know how to catch crabs and how to sail a boat and you can tell me the batting average of every one of the Dodgers. There's lots that you know."

But he's not listening. I don't understand why he wants to come back here so bad. All he did before his accident was complain about work, and now all he talks about is going back. Maybe it's one of those things that seem better than they really are, like the smell of hot dogs from the hotdog stand, or houses that seem cozy when you look into their windows on a cold night. Maybe he just *thinks* he wants to go back to work.

Dad doesn't move, just looks down at the guy in the olive hat for a long minute. Then he turns and shuffles slowly down the walkway. I follow him, but not before I do something I've been wanting to do since we climbed up here. I spit over the side. It takes a long time to reach the bottom.

28

L O R E N A

LORENA TURNS THE record player up loud, sings along with it as she watches herself dance in the bulb-lit mirror of her dressing table. Nobody's home. Cassie's at Molly's and Pete's at work. His first day back, glory hallelujah. She had fixed him an extra-special lunch: not only his usual bologna sandwiches, but leftover fried chicken she had made especially for last night's back-to-work celebration dinner. She added a leg and a breast to his lunch box as a surprise.

She gave him a good-luck peck on the cheek this morning, and was puzzled at his seeming reluctance to go. After all, he claimed he wanted to get back on the job, so what was this, standing stock-still on the porch, not moving until she asked him what was the matter? He had muttered a few things last night, something about if this didn't work out he'd have to work inside the welding shop instead of outside on the ship itself, but when Lorena had said, Big deal, what's the difference? he had fallen silent.

Now he's gone. Out. Back to work. Back to normal. Lorena

revels in her solitary state. The house is hers again. She can concentrate on reaching her goal. She's already planned what she'll do now that she's perfected her dance routine. She'll ask Binky—nothing personal, of course—for Wally's number. That's all. Very businesslike. Let him know that all her practice has paid off and she's ready for The Big Time.

Once she's a star she'll still be a good wife and mother. She won't let fame change her. She'll stay a regular person, won't get snooty, even when she makes lots of money. Of course they'll move to Hollywood or New York, the only places anything happens, can't keep living in Newport News, nobody in show business lives in Newport News. Stars can *come* from Newport News, like she heard Ava Gardner did. Hey, she and Ava have something in common—maybe they can be friends once she's famous.

Lorena poses in front of the mirror, waiting for the needle to connect with the record. Once again from the top: And she's off in a frenzy, loose as a goose, limbs swinging, hips swaying, toes tapping in total timpani with the music swelling from the 45 player. ". . . Dinner in the diner, nothing could be finer," she sings to her image in the dressing-table mirror knocked crooked from the vibration of her energetic pounding, "Woo woo Chattanooga, there you are."

Got to do something with this hair, she thinks, fluffing it as she gyrates before the mirror. She's let it go since Maybelle's funeral. Della is going to a new person, a male hairdresser downtown, Mr. Ralph, but Della's got that wild kind of hair that a chimpanzee could cut and it'd still look good. Lorena watches her hair flop as she taps ferociously, flinging her head from side to side. Oh, Maybelle, she mourns, why'd you go and die on me before I could change this style? She's tired of her proper "Mama" cut, the mousy color, the limp, lank strands that hang down her neck like fringes from an old bath mat. Well, she'll just have to make an appointment with Mr. Ralph even though she wonders about men who like to fuss with women's hair.

Whap. She hears the mail slot open, the whoosh of mail sliding through, the final slap shut. She looks out her bedroom window, shoves up the sash, waves frantically at the gray figure slinking away.

"Yoo-hoo," she calls. Mize well do it now as later, just be spontaneous, ask him right this minute, Does he know Wally's number? "Yoo-hoo," but Binky is already down the sidewalk, furtively glancing behind him as he scurries off.

Well. Another time. Maybe it's just as well he didn't see her with her looking so frizzy and all. She decides to give Mr. Ralph a call.

She's looking in the phone book when the telephone rings.

"Miz Palmer?" says a vaguely familiar voice.

"Yes?" She gets a feeling of—what do they call it?—dayja voo?

"This is Dwayne, Pete's foreman. Remember me?"

That's it. Dayja voo.

"Miz Palmer? You there?"

"I'm here," she whispers.

"I'm afraid Pete went and set hisself on fire."

"Far?" That's how he pronounces it. That's how she repeats it. "Set himself on far?"

"Yessum. Actually, it's just his hair he set on far. Rest of him's okay. 'Cept for his hands. He used them to beat out the far in his hair."

Lorena closes her eyes.

"Doctor said he'll be okay once he heals up," Dwayne continues. "Might be bald, though."

"Bald?" Lorena's eyes pop open. "You mean, no hair?"

"For a while, anyway. Maybe not permanent."

She tries to picture that: Pete with no hair, his black, curly, Clark Gable hair fried to a frizzle. Bald as a bean.

"Um." She hesitates, afraid to ask the next question, the question whose answer might determine her sanity. But she does. "Think he'll be going back to work soon?"

"Well, Miz Palmer." She can almost see him squirm before he says, "I wouldn't wanta speckalate on that quite yet."

"Why *not?*" Lorena asks in a strangled voice.

Silence. Dwayne is clearly groping for words. "I think your hubband's got some . . . problems," he says finally.

Well, thinks Lorena. So do I. So do I.

C A S S I E

D AD HAS A Frankenstein head, all wrapped up in bandages, and big white-mitten Al Jolson hands. I can tell he
doesn't want Mom to visit him in the hospital because
he says "Go home" when she taps on his door to come in. But
here she is anyway, sitting on the chair next to his bed while he
pretends to sleep.

I read my Nancy Drew or play cat's cradle with a piece of
string. I hate hospitals, the way they smell like Lysol and cafeteria
food, but I make Mom bring me. I have to keep an eye on Dad,
make sure she doesn't try to hurt him again. First the soup, now
this.

Dad won't say it, but it's all Mom's fault. I figured out what
happened. He was checking out his welding torch, hadn't put on
his gloves or shield yet, had to adjust the valves. He was thinking
about something else, he said, somehow turned it on, and the
torch just jumped out of his hand. Before he knew it, he had set
his hair on fire.

Jumped. Welding torches don't jump. He said it was like it was greased or something. And then he remembered he ate fried chicken for lunch and there were no napkins.

Mom planned it. She never gave Dad anything but bologna sandwiches for lunch before. But this time, she gave him fried chicken. Greasy fried chicken with no napkins.

Mom says that Dwayne, Dad's foreman, said he thinks maybe Dad does these things to himself, not on purpose but for some reason Dwayne can't figure out. He thinks Dad's got problems, whatever that means, and that Dad is a danger to himself. Worse, he says, Dad's dangerous to the other people he works with, and Dwayne's going to recommend that Dad should do some other kind of work.

But I know who the dangerous person is. It's Mom.

THE HOSPITAL ROOM is hot. Dad is sweating big milky drops that slide from underneath his head bandage, down his cheeks and nose. Every now and then Mom reaches over and pulls a Kleenex out of the box to mop his face, but he won't look at her, just studies the wall like there's something important written on it. She sits there dab, dab, dabbing at his face until the Kleenex is shredded and then she reaches over, pops another one out, and starts all over again. Nobody talks. All I hear is nurse noise down the hall or long slow farts from the guy on the other side of the curtain.

I don't know whether to warn Dad now that Mom's trying to kill him, or wait until he comes home. Maybe this time he'll believe me. I don't know what he'll do if I tell him about Mom and the mailman, but now I feel like I have to tell him because he'll want to know *why* she wants to kill him. You have to have a reason to want to do something like that.

When they bring his dinner tray Mom looks at her watch and says to me, "Mize well take you on home now. I'll come back later." But I won't go, I won't leave her alone with him. I'm scared of the way she stares at Dad, scared at how good she can fake looking sad, her eyes all droopy and her nose runny. It's like *Dragnet* where Sergeant Friday says, "Just the facts, ma'am," and she thinks she can fool him with her sad droopy eyes but he's too smart. If I could tell Sergeant Friday what I know, he'd arrest her just like that.

When I told Molly, she looked at me like I was crazy. "Your *mom*?" she said. "I mean, just because she did sex with the mail guy doesn't mean she tried to kill your dad. People only do stuff like that in the movies."

Well, it happens all the time on test-pattern TV. Like this show I told Molly about, where this really rich guy named J.R. got shot and you thought it was his wife and then you found out it was really her sister because she did sex with J.R., but Molly interrupts with "There you go again, making stuff up. Sex sex sex, like they really talk about that on television. You think about sex too much. I'm sorry I told you about it in the first place."

Even if Molly doesn't believe I see these things, she listens because she likes to hear weird stories. Mr. Finkelstein sometimes listens, too. He never says he doesn't believe me but at least he doesn't interrupt like Molly does. Instead, he'll ask me things like "Tell me again what a 'slam dunk' is," or "What's that record player you say people wear on their heads?"

I memorized the beginning of one of my favorite test-pattern shows. It's about this sixth dimension beyond that which is known to man, the one that's as vast as space and as timeless as infinity. Each time I watch the show, it sticks with me and gives me the same tingly feeling I get with the test pattern.

Today, when I'm reciting the show's beginning to Molly in a spooky voice like the one on TV, Mr. Finkelstein comes into the room. He stops and listens all the way through the part about the dimension of the imagination that's called the Twilight Zone. When I'm finished, he pets his beard, then says, "That's very sophisticated language for someone your age." He looks at me quietly for a minute as if he's studying me. Then he asks me—no, not asks—*tells* me, like he really believes me for the very first time: "You didn't make that up, did you."

"No. It's real. I heard it on my test-pattern show."

"I figured you did," Mr. Finkelstein says. Molly gives me a look, says, "I'm getting some Kool-Aid," and leaves for the kitchen. Mr. Finkelstein crouches down to where I'm sitting on the floor. "Tell me this," he says. "What is it you think you're seeing?"

I think hard, because lately I've been wondering a lot about that. Sometimes, when I watch test-pattern TV, I feel like it's watching me. I scare myself when I think about what all this could mean, but I tell him anyway. "Maybe, since nobody else sees these things, I'm not seeing anything either. Maybe Mom's right. Maybe I'm like my aunt Lula."

"How's that?"

"Crazy."

"Crazy?" He shakes his head. "Nope. Don't think that's the case," he says, which makes me feel better. Then he looks real serious and asks, "What else do you think it could be?"

I shrug. Why not tell him what else I've been thinking, especially lately since I've been watching that spooky show I was just telling Molly about. "Well—I guess this *will* sound crazy—but sometimes I think that what I'm seeing hasn't happened yet."

Mr. Finkelstein nods his head like he's not surprised, but like he's been wondering about that himself. "Hmm," he says. "And, let's say that *is* what you're seeing. How do you feel about that?"

I think for a minute. "Scared," I finally say. "I don't think I'd want to know bad things that could happen."

"Well, let's suppose you did see something bad. Is there anything you could do about it?"

I don't know what he's talking about. What could *I* do to change the future, if that's what I'm seeing? It's not like I'm Superman, or even Wonder Woman. I shrug again. "Nothing, I guess."

"Mmmm," he murmurs. "Maybe so, maybe no. And if it's so, who knows if it's for better or for worse?" He's quiet, like he's listening to some invisible person. Then, his bones crackling like Rice Krispies, he stands back up again. He pets his beard and says, "I guess it's best to let things be."

He's right. If you could change the future by making things happen, or by stopping them from happening, it might make new things happen and you'd see a whole *other* future, and then do you get to change that, too? It's all too complicated. Mr. Finkelstein is so smart. I don't know why Dad doesn't like him. That's one of the things I would change, if I could change things.

DAD'S HOME AGAIN. His head and hands are still bandaged but not in fat bandages, just thin ones that Mom has to change every day. Dad's hair is gone but he says maybe it'll grow back. When he's got the bandages off, I don't mind that his head is bald like that. It makes him look like an elf.

When he first got home, he'd spend a lot of time staring at the model he made of the battleship *Missouri* that he kept by his bed. The other day I heard this crash and I went running to see what happened and there's his battleship, all in pieces on the floor. It didn't look like it fell. It looked like it was thrown. Dad didn't say anything, just looked at me with big, wet, scary eyes.

Mom stays away from Dad now. If he's upstairs, she's downstairs. If he's downstairs watching TV, she's upstairs. She quit practicing her routine because he yelled, "That's all I need, you're driving me nuts with that racket!" She has to bring him food, but that's the only time she sees him except when she has to change his bandages. She doesn't talk much, and when she does it's like she's not really there.

Now we always have TV dinners. Turkey on Monday, fried chicken Tuesday, roast beef Wednesday, pot pie Thursday, and then start all over again. It's not so bad because I get to eat dinner while I watch *Mr. Peepers* and *Dinah Shore* and I don't have to talk to Mom. I don't have anything to say to her. I keep thinking, She tried to kill Dad. She doesn't know I know. I keep an eye on her all the time to make sure she doesn't try it again.

Sometimes she just sits in front of the TV and cries. Not during sad things, but when she's watching *Arthur Godfrey's Talent Scouts* or the June Taylor dancers. She even cries when she sees the dancing Old Gold cigarette packs.

I wish we could go back to the way it was before, when we were just a regular family and there wasn't any mailman and Dad wasn't all wrecked up. I wish I could just close my eyes, click my ruby slippers three times, and say "There's no place like home." And when I open my eyes again, everything would be the way it used to be.

30

L O R E N A

IR COOLED READS the sign over the ticket window of the Paramount, each letter dripping with frosty blue icicles. Lorena pushes a quarter and two dimes under the window opening, gets her pink ticket in return, doesn't even ask the soporific ticket taker what time the show starts. She just wants to escape.

Escape from heat as smothering as a deadly cloud dropped from the white-hot sky. Escape from meaningless tasks she performs on automatic—matching socks, bleaching sheets, emptying the Hoover's dust bag. Escape from the accusatory silences of Pete and Cassie.

It's Wednesday, the middle of the week. Della's at work, so Lorena is alone. It doesn't matter. She just wants out. Someplace cool, someplace dark, someplace that will take her somewhere else.

The movies.

She looks up, reads the marquee: THERE'S NO BUSINESS LIKE

SHOW BUSINESS. She feels electrified, not just because it happens to be a movie she wants to see, but because she is zapped by a premonition that it's a signal, a sign, a message from above. There it is in black-and-white, placed as if by the hand of God in big plastic letters on the marquee overhead: *THERE'S NO BUSINESS LIKE SHOW BUSINESS.*

She scans the poster at the entrance to see who's starring. Ethel Merman, Dan Dailey, Donald O'Connor, Marilyn Monroe, Mitzi Gaynor . . .

Mitzi Gaynor?

Lorena's head spins with revelation. God *is* telling her something, throwing her this double whammy: *There's No Business Like Show Business* and Mitzi Gaynor, too. It's more than just coincidence that this movie is showing today at the Paramount, at the very moment she's desperate for some sign. It's Fate in the guise of Mitzi Gaynor, a validation of all her hopes and dreams.

She stumbles in exaltation down the aisle of the darkened theater. The show has just started. She takes a deep breath of Air Cooled air and a bite from her Hershey bar. She's almost alone in the theater except for a couple of fellow loners and a clot of kids at front row center, feet propped up on the rail.

"There's *no* business like *show* business," bellows Ethel Merman in the opening number, and Lorena almost weeps with longing. Ethel Merman should have been her mother, the Five Donahues her family—a singing, dancing, tappety-tapping family who hold hands and take their bows before a curtain sparkling with billions of tiny stars. They have it all: a happy family *and* fame.

Lorena gapes in openmouthed envy as, with a wink of an eye and the wrinkle of her upturned nose, Mitzi Gaynor bursts on-screen and whirls into a leg-flashing skirt-flouncing tap-dancing cancan. Lorena can hardly sit still. In her mind, she is Mitzi's shadow. Her legs and arms twitch as she mentally mimics Mitzi's moves, shimmies her shoulders, peels off a glove, balances those feathers on top of her head.

Oh, she could do that, she knows she could do that. It's a gift as natural as breathing Air Cooled air. Why isn't that me up there? she agonizes. And then it hits her: Why *isn't* that me?

As if in answer, Marilyn Monroe, in her role as an aspiring singer, says in her breathless baby voice, "This show is my big chance. It's make or break!" Lorena's head clears as suddenly as the drain when she extricates a hairball, a gush that flushes all doubt and uncertainty. Of course, she thinks. My big chance— my *only* chance—is *Talent Scouts.* That *could* be me!

Her future dances before her in CinemaScope. Pinwheels spin and banners fly as the Five Donahues sing and dance down a star-studded stairway in a grand finale that ends with a choral command: "Let's go-o-o on with the show!"

It's a sign. It's all a sign. Yes! She must go on with the show.

When the lights come up and the sparse audience straggles out, Lorena doesn't move. She stares as the purple curtain, shabby and threadbare in the harsh light, draws majestically to a close across the screen still alive with afterglow.

The sun is high in the sky, the heat an unrelenting presence when Lorena finally leaves the theater, but she strides down the simmering street as cool as a penguin on ice. The chill air of the theater has left her with a glacial glow that frosts her walk with purpose.

She's got to do what she's got to do.

SHE WAITS FOR him at the corner. Watches as he makes his rounds at the next court before he heads for hers. A gray blur in the distance, the familiar stride, head down, shuffling through his bag for the next stack of mail. Getting closer. Still doesn't see her, brim of his hat shading his eyes, the same hat she danced with, none the worse for wear.

"Hey," says Lorena, blocking Binky's path up the sidewalk as he approaches.

He blinks. Knows it's her but she can tell he's disoriented, the way he's stopped in mid-stride, one dusty black shoe planted firmly on the ground, the other frozen, toe bent, heel lifted, on its way up.

"It's me," she says, knows he knows it's she, knows she looks good because she planned it that way: white shorts, halter top pulled low, makeup just right—patch of blue over the eyes, heavy on the mascara, frosted tangerine mouth. Tan. She worked on that all week, lying out on the sticky webs of the lounge chair beneath a burning sky. Gradual, a little bit at a time so she wouldn't peel, slathered on that baby oil and iodine until she looked like she was dipped in caramel.

And her hair. Mr. Ralph outdid Maybelle. Rhonda Fleming Red, he called it as he happily squished it through her hair—still pretty short, nothing to be done about that until it grew out—but curled and wild and red red red. That, if nothing else, should get Binky's attention.

"Wow," says Binky.

"It's been a while," says Lorena.

"Yuh." He shifts his bag forward on his hip, clears his throat. "So. What ya been up to?"

"Oh, where to begin?" She rolls her eyes prettily to the sky. "So much has happened," she hurries on as he glances at his watch, "Pete had an accident and was laid up and then he had another, um, accident so he's still at home and Cassie, well, Cassie . . ." She pauses. "Anyway, I've been doing a lot of thinking and well, I wanted to talk to you about this—"

Binky looks acutely uncomfortable by now, no longer glancing but staring pointedly at his watch. "I've gotta keep on schedule, you know how it is with the post office." He backs away but gazes appreciatively at the way her plunging top reveals her sharply delineated tan line, among other things. "But," he adds, clearly torn, "you look great. Really. Just great."

"Wait," she says, a tiny note of panic in her voice at his hasty retreat. Not that she expected him to fall panting at her feet, at least not out here in public, but she didn't expect the look of fear that shared the loose-lipped look of lust on his face. "It's not what you think."

"I'm not thinking anything," he says, shaking his head nervously. "It just all got too complicated."

"You mean Cassie?"

"Well, yeah."

"You think I meant for that to happen?"

"Well, no. But it did."

She has no argument for that. She needs to make her point and make it fast before he gets to the Hutchinsons' house, which he is rapidly approaching, albeit backward. "All I want is to ask you if I can meet your cousin."

"Cousin?" He looks perplexed.

"Your cousin Wally you told me about."

"Wally?"

"The talent scout? For Arthur Godfrey?"

Binky's blank look melds into comprehension. "Oh. *Him*."

"Yeah. Remember? Remember you told me he's always looking for new talent?"

Binky looks blank again. "Talent?"

"Well," she says, exasperated, "I dance!"

Binky's mouth opens but nothing emerges.

Lorena clenches her fists, resists the urge to reach over and give him a whack on the head. It's one thing for Binky to reject her sexually. It's another to reject her talent.

"Uh, I only saw you dance once." He's at the Hutchinsons' door, looking not at Lorena but down at the bundle of mail he's fumbling through. He feeds several letters, a *Saturday Evening Post* and a *Colliers* through the mail slot, shredding the edges of the magazines as he rams them in.

Lorena watches from the sidewalk, then follows him as he hurries to the next door. She wants to forget that particular dance, but of course she hasn't, he hasn't, it won't go away. But, she realizes with a little jolt, of *course*, that *is* the only time he's actually seen her dance. So even though the consequences of that dance were so horrendous that the memory makes her wince, she still has to know: "What did you think?"

"About what?" He shuffles busily through his mailbag now, scattering letters and magazines at random, avoiding her eyes.

"About the dance," she persists, scooting after him. "The dance itself, not . . . you know. After."

He whirls, almost knocking her down with the mailbag. "You wanta know what I thought?" he rasps with sudden fervor, his eyes hooded and dark with remembered lust. "I thought about your tits. About how they were bouncing and jiggling all around. About how I wanted to squeeze 'em. And about how I would throw you down on the bed until those stupid shoes were waving at the ceiling while I . . ."

This wasn't what she expected to hear.

But it does make her think.

Now that she's got his attention, she decides to grab it and run. She undulates her hips in their short white shorts, leans forward so the halter top reveals even more, lowers her eyelids, and pushes her lips out in a Marilyn Monroe pout. "I didn't realize," she says breathlessly, "my dancing had such an effect on you."

He gawks at her, stupefied. "Well, that. And also you were buck naked."

"I was not," she huffs. "I still had my panties on. And my stockings. And my shoes." Which reminds her. "That dance I did—you know, to 'Chattanooga Choo Choo'?—that was my routine."

"Routine?"

"I've perfected it. It's better now."

"Better?"

"Well, you didn't get to see the whole thing because . . . you know." She doesn't want to mention, even think about Cassie's role in any of this. She's excised that part, mentally lifted it out of the scenario. She's thought about it too much already and it's gotten her nowhere. It's time to move on. "The rest of the routine is very difficult to perform, lots of complicated footwork before I get to the grand finale."

"Grand finale?"

"I do a split."

Overcome with enthusiasm, she demonstrates, *tappety tappety tap tap tap,* spin and a tap, spin and a tap, then, whooom, arms up, she collapses on the sidewalk with her legs splayed forward and back beneath her. "Ta-da-a-a-a!"

Binky takes several steps backward, looks around furtively. "Get up," he pleads, and she does, struggling to her feet and dusting off the seat of her shorts.

"Well, you get the idea," she says. "So what do you think?"

Binky is backing off again. "Uh. Very athletic." He hoists his bag meaningfully. "I gotta get going."

Oh, no. She's losing him. Heels clip-clopping, she minces after him as he hurries up the sidewalk, yanks a fistful of mail from his pouch, then bends to stuff it into the mail slot at 1226. Desperate now, she comes up behind him, grinds her hips into his butt, reaches around to clutch at his fly. He straightens abruptly with a gasp and spins around.

Now she's got him. Before he can protest, she pulls him behind the hydrangea bush and gives him a wet, openmouth kiss that makes them both sink with passion among the fat purple blooms.

"Oh, God," he groans, raking at the halter top until it comes loose and falls to her waist. She nimbly yanks it back up and rolls out of his grasp.

"Not here," she admonishes him, pointing to the window just above them. "Meet me somewhere."

"Where?" he whimpers.

"Your place?"

"Um." He hesitates. "I live with my mother."

"Your *mother*?"

He gives an embarrassed shrug. "Haven't found my own place yet."

Now what? Clearly she's going to have to offer him more than just promises before she can bring up cousin Wally again. "Where's your mail truck?"

"My truck?" He looks puzzled. Then, "My truck!" as it dawns on him. "Not my *truck*."

"You got any other ideas?" She sways above him, straddling him with her caramel legs, taunting him with her bare shoulders. She feels wicked. She likes that. She's never felt wicked before. Plump purple blossoms spill all about them, shading them in lavender light. Surrounded by flowers, her knees on the earth, she could be Hedy Lamarr or Dorothy Lamour: exotic, tropical, wild, and forbidden. This is who she wants to be. This is the real Lorena.

So taken is she with the idea of seduction *al fresco* that she almost succumbs to his suggestion: "How about right here?" as he lunges again at her top before she gets it properly tied. But the thought of Cassie and Pete so close—Lorena can almost see their house from here—sobers her. She tugs the top primly back into place and shakes her head. "Where's your truck?"

"Down the street." He points south. "Two courts down."

"I'll meet you there," she says, backing out of the bushes. "Hurry up."

She spots the boxy, snub-nosed truck, looks around to make sure no one sees her, slides open the door to scramble inside. She crawls behind the driver's seat and scrunches among the bags of mail. There is an animal odor to the truck, steamy and redolent with the aroma of cowhide. She leans back against an envelope-stuffed bag and imagines herself as the Farmer's Daughter—no, better yet, a cowgirl. Dale Evans. Dale Evans and Roy Rogers. In bed. She pictures Dale, dressed only in boots, teasing Roy, dancing with his white cowboy hat. Does Dale dance? No. Dale sings. Oh, well.

She hears the clomp of footsteps. Binky leaps onto the stand-up seat and hastily starts the truck. "Where are we going?" Lorena asks, peering around the seat from her perch in the back.

"Couple of streets over. Dead end," he mutters. "Not here."

Okay with her. She hangs on as they career down the street, invisible to her from the windowless back of the truck. She is thrown against the bags as the truck takes a corner and bumps crazily over what feels like rocks before coming to a sputtering stop. She sits up and looks through the windshield, which is veiled by a splay of branches and leaves. "Are we there?"

"Yeah." He turns to her, takes off his hat, loosens his tie. "Boy. I'll tell you, I never thought this would happen again. After before."

"Me neither." She struggles to arrange herself more seductively among the mailbags. He tumbles onto her from his seat and hovers just a moment before sinking his face into hers, almost suffocating her with a prolonged tongue-thrusting kiss. She feels his hand pawing at her top and lets it fall down this time, lifting her back to help it along. And then his mouth moves to her breasts, tastes one, then the other, back and forth, back and forth, as if he can't make up his mind which one he likes best.

Lorena grabs his Vitalis-slick hair, moans, moves her hips, and opens her legs. She likes this, she really does, feels like forbidden fruit devoured by a starving man—juicy as a plum, tart as a persimmon, wicked and inviting as Eve's red apple. She's a red-hot flaming redhead, wild in a Rhonda Fleming kind of way, and she tosses her russet ringlets for emphasis as Binky nibbles down the path that she clears for him, hooking her thumbs in the waistband of her shorts, inching them down to her thighs.

But. "Wait," she says.

"Huh?" Binky looks up for a second, then resumes.

"No, wait."

"What?"

"I have to ask you something."

"What?" He shifts gears, biting and licking with increased rapidity. "Zat better?"

"No, no, it's not that." She tries to wrest herself away, just for a moment, just until she can ask him. "I need to know—"

"Okay, I love you," he says, not losing momentum.

Hmm. "You love me? Really?"

"Oh, yes, yes, I love you, I love you," he murmurs into her belly as he attempts to pull her shorts free of her feet.

"How much do you love me?"

"Oh, *so* much do I love you." He sits up to unzip his pants.

She takes the opportunity to cross her legs tight. "Why should I believe you?"

"I swear it," he grunts as he attempts to pry her legs apart. Frustrated, he rears up and cries, "I swear, as Arthur E. Summerfield is my postmaster general, I love you!"

That does give her pause.

"Well," she says, sure now of her powers, "if you love me, then will you do me just a teensy-weensy favor?"

"Anything. Anything."

"Introduce me to your cousin?"

"What?"

"Wally. Your cousin Wally."

"Wally?" Binky looks dazed.

"All I need is a chance," she wheedles. She pulls him closer and wraps one leg around him. "That's all I ask."

"Oh, yes," he agrees. "Yes."

"Swear?"

"Yes, *yes*," he whimpers, and raises his right hand. "I *swear* it."

Now she can relax and enjoy herself. And so she does.

31

LAST WEEK MOM went to the movies in the middle of the week and since then she's been weirder than ever. The next day she went to a new hairdresser and came home with hair the color of tomato soup. She wears this goopy orange lipstick even when she's home, and dresses like she thinks she's in high school. Shorts, fluffy blouses, high heels. I could die when the kids from the court come over to ask if I want to play kickball. They look at her like she's a freak.

She barely has time now to put TV dinners in the oven, she's so busy trying on makeup, curling her hair, practicing her stupid routine. She put the record player in the kitchen so she can practice away from Dad. She closes the door but I can still hear that music, that tapping. I hate it I hate it I hate it.

It's raining, so I can't escape outside to play No Bears Out Tonight. I go into the living room and sit with Dad. All he does now is watch TV, listen to baseball on the radio, or look at his star maps.

He says he's going back to work but he has to wait till his boss tells him it's okay. I don't know what that boss is waiting for. Dad's okay now, he's got all the bandages off and he's even got a few sprouts of hair pushing through his scalp like onion grass does in April: tough little tufts that boing up before the real grass starts growing again. His hands are bald, too, but they work okay.

Dad and I are watching wrestling on TV, trying to ignore the sounds of Mom practicing, but we can hear her over the rain and the noise from the crowd as Gorgeous George comes into the ring. Dad goes "boo hiss" because he doesn't like George being so gorgeous with his long curly blond hair and his glamorous satin movie-star cape. I like it. It's something Mrs. Superman would wear. They even have to spray perfume—Chanel No. 5, the announcer says—into the ring before he'll wrestle.

I think he's funny but Dad says, "He's not a real man. A real man doesn't do sissy stuff to his hair or wear perfume or dress in ladies' clothes."

"He's just pretending, Dad," I explain. "All the wrestlers just pretend." That's what I like about wrestling, they're acting like they're hurting each other but they don't really do those things, banging heads together, pinching ears and noses. And they do neat flips when they throw each other around.

But Dad thinks it's real. "Watch. He's gonna get pulverized. That guy's gonna make mincemeat outta him." He points to the other wrestler, a snarly bald-headed guy with gnashing teeth beneath a big curly mustache. His helpers are holding him back from getting to Gorgeous George but George isn't worried, he's prancing around like he's at a ballet or something, fluffing his hair and sweeping his cape.

The crowd roars when Gorgeous George tackles the other guy but over the roar we can hear Mom in the kitchen, tapping away as usual to "Chattanooga Choo Choo." Dad turns the TV up real loud and yells "Kill him, kill him!" except he's not yelling at the

TV, he's yelling toward the kitchen, his eyes popped out, his neck all red.

I feel like everything's crashing, all the noise, all the yelling, all the music, all the tapping, and I put my hands over my ears and scream "Stop!" I don't realize it but I'm crying and Dad's looking at me like he forgot I was there.

"I'm sorry. I'm sorry." He pulls me to him, lets me sniffle into his shirt while he rumples up my hair, soft, like he used to do. Then he turns down the TV. We hear Mom and the music, loud and clear now. He runs his hand over his head and looks sad and droopy. "I gotta get back to work. She's driving me to the nut-house. I gotta get outta here."

That's how I feel. I gotta get outta here, too.

BECAUSE MOM DOESN'T seem to care anymore, I can go off where I want and she won't ask where I'm going. Sometimes I dig for treasure on the beach, sometimes I wade into the water up to my knees. The sand squishes between my toes and the water is cool on my legs and I wish I could just keep going, wade out into the lizard-green water until I get to Norfolk. But then I think about Edgar in the iron lung, think about what it must be like to look at the world through a mirror, upside down and backward, and I wonder if you can get polio through your toes.

I wish I was a little kid again when I didn't worry about things like Mom and Dad, or school, or getting polio, or the H-bomb. On TV, they showed the Bomb blow a whole island into smith-ereens, just disappear in this gigantic mushroom cloud. I think about the Bomb a lot, especially now that school's started again. We have air-raid drills where we practice ducking under our desks in case they drop the Bomb. During our practices, I think, Fat lot of good this'll be if we're on the playground when the Bomb hits, and then I look up and wonder if any of the old chewing-gum blobs stuck under my desk still have any flavor left.

When I tell Mr. Finkelstein I'm worried about polio and the Bomb, he says there's no sense in worrying about things you can't do anything about. He says if you live scared all the time, the world becomes a very small place.

My world is very small. My house, school, the court. I want to do the things I read about or see on television, especially test-pattern TV. I want to meet people who are different from me, find out things that I don't even know exist. I want to have adventures before I'm a smithereen.

Today my adventure is to ride my bike in the street. I decide to go to the woods where Molly and I had our picnic. That day wasn't fun because I was scared Mom would find out, but since then I've thought about those woods a lot. I need a secret place where I can sit and think about things.

I fix me a peanut-butter sandwich, stash it in my shirt, yell "I'm going out" to Mom but she doesn't answer. I don't know where she is. Dad just nods and waves me off because he's listening to some game on the radio. I run down and jump on my bike. It's good as new since Mr. Finkelstein unbent it for me after I fell. I hurry to make sure I'm gone in case Mom pops out and asks me where I'm going because then I'd have to lie.

I feel my heart banging around my chest as I pedal slow and easy to the next court over, then I ride the sidewalk till it ends. The curb bumps under my wheels and then I'm riding in the street, pedaling fast and hard past houses with fences and yards. Kids are playing outside and I wonder, What are their families like? Do they fight? Do I want kids myself someday? Maybe some people just shouldn't have kids.

I think about all kinds of stuff while I'm riding, not worrying, just riding like a normal person. After a while I see the patch of woods behind some of the houses and I turn onto the path Molly and I took that leads into the trees.

The woods are dark and cool. I lay my bike down on the grass. My bike looks happy to be here, happy it's not riding on a hot sidewalk, happy to be in the shade with buttercups tickling its tires. I sit with my back against a tree, listen to the wind ruffle the leaves over my head, unwrap my sandwich, and take a bite. Peanut butter tastes better in the woods.

Once in a while I hear a car pass in the distance, but mostly what I hear is the scritching of birds in the nest over my head, the wind like somebody humming through a comb, the card-shuffle sound of leaves. It's easy to pretend I'm someplace far away even though my house is just a few streets over. It even smells different here, like lettuce smells when you stick your face into the vegetable bin at the A&P.

I hear a noise, a crunching in the woods, but when I peek through the trees I can't see anything, and it's quiet again. Some ants are parading back and forth and I wonder, Do bugs recognize each other? I lean back and watch leaf shadows shift and change, and I think about how this will be my special place forever.

I'm drifting, almost asleep, when I hear voices way off. Somebody's in the woods down where the street stops. I don't want company, so I get on my bike and start to ride down the path until I see what made that crunching sound I heard before. It's a truck. A mail truck. I get this uh-oh feeling.

I get off my bike, sneak it behind trees and bushes to where the truck is. Then I hear the voices clearer and I see a head of tomato-soup hair and there she is: Mom, bending over, her bare white butt like a fat mushroom in the forest, pulling her shorts on while this guy tries to grab them away from her. They giggle and I know before I even see his face that it's the same mailman I saw in Mom's bedroom.

The first thing I want to do is run out and tell them I hate them, but then she'll know I rode my bike in the street. I crouch behind a bush trying to make up my mind and before I know it they've climbed up into the truck. It backs up and bumps hard over the ground and they're gone.

I stay in the woods for a long time. I don't care if I never go home. I think a lot about what Mr. Finkelstein said, about the world becoming a very small place, and I think I know exactly what he meant.

THE HOUSE IS silent, frozen in the black ice of night. I can't sleep. All I can think about is Mom's mushroom butt and the mailman in the woods, about her dancing for him in the bedroom, and I wonder if this time I should tell Dad. Then I think about what might happen if I do, bad things like I see on TV, all those guns, all that blood, and I can't think anymore.

The stairs creak as I tiptoe down into the blackness. I click on the TV.

Test pattern.

I wait, toes and fingers tingling. The bull's-eye shifts and changes, begins its spin, faster, faster until it dissolves like Kool-Aid powder in water. And then a picture appears, black-and-white. A man behind a desk. Crew cut. Bow tie. Prissy little mouth.

Hey, it's the same guy who reports the news on Channel Four. What's he doing on test-pattern TV?

"A Newport News shipyard worker home on disability was shot and killed last night," he says. "Pete Palmer, a welder, was killed by a blast from his BB gun as he and his wife, Lorena Palmer, struggled over it during a domestic dispute."

What?

"The BBs penetrated Palmer's skull right between the eyes. The scene was witnessed by their eleven-year-old daughter, Cassie, who is now being cared for by friends of the family. Lorena Palmer was taken into custody. She has pled not guilty by reason of insanity."

My eyes are stuck to the TV screen. The newsman fades and fades until nothing is left but the test pattern. "Liar!" I yell at the TV. "Liar, liar!"

I run upstairs and open the door to Mom and Dad's room and there they are, asleep like always, Dad snoring, Mom curled up on the edge of the mattress. She picks her head up, mumbles, "What's wrong?"

"Nothing," I say. "Bad dream." Even if I told them what I had seen, they would never believe me. I shut their door and go to my room. Climb into bed. Pull the covers over my head and scrunch into a ball.

I don't know what to do. None of this makes sense. Maybe this *is* a bad dream.

What if it's not? What if I'm as crazy as Lula?

Or, even scarier: What if it's true? What if the things I see on test-pattern TV haven't happened yet, but will?

And if that's so—what can I do to change it?

I'VE NEVER TOUCHED Dad's BB gun before. I unsnarl it from the tangle of coats and umbrellas in the closet. It's heavier than I thought it would be. I need two hands just to lift it. Dad makes it look so light on those mornings when he swings it up on his shoulder, squinches up one eye, and takes aim at the cans he shoots off the fence at the beach.

He's never let me hold it because I'm a girl, but I've watched him load and unload it, so I know what to do: snap the little metal piece back, hold the cold steel barrel in my hands so the gun is upside down. I hear the BBs rattle like hailstones, and before I can catch them, out they spill. They bounce, they roll, they tumble over the floor and under the couch, they catch the light, they shine and spin like tiny planets orbiting the coffee table. Shh-shh, I whisper. I fall to my knees, spread my arms to capture them, to silence their clatter in the cold still darkness.

Shh-shh. I listen for the sound of creaking upstairs, the sound of Mom and Dad getting out of bed. Nothing. The BBs have stopped bouncing. I feel around the floor to gather them up, my hands gritty from pretzel crumbs and dried-up bits from old TV dinners. I stuff the BBs into the pockets of my pajamas. Heavy with the weight of metal, the bottoms creep down my butt.

I tuck Dad's gun back into the closet, hide it under Mom's beaver coat. Its furry whipped-cream softness folds around the cold barrel of the gun, now just an empty tube filled with air. But my pockets are full of danger.

Before I get back into bed, I pour the BBs into an old sock, hide it way up in my closet. When I close my eyes, I still see them shine, round and smooth, silver as the moon.

32

L O R E N A

'VE GOT A secret, Lorena sings to herself as she tears open a
TV-dinner box. She does a shuffle-ball change and tears off
the end of another Swanson's, lunges into a double-time step,
ends with a flourish as she tears open another box. She throws
the trio of pans into the oven and does a shuffle-off-to-Buffalo
out the kitchen door. She's all a-tingle, sizzling with anticipation
of the audition Binky had sworn she would get with Wally.

Yesterday, as they sped back in the mail truck after their tryst
in the woods, she had reminded him of his promise. "When?"
she persisted before climbing down from the truck.

"I dunno," he replied, adding hastily when her expression hard-
ened, "Soon. I'll ask my aunt Edna when's the next time he'll be
in Norfolk." To seal the deal, she left him lustful, kissed him with
all the passion she could summon up, rubbed her body against
his gray uniform until he was electrostatically charged. She could
see him still quivering in the truck as she strutted down the street
with a saucy wave.

Last night at dinner Cassie was even more sullen than usual but Lorena didn't dwell on that. Her head was filled with fantasies of fame that jostled each other for space like kittens in a basket. She had caught Cassie staring at her over the chicken pot pie, her mouth moving as if there were words inside instead of chicken and peas and carrots. As Cassie chewed and stared, Lorena dismissed it as yet another symptom of puberty, a word which startled her when she heard it on television the other day. She had accidentally turned on *Answers for Americans* instead of *My Little Margie*. Puberty. Of course! That explains everything.

So while last night was merely a typical night with a moody pubescent daughter, tonight will be special, a TV milestone. For the first time ever, the Miss America pageant is going to be telecast. Lorena will be able to watch it as it happens, live on TV. Until now, she's only seen it in bits and pieces, on Fox Movietone News, in the *Daily Press,* in *Life* and *Look* and *Time.* As she studied the grainy photos of each year's anointed, she would instinctively change her posture to a more queenly stance and think, That could have been me. I was once Miss Buckroe.

She recalls the sensation of balancing the crown, wobbly yet regal, upon her head, feels once again the satiny slide of the winner's ribbon weaving over her head and under her arm. Miss America has become Lorena's own mythology. She knows what it takes to be the chosen one, and—as only the once-chosen may—anticipates surveying and judging tonight's aspiring contestants with a practiced eye.

The promise of Wally has transformed her mood. Fame beckons. Life will change. Nothing can stop her now. She wants to share her ebullient mood, make tonight a special occasion. Pete's recovery is almost complete. The first tentative thrusts of fuzz are scattered across his scalp, and Lorena even entertains thoughts of their being sociable again. She plans a festive meal tonight, all three of them gathered around the TV set just like they used to do. As a special treat, she bought flag-studded cupcakes from the A&P to eat during the pageant itself.

"Dinner is served," Lorena sings as she retrieves the warmed-up trays from the oven. Pete parks himself on the couch and begins scraping the compartments of the aluminum tray with his fork before Lorena sits down. Cassie watches warily, gnaws the crust off the chicken, leaves the rest. Bathed in the glow of the TV, they finish dinner quickly.

"Through?" Lorena asks as the processional music of the Miss America pageant begins. Not waiting for a response, she hurriedly gathers the empty trays, dumps them on the kitchen counter, then settles into her corner of the couch. She doesn't want to miss a moment.

Pete is restless during the evening-gown portion of the pageant, shoots annoyed glances at Lorena as she provides a running critique on the fashions: "Too frilly." "Puffy sleeves are out." "That bow in her hair makes her look like Minnie Mouse."

Cassie stares at the screen, never acknowledging Lorena's presence even when she scurries to the kitchen during the commercial, singing, "I have a surpr-i-i-ise for you." She emerges with three proud and patriotic cupcakes on a plate just as Miss Oklahoma begins a stunningly off-key version of "O mio Babbino caro," but Pete turns down dessert. Taking his cue, so does Cassie.

"More for me, then." Lorena removes the flag from her cupcake, waves it, pokes it rakishly into her nest of robin-red hair. "Sure you don't want it?" she teases Pete, then peels away the cupcake paper and sinks her teeth into the snowy frosting. The cupcake vanishes in three hasty bites. Licking her fingers, Lorena draws closer to the TV as the parade of talent marches on: pianist, juggler, the obligatory baton twirler, a halting recitation of "O Captain, My Captain."

Pete snoozes, slumped down in his chair, gathering his energy for the swimsuit competition. The cupcake has proven too much of a temptation for Cassie, who surreptitiously pinches pieces from it and reduces it to a sticky heap of crumbs. She gazes, bored, at the screen.

Lorena's never-flagging attention climbs several notches when the spotlight zeroes in on the next contestant, Miss Ohio. Her talent, genial host John Daly announces, is tap dancing. Miss Ohio poses perkily in the spotlight, one arm up, hip cocked. Her shiny tap shoes start their *rat-a-tat-tat*. Taut shapely arms begin a churning rotation. And—WOO WOO-O-O—the first notes of "Chattanooga Choo Choo" accompany Lorena's high-pitched wail: "That's *my* routine!"

Cassie's hands fly to her ears. *"Turn it off,"* she shrieks, but Lorena is transfixed by the choreographic nightmare unfolding before her on twenty-one inches of screen. WOO-WOO-O-O. Miss Ohio's arms rotate faster, faster, moving in rhythmic circles from shoulder to hip and back again, WOO-WOO-O-O, neat feet tapping in complicated counterpoint to her chugging arms, WOO-WOO-O-O in a forlorn chorus harmonizing with Lorena's wail and Cassie's cry.

"Shut up!" Pete shouts into the cacophony, but not until Miss Ohio's number is over and the patter of applause for her efforts dies down does his demand get results. Cassie shuts up but her eyes narrow with revenge. She turns to Lorena, whose dismay over Miss Ohio's dance selection evolves to slow comprehension, then fear.

"I'm telling," Cassie announces.

"Telling what?" Pete's blank look Ping-Pongs between Cassie and Lorena.

Lorena stares at Cassie, willing her mute.

"I'm telling. I wasn't going to tell but I saw you with him again yesterday."

"Him?" Pete's gaze fixes on Lorena. "Who's 'him'?"

Cassie answers for her. "The mail guy."

"Mail guy?" Pete looks as if she said Man in the Moon.

"That's why she keeps trying to kill you."

"*Kill* him?" Lorena's mouth goes slack with shock. "I never tried to kill him."

"Yes you did! You made Dad so mad he fell off the ship." Cassie's words slosh around in a sea of tears. "You burned him with soup and you gave him greasy chicken so he'd set his hair on fire. You want to kill him so you can do sex with the mail guy."

"Sex?" Pete asks. "Mail guy?"

Lorena glares at Cassie. "Those were *accidents*."

"What mail guy?"

"Yeah, right, accidents." Cassie sniffs wetly. "Nobody has that many accidents." She turns to Pete. "Right, Dad? And then she blamed them all on you."

"What mail guy, dammit?"

"The mailman who comes to our house, the one she does that stupid dance for without any clothes on," Cassie volunteers.

"Dance?" Pete's neck is very red.

"I did *so* have clothes on," Lorena protests.

"And yesterday in the woods I saw your butt. Your shorts were off."

"What?" Levitated by rage, Pete jumps up, loses his balance, and plops back into his chair.

"What were you doing in the woods?" Lorena yells at Cassie.

Cassie folds her arms, looks away, defiant. "Riding my bike."

"What were *you* doing in the woods?" Pete barks at Lorena.

"Riding your bike?" Lorena asks, waving Pete off. "You rode your bike in the street?"

"*Who gives a good goddamn?*" Pete bellows. "I wanna know just who is this mail guy?"

"Nobody," Lorena mumbles.

"Oh, no. He's somebody, and I'm gonna find out." Pete rushes to the closet, burrows through coats and umbrellas, emerges with the BB gun gripped under his armpit. "Tell me who that sonuvabitch is so I can shoot his pecker off."

Cassie throws her hands over her mouth. Her eyes widen more in astonishment than fear. "It's true! It's not a bad dream!"

Lorena grabs at the gun. They grapple for it in a lurching dance around the coffee table accompanied by Cassie's screams and the ensemble chorus of Miss America contestants warbling "God

Bless America" from the TV screen. Having the advantage of fancy footwork, Lorena trips Pete, sends him soaring over the coffee table and onto the floor. His sweat-slicked hand loses its grip on the BB gun.

Lorena snatches it away, holds it in both hands like a fishing rod. What now? She's never held the BB gun before, only imagined herself doing so, and now that she feels its heft between her palms, she's stupefied.

"Whattaya gonna do now?" Pete taunts her. "Shoot me? For a mailman?"

"He's not just a mailman. He understands me." She waves the gun around for emphasis. "He appreciates my talent."

"*What* talent?"

Something snaps, something burrowed so deep in her brain that what she does next shocks but doesn't stop her: She points the gun at Pete's forehead. Sees his eyes go big and round. Sees the dent where barrel meets skin. Cold metal bites into her flesh as she wraps her finger around the trigger and pulls it.

Click.

It sounds puny, that hollow sound, as unexpected as a hiccup from a bear. Stunned by what she almost did, Lorena's face goes as blank as the unfired shot. She barely reacts when Pete knocks the rifle out of her hand. He grabs it, opens it, looks down its chamber for BBs.

"Empty!" he crows. Then, as if it just occurred to him, "You woulda shot me." He plunks down on the couch, clutching the rifle. "You woulda shot me," he says softly. "Right between the eyes."

Lorena doesn't know what to say. Yes. She would have shot him. Right between the eyes. She looks at his forehead, sees the faint indentation of an O where she had pressed the barrel of the gun. Zero. She shudders at the image of what might have been: Pete on the floor, BBs embedded inside his bald head. Blood drenching the Naugahyde chair. Cassie screaming. Police. Sirens.

Jail. Detectives grilling her in a smoky back room, just like they do on *Dragnet*.

"You calling the police, Dad?" Cassie peers around the corner from the safety of the hallway.

"Police?" Lorena is stunned. "What for? He's not *dead*."

Pete is very much alive. He leaps up, jabs a finger in her face. "Who is it?" he yells. "What's his name? You better tell me who it is you'd shoot me for."

Lorena hesitates, just for a second, then lets it spill out, why not? Why not bare herself to the bone after all that Pete has done? It'll serve him right. "Binky," she says in a burst of truth. "Binky, Binky, *Binky*."

A shadow of disbelief crosses Pete's face. "What kind of dumb-ass name is Binky?"

Lorena shrugs. She never gave Binky's name much thought. In high school, it seemed such a manly name: Binky the football player. Binky of the padded shoulders. Binky of the strutting walk, the slow gray gaze, the shifting grin. "Binky" she used to write all over her notebooks, and never once thought it was dumb-ass.

"What's his last name?"

"Never you mind," she says. The combination—Binky plus Quisenberry—suddenly strikes her as the wrong name for the hero of what she sees as a tragic romance of movie-epic proportions. Binky is her hero, she wants to believe that's so. He's her savior from a life as dull as dog food.

She must have gone crazy, almost shooting Pete like that. Not Lula-crazy, where it's built into your brain, but regular crazy, where somebody else makes it happen.

Pete. It's Pete who makes her crazy. "*What* talent?" he had said, like she was a big nothing. Because of Pete she has no life, no one has discovered her, she's doomed to biscuits forever. Who wouldn't have been driven loony from that?

"It's all your fault," she tells him. "You made me go bananas.

If you hadn't made me so crazy—not just today, but crazy for a long time, what with your moping around and not ever paying attention to my talent—"

"Here we go again."

"I *dance*," Lorena reminds him, "but do you care? When you've got talent and somebody squashes it like a bug, well, you start looking in other places for appreciation."

"Yeah, I just bet Binky the mailman appreciates your talent." Pete peers down the barrel of the BB gun. "If there'da been BBs in there"—he marvels, still dazed—"I'd be dead as roadkill." He shakes his head, sticks his finger down the barrel. "It's like God or somethin' emptied it for me."

"It wasn't God," Cassie confesses. "It was me."

"You?" Pete looks at Cassie as if she had just materialized. "What were you doing messing with my gun?"

Cassie hesitates. "I knew something bad was going to happen."

"You knew? How'd you know something like that?"

Cassie starts to say something, presses her lips together. After a moment, she whispers, "I just knew, that's all."

C A S S I E

T'S TRUE. IT wasn't a bad dream. And I'm not crazy, either. Now I know for sure what I saw on test-pattern TV. It was the future.

And then I changed it.

I don't understand any of this. But it doesn't matter. I changed the future: Mom didn't kill Dad, and that's all that matters.

The BBs are still in my sock, way up in the back of my closet. Dad didn't ask for them back. He didn't even make me tell him how I knew Mom would shoot him, didn't say much at all. Just flopped down on the couch when Mom went up to bed, then lay there and stared up at nothing.

So now I'm lying on my bed with all my clothes on, afraid to get undressed in case something else happens. But nothing is happening. The house is so quiet I can hear the chinaberry's leaves swishing the wall like a broom in the summer-night breeze. Now and then I hear the bedsprings squeak in Mom's room, *eek eek* like a mouse. She's probably not asleep. She's probably mad at me.

I don't know what will happen, now that Dad knows about the mailman, now that Mom tried to shoot him between the eyes. I just know that nothing will ever be the same again. I can't think about tomorrow, so I listen to the tree's leaves swish and the mattress squeak, and wonder about all those things I saw on test-pattern TV.

Were they real, too? As real as the newsman who announced that Mom shot Dad? Will all those things I saw really happen someday—the spaceman up in the stars, the painted dancing ladies, the president who got shot? And going to school with colored people? And the scary stuff with guns and wars? And the guy who got his penis cut off?

And then I remember the spooky thing I memorized: "There is a sixth dimension beyond that which is known to man . . ." Maybe that's it. Maybe I did see the dimension of the imagination. Maybe what I saw was the Twilight Zone.

I never want to see it again.

Mr. Finkelstein said that if you could change the future, who knows if it's for better or for worse? If it's true that I *did* change it for the better this time, maybe next time it would be for the worse. Maybe, like Mr. Finkelstein said, it's best to let things be.

34

L O R E N A

L ONG HOURS AFTER Miss America's crown has been bal-
anced upon the dark shining locks of Lee Ann Meriwether,
long after Pete has fallen into twitching slumber on the
living-room couch, Lorena lies awake in her solitary bed and
plans her next move. When morning comes, she makes that move.
She reaches over, picks up the phone, and dials up Binky at his
mother's.

He's left for work already, but Lorena, undaunted, plows on:
"Oh, Mrs. Q, I bet you don't remember me—Lorena? Lorena
Wythe-but-now-it's-Palmer?" And though it's clear that Mrs. Q
has no clue, Lorena proceeds to confess her hopes, her dreams,
and especially her need to meet Wally. She so charms that befud-
dled lady that Mrs. Q agrees: "Why, sweetie, of course I'll tell
Binky you called. Why, my goodness, I had no idea you were so
talented! Wally'll love you. You know he's my sister's oldest boy,
a little peculiar but made a real name for hisself with those TV
people."

When Lorena calls him from Della's that night, Binky sounds slightly crazed. "Who told you to call me here?"

"You promised I could meet Wally."

"My *mother* lives here."

"I know. We had a nice talk."

"Why did you tell my *mother*?" His voice escalates to a croak. "She's already called my aunt!"

"Well, you promised. No," she corrects herself, "you *swore* it. You swore I could get an audition with Wally."

"You know what this means? It means I've gotta take off work and get you to Norfolk on Thursday because that's the day Wally'll be there. It's my aunt's birthday. He'll just be there for the day."

"Perfect," says Lorena.

"Perfect? Perfect? You think the post office is going to think it's perfect? My *record* was perfect. Not one day off, not one missed day, always on time, always there, rain, snow, sleet, whatever, I forget how it goes. And now this."

"I'll make it up to you."

Binky is silent, then, "Yeah?" he asks. "How's that?"

"Remember in your truck? That little trick?"

"You mean, that thing with the rubber bands?"

"Mmmm-hmmm." She lowers her voice to a purr. "Any time. Any place. You name it."

She can almost hear him thinking. "Thursday," he finally agrees. "In my car. On the ferry home."

"It's a deal."

"WELL? DO YOU love it?" Lorena twirls for Della in her new dress, an explosion of red poppies gathered at the waist by a wide red cinch belt. On her feet are new red shoes, three-and-a-half-inch heels, she tells Della, three-and-a-*half*. She's never worn such high heels before because they'd make her taller than Pete. Now that she's left him, it doesn't matter.

Della surveys Lorena from her perch on her kitchen counter because there's no place left to sit. Lorena's clothes are scattered everywhere, over the couch, the chairs, even over the TV set, where she's hung several pairs of stockings to check for runs against the light from the screen. She's moved in with Della—just temporarily, just until she can get herself together for her audition with Wally.

When she's not shopping or undergoing hair transformation at the hands of Mr. Ralph, Lorena practices her routine, tapping away on Della's kitchen linoleum until its surface has become as pitted as the moon. *Tappety tappety,* she perfects her routine, *tap tap tap,* adds flourishes to the steps she learned from Cassie—the monkey step, the swimming step, that backward-forward sliding step. She doesn't stop practicing until she hears "The Star-Spangled Banner" signal the end of the broadcast day and Della call "Nighty-night" on her way to bed.

After three days of this, Lorena feels she's ready. She leaves for Norfolk tomorrow on the early-morning ferry. She knows her costume for the audition itself is perfect. But . . . the dress. Will it do?

"It's a great dress," Della says.

"So why do you look like you just ate a pickle?" Lorena twirls again. "Be honest. Is it too sexy? Should I wear something a little more . . . *church*-y to meet Wally?" She flips up the hem of the dress to reveal a crunchy crinoline, flirtatiously points the toe of one red-clad foot. "Maybe I shouldn't dazzle him too much at first." She fluffs out her newly dyed curls with Flame Red–lacquered fingernails that almost match her hair.

"I don't know." Della is quiet, for Della. She dangles her legs over the counter and studies Lorena.

"You hate it." Lorena folds her arms and pouts. "I can tell. What is it? Too low-cut? Red's not my color? What?"

"It's not the dress." Della shifts uncomfortably on the hard countertop. "It's just . . . this is such a big step. Leaving your family and all. I mean, it's one thing to develop your talent. But . . . what about Cassie?"

Lorena's pout deepens. "I'm not *leaving* leaving. I'll come back for Cassie." She releases the cinch belt, exhales with relief. "This could be my only chance to be discovered, to follow my star. Would you let opportunity pass you by?"

"What opportunity? My only talent is being able to type sixty words a minute."

Lorena pulls her skirts up like a cancan dancer, gives a little kick with one black-stockinged leg. "Now don't you go talking about yourself that way. You've got loads of talent. What about your art? That *Twin Scotties* painting you did for your bedroom, well, nobody would even guess it was from a kit."

"Well, yeah, but—"

"And that adorable little toilet-paper cover you crocheted for my birthday, the one that looks like a hat? You could go into business making those things, that's how cute it looks sitting on my toilet tank."

Della ponders that possibility for a moment. "Nah," she decides. "That's not what I really want to do with my life." She sighs. "I don't know. Maybe if I had your talent, I'd do what you're doing, leaving and all. But . . . I still think it would be hard to leave a kid, if I had one."

"I told you, it's Pete I'm leaving, not Cassie. If I don't get away from him, I'll wind up crazy as Lula."

"Well," Della says after taking a deep breath, "as your very best friend, I got to be real honest with you. When you told me what happened last night with you and Pete and the gun, I thought to myself, Lorena's gone bonkers. Nuts. Crazy as Lula."

Lorena opens her mouth to protest, but Della plows right on: "You coulda *killed* him, Lorena. If it wasn't for Cassie, you'd be sitting in jail right now, wearing stripes 'steada that fancy dress. How do you think Cassie feels with her family all broke up? And still, all you want to talk about is your stupid routine."

"It's not stupid!" Lorena says, lip quivering.

Della looks contrite. "Yeah, okay, I'm sorry. It's not your routine I'm talking about. It's your family. Seems like you just forgot about them, forgot about Cassie and what she's going through."

"I haven't forgot Cassie. I saw her yesterday."

"And . . . ?"

"She's not ready to talk to me yet. Crimminy, it's not like I haven't tried, you know." Lorena makes a pouty face.

"Well, try some more," Della says. "She's the only daughter you've got."

Lorena's ebullience deflates at Della's forlorn expression. "I'm not *leaving* leaving," she says again, more to herself than to Della. And this time she thinks she really means it.

LORENA FEELS ENERGIZED. Wind off the water—wind crisp with a touch of autumn, crunchy as her crinolines—kicks up her skirt as she stands on deck. Waves lick the ferry with black tongues in the predawn darkness. There had been no moon that night.

As Newport News fades into the watery distance, she sees, like a fragment of dream, the image of Cassie's face last night when Lorena came over to pick up her top hat, forgotten when, a few days earlier, she hastily packed her costume with her clothes. She had tried to hug Cassie, almost said "I love you," but Cassie's tear-streaked face was a mask, her body stiff as a mannequin. She didn't hug her back.

Lorena yawns and stretches. Oh well. You don't have to tell somebody you love them for them to know it. She's sure Cassie would have hugged her if Pete hadn't been skulking in the darkened living room, trying to make her feel guilty. He hardly looked at Lorena when she came inside. She could barely make him out in the shadows, his polished head the only gleam of light aside from the flickering TV.

The wind is whipping her hair like an eggbeater. She'd better get back in the car. She looks over at Binky's Henry J hunkered among all the other cars on the ferry deck, their owners snoozing away like Binky is, slumped against the door like a bag of laundry. He wakes up with a snort when she climbs into the car and flicks on the overhead light.

"Are we there yet?" he asks.

"No. It's pitch-black out. I still don't understand why we had to leave so early."

"I told you. I gotta be back for the late shift. I traded hours with one of the guys. Thanks to you, I'll be working till midnight tonight, shuffling mail in the back room."

"I'll make it up to you," she promises. "On the way back." She slides her hand over his orange-and-green plaid shirt and down one leg of his shiny brown slacks. She's never seen him out of uniform before—at least, not when he was wearing clothes. She turns to examine him. Clumps of lubricated hair from his hatless head cling to the low ceiling of the Henry J. A spot of blood targets the shred of toilet paper on his chin. He picks at a tooth with his little fingernail.

Lorena gasps at the sudden revelation which rides in on a high tide of nausea: Out of uniform, Binky looks a lot like Uncle Rudy.

The more she stares, the less he resembles Errol Flynn. His eyes aren't the color of rain; they are pavement gray, crusted in the corners with sleep. There's a blob of doughnut custard on his mustache. Binky catches her glance and grins—not the slow-moving grin that made her heart turn quick flips, but the maniacal chimp grin of J. Fred Muggs.

"Rubber bands," says Binky, and gives her a wink.

She stumbles out of the car, scurries to the railing, inhales the sharp seaweed scent of the bay. Way off in the darkness glimmers the vanishing aurora of the lights of Newport News. Lorena's whimper harmonizes with the ferry's mournful toot, a wail that ends in a melancholy woo-o-o.

She bends her head and presses her face to the cold metal railing. What was that commercial? "Don't trade a headache for an upset stomach"? Is that what she's doing? Trading a Pete for a Binky?

She snaps her head up at the next toot of the ferry—a proud toot, an insistent toot, a toot that announces, rather than mourns. Splashed against the sky, twinkling upon the water, a dazzling array of lights dispels darkness and regret. The ferry glides into the harbor. Norfolk rises before her, a shimmering crown of neon that illuminates the heavens and heralds her arrival. She opens her arms and embraces the light.

BY THE TIME they get to Binky's aunt Edna's house, the sun is up and so is Aunt Edna. She waves at them from the porch, where she's drinking something from a cup the size of a mixing bowl. "Hey, y'all," she cries, "come on in, take a load off." Lorena swivels the rearview mirror for one last makeup check, although she had freshened up in the ladies' room at the ferry landing.

"Lawdy mercy," says Edna as Lorena wobbles up the porch steps in her three-and-a-half-inch heels. "You showbiz people sure know how to dress."

Lorena bats down her flyaway crinoline. "Oh, this old thing," she says, and reaches out a white-gloved hand. "You must be Edna. The birthday girl!" She cranes her neck around Edna's girth. Where is Wally?

"Postum?" asks Edna, waving them inside. "I got a potful in the kitchen. Lemme go see if Wally's got hisself up yet."

Wally stumbles into the kitchen several minutes later, bleary-eyed and cranky in a silk dressing gown. "What time is it?" he wants to know, then, "Binky? What are *you* doing here?"

"This is Lorena," Binky blurts. "She's going to dance for you."

"Huh?"

"Oh, Wally honey, I forgot to tell you," Edna says as she sloshes Postum into bowl-sized cups. "Binky's mom called, said Binky wants you to meet this real talented person"—she indicates Lorena with a cheery nod—"who wants to try out for *Talent Scouts*." Lorena gives a little acknowledging curtsy.

Wally closes his eyes, seemingly in pain. "Thanks, Mom," he says.

"I just want you to know how much I really and truly appreciate this," Lorena says, fluttering. "If you'll wait just a teensy moment, I'll change into my costume." She turns to Edna. "Can I borrow your bathroom just a teensy moment?"

"Make sure you give it back when you're done!" says Edna, slapping the counter in her mirth.

Lorena wiggles into her tap pants, buttons up the tuxedo top, ties on her tap shoes, slaps on her top hat. This is it. Her big chance. All those months of pain and practice have come down to this moment. Feet, she says to her beaming reflection in Edna's bathroom mirror, don't fail me now.

"I brought my own accompaniment." She plugs in the record player, plunks the record on the fat spindle. Wally nods warily. Wally is a crab of a man, hard round body perched on a stool, hands clutching his scrawny knees like claws. His tiny black eyes are so close together they almost seem to touch, and they stare, unblinking, at Lorena as—WOO-O-O—she begins her routine.

Chug-a-chugga *chug*-a-chugga. She's a little nervous, but the music revitalizes her and she mouths along with it: "Pardon me boy, is that the Chattanooga choo choo?" Faster now, arms and legs churning, "Track twenty-nine, boy, you can gimme a shine." Wally sits up attentively, little crab eyes bulging, shiny as buttons. "Woo woo Chattanooga, there you are."

There's a change in Wally's face. It softens, it smiles, and before she finishes the monkey step, laughter beads his tiny eyes with tears that roll down his cheeks. His laugh—more creak than laugh—puzzles her, but his delight impels her to head full throttle into her grand finale. "So Chattanooga choo choo," Lorena plunges into her split, "won't you choo choo me ho-o-me," leaving Wally crumpled in breathless hysterics.

Edna takes a sip of Postum and lifts an unplucked eyebrow at Binky. "Your momma been feeling okay lately?"

"HE LIKED ME. He really liked me." Lorena squiggles happily in the seat of Binky's car as the ferry pulls away from the dock.

Binky shakes his head, looks bewildered. "Wally always was strange," he says, then retracts at Lorena's angry glance. "I mean he did, he really did like you."

Lorena leans back, kicks off her heels, closes her eyes. She sees Wally, tight face stretched into a lipless grin, beady eyes shining as he grasped her hand in his. "I'll be in touch," he had said, and before he let go, scraped his thumbnail along her wrist in a strangely sensuous motion.

She feels exhausted, exhilarated, and somehow redeemed. "*What* talent?" Pete had said. She'll show him. She's on her way to stardom. Behind closed eyes, she pictures herself in her new life: a night on the town with Gene Kelly, an intimate lunch with Lucy. She's just drifting off into self-satisfied sleep when she feels a hand shuffle her crinolines and land on her leg. She gasps and jerks away. "Rubber bands," murmurs a voice in her ear.

"What?" Her eyes pop open. It's Binky.

"Remember? In my truck? That little trick?"

"Oh. That." She edges away.

He reaches into the pocket of his shirt, pulls out a nest of thick, postal-issue rubber bands. "I picked the stretchiest ones," he says, sproinging them between his fingers.

"Forget it." She squints out the window of the car. Sunlight glances off the roofs of cars, paves the bay with diamonds.

Binky's face falls into a frown. "We had a deal."

"Well, I didn't mean *here,*" she says. "Not on the ferry, in your car. Not now." Or ever, she adds to herself.

"I thought of that." He reaches into the backseat, pulls out an army blanket. "We can make a tent. Cozy, huh?"

Lorena turns and gives Binky a hard, cold look. How could she have imagined he looked even remotely like Errol Flynn? She must have been crazy. Without a word, she slides over the seat and out the door, ignoring his plaintive, "But we had a *deal*."

She leans on the railing, lets the wind whip her hair into a wild red froth. As the ferry pulls into Newport News, Lorena feels herself recede. Lit by the glaring sun of noon, the city seems flat and dull, a black-and-white image that pales in the glow of her Technicolor dreams. Soon all this will be part of her past, a history she plans to recount with teary-eyed nostalgia when she's interviewed on TV.

35

CASSIE

MOM LEFT. I don't know if I'm glad or sad. I feel like a big hole's been punched where I'm supposed to be feeling something. She tried to hug me good-bye but I didn't want to hug her back, even though somewhere inside there was my little-kid self saying, "Don't go, Mommy!" like when she left me at school on my very first day.

Maybe it was that fake kiss she gave me, smacking those candy-apple lips at the air when she touched my cheek to hers. Maybe it was because her hair matched her shoes and her perfume smelled like the ladies' room at the Paramount. Maybe it was because she said, "Just wait, you'll see me on TV and you can tell all your friends, 'That's my mom!' " All I know is I couldn't wait for her to go, and next thing I knew she *was* gone, her high heels tapping down the sidewalk. *Tappety tappety. Tap tap tap.*

Sometimes I wake up in the middle of a dream—the same dream I keep having, the one where Mom's coming home—and think I hear that tapping. But it's only the chinaberry tree tapping witchy fingers at my window. And I lie awake, wondering just what it is that I really feel inside.

DAD AND I are outside lying on the lawn chair, comparing feet even though we're wearing shoes. It's chilly out. The stars are crisp and clear over our heads and the leaves are turning on the maple tree. My saddle shoe comes up to where the laces start on Dad's work boot. His hair's growing in good now. It looks like teddy-bear fur, and he smooths it down as he talks about how he's going back to work, soon as his boss gives him the word.

"My daddy worked in the shipyard," he says. I nod. I know that. "I always worked in the shipyard, too." I know. "It's all I ever wanted to do. Except"—he smiles a little—"once upon a time, I thought I could play in the big leagues." I didn't know that.

"You played baseball, Dad?" And then I remember the newspaper clipping in his night-table drawer. "Were you a star?"

"Yeah," he says, laughing with his voice but not his face. "A shooting star."

"What happened?"

"I hit a home run. It won the game, but it was just an accident."

"Home runs aren't accidents, Dad. You musta been good."

He shakes his head and says, almost to himself, "I'm not much good at anything."

"Sure you are, Dad," I say, and then I remember what Mrs. Finkelstein said: "Everybody's good at something. The hard part is knowing just what that something is."

When I say that to Dad, he gives me a look. "Where'd you get that?"

He doesn't even get mad when he hears the word "Finkelstein." "Well," he says finally, "if my something's not the shipyard, I don't know what it is."

"Maybe it's not the shipyard that's the problem, Dad. Maybe it's what you *do* there."

"I do what my daddy did."

"But your daddy got killed doing that. And," I say, shivering in the chill, "I'm scared you will, too."

He doesn't say anything, just looks up and seems to study the stars. Then he says, "Yeah. Me, too. I've been thinking about that a lot."

WE HAD DINNER at Della's tonight. She's been extra nice since Mom left, inviting us over, taking me shopping for school. At first Dad didn't want to have anything to do with her, but the more we see Della, the friendlier he gets. Tonight Della made real fried chicken, not as good as Mom's but not bad either. I brought the biscuits. I've gotten better at making them. They don't look like hockey pucks anymore.

Dad's been different. Quiet—not the kind of quiet he was when Mom was here, that creepy kind of quiet like when the Lone Ranger and Tonto are clopping along the canyon and the bad guys are around the bend—but a thinking kind of quiet. We watch a lot of TV together. When he goes outside to look across the water at Norfolk, I know to leave him alone.

Tonight when we got home from Della's, he asked me how I knew to take the BBs out of his gun. I knew he'd never believe me about the newsman on test-pattern TV, so I just told him that their fighting all the time scared me and I didn't want a loaded gun around. He didn't say anything for a minute, then reached out and hugged me hard against his chest. "It's been real sad for you, hasn't it?" he said, and I nodded yes. Then he kissed me on top of my head and for a minute it felt just like it used to before everything started getting weird.

The other day he got a whole bunch of things together—old photographs of Mom and him, some letters, a bow tie with yellow dots Mom gave him for Christmas—mashed them into a grocery bag, stomped it flat with his foot, and threw it in the garbage can. When he went inside to watch TV, I fished out a couple of the photographs that weren't scrunched too bad and put them in my secret treasure box under my bed.

Mom's called a few times from New York. She says some guy named Wally is going to make her a star. Dad doesn't talk to her but I feel like I should, since she's my mother and all. Like Mr. Finkelstein says, you only get one mother in this lifetime, and she's mine.

So I listen and act like I believe her when she says she'll be back to see me soon. The truth is I don't care about her dancing thing, don't care that she's not with the mailman anymore, don't care if she'll be famous when she goes on *Talent Scouts*. All I know is that she's with that Wally guy now, and I don't even want to know what it is they're doing.

Tonight while Dad and I are outside, I hear the phone ring and it's Mom calling to remind me to watch *Talent Scouts* at eight-thirty because she's going to be a contestant. When I tell Dad, he says he never wants to see that show again in his entire life, that if I want to watch, go ahead, but he's staying outside until it's over. I decide to watch, not just because Mom wants me to, but because I can't believe Arthur Godfrey would have somebody like Mom on his show.

I go inside and turn on the TV. Arthur Godfrey introduces the first act, a juggler who's great, and a singer who's sort of good, and next thing I know, he's saying, "So let's have a big hand for this little lady: a bright new comedy dancer—Miss Lorena Palmer!"

The curtain goes up and there she is posing in the spotlight, wearing those stupid red tap pants and a top hat on her Mr. Ralph curls. And then I hear it: WOOO-WOOO-O-O, like an arrow through my head. WOOO-WOOO-O-O.

I put my hands over my ears but my eyes can't stop watching. I can't believe this is happening. I must be dreaming.

But it's not a dream.

It's a nightmare.

L O R E N A

LORENA'S COSTUME ITCHES. The satin tap pants are caught in the crack of her butt. She extricates them with a flip of her thumb, scrunches the top hat more firmly atop her springy red curls. She can hear the studio audience applauding for the previous contestant on the other side of the curtain. The heavy velvet muffles the sound, reduces it to the staccato of a rainstorm.

"Don't be nervous, now," whispers the *Talent Scouts* assistant, a motherly gray-haired woman who just a few moments ago retouched Lorena's makeup, pressing on a new layer of powder with a gigantic puff.

But Lorena isn't nervous. She feels electrified, toes and fingers tingling with anticipation. Her time has come, ticking closer and closer to fame as she awaits her cue. Her gaze rises to the heaven of rafters that crisscross the backstage area, to the multiple curtains rigged to rise and fall on command, to the complexity of lights overhead awaiting the flick of a switch. Suspended in this moment between two worlds, she knows she is truly blessed.

The curtain shudders and begins to rise. She hears her name spoken in the sleepy voice of Arthur Godfrey himself. She is prepared, poised in position, as the curtain ascends and disappears into the rafters. Momentarily blinded by a galaxy of lights, she recovers and instinctively turns toward the TV camera with a pert hip flip. The first note wails—WOOO-WOOO-O-O-O—and infuses her with energy. Bathed in the golden beam of the spotlight, she slides easily into the familiar routine, arms rotating *chugga*-chugga-*chugga*-chugga, feet accelerating into a blur of smacking, cracking, tapping rhythm.

"Pardon me, boy . . ." She feels the studio audience breathing like a great silent beast. ". . . is that the Chattanooga Choo Choo? . . ." The spotlight gilds her pale legs as, arms flailing, she tappety-taps across the stage. ". . . Shovel all the coal in . . ." She beams a red-lipped grin after a particularly inventive twirl. ". . . Gotta keep a-rollin' . . ." Now a big wink. ". . . Woo woo Chattanooga, there you are."

She hears a ripple of—what? Applause? Giggles? After a hip-twisting series of moves she learned from Cassie, Lorena revs up for her finale, letting go with an abandon she's never before experienced, legs loose as a puppet's, head swinging gaily as the applause becomes a roar. ". . . So Chattanooga Choo Choo . . ." Her top hat flies off as *whomp* she lands in a crotch-bruising split, ". . . Won't you choo choo me ho-o-ome." Arms way up. Now *big* smile.

The studio audience goes berserk, clapping, whistling, hooting with laughter. Arthur Godfrey applauds from the wings looking happily bemused, a living Howdy Doody. Lorena struggles to her feet and throws kisses like candy to her wildly adoring fans. Their love washes over her in escalating waves. Somehow, she always knew it would be this way.

It's like a dream. Not just any dream, but *her* dream. Now she understands its meaning—the dazzling lights, the black-glass sea, the babbling creatures in the darkness. They are the fans beyond the footlights, sensed more than seen. She hears their voices rise, not in speech but in laughter, hears their hands beat together in a frenzy of adoration. She needs no vocabulary to interpret that sound, for applause is the language of fame.

37

C A S S I E

T'S WORSE THAN a nightmare. Nightmares are scary, but they don't make you want to throw up. That's how I feel now watching Mom on TV, like the Dinty Moore stew Dad fixed for dinner has changed its mind and is going up instead of down. The feeling started as soon as I heard that first WOOO, and just gets worse as I watch.

And then I see Dad in the doorway. He's come inside to see. His face is gray in the light from the screen, and his lips look sewn together. He's staring at the TV screen as if it were John Cameron Swayze announcing the end of the world instead of Mom dancing in those silly shorts that show off her Jell-O butt.

"What's that thing she's doing with her arms?" he asks. "She looks like a gorilla."

It looked neat when I saw those kids do it on that teenage dance show on the test pattern. But I don't say that. I say, "I hope nobody is watching this."

"Everybody is watching this," he moans. He plunks down on

the couch. Mom's doing the backward-forward step now, holding her top hat above her head and grinning like Charlie McCarthy. Dad's face is scrunched up like he's getting a shot but he can't stop watching. "Where the hell did she get *that* from?"

"From me," I blurt out of guilt.

"You?" He tears his eyes away from Mom and glares at me.

"Yeah. I saw it on . . . on TV." I feel rotten. "It looked a lot better when this guy did it. He—"

"Oh, God," he interrupts as Mom's face fills the screen in close-up, so close that all you see is her big wink and that stupid grin that shows all her teeth. She's going into her finale. The camera moves back. She's winking, she's grinning, she's flying across the stage. And then—oh no, please please please, don't let anyone I know be watching—she flings herself into a split.

"I don't believe it," Dad says. He looks as sick as I feel. "Those morons are actually applauding for her."

I watch Mom throw kisses to the morons. And then I ask Dad, "Does this mean Mom is famous?"

EVERY NOW AND then I get a postcard from Mom. After she won third prize on *Talent Scouts*, she tried out for the June Taylor dancers but didn't make it. She says she's working up some new routines and she's practicing all the time, which I guess that Wally guy got tired of because she says she's not with him anymore.

Last time I got a postcard it was from Hollywood, California, a picture of Graumann's Chinese Theater. Mom wrote that Hollywood was her destiny, her talent was meant for the big screen, not TV. That's what Raoul, her new friend who's going to be a movie star, told her. She met him at the restaurant where they both work, and she said that on their breaks they rehearse in the alley outside the kitchen. She says she's ready to find an agent.

Dad's gone back to work at the shipyard. He works in an office now. He says it's a better job, that he got a promotion and maybe next year he'll get a raise. He had a talk with his boss and they agreed that he shouldn't work outside anymore, that he's better suited to keep track of inside stuff, like who's working where and things like that. If I call him at work, he answers the phone, "Personnel." He sounds very important. He even wears a real hat to work.

I think he sees Della there. When we have dinner at her house, they talk about the same people. They go out, too. The other night they went to the Moose Ballroom to dance to the Rhythm-airs. I have a feeling they smooched a little because Dad's face was the color of Della's lipstick when he got home. It's weird to think they might do that because I still think of Mom as my mom, but then I think if she weren't, who would I want? I can't have Mrs. Finkelstein because she's already Molly's mother, but Della wouldn't be so bad. She's funny, she makes me laugh, and the best part is she makes Dad laugh, too. So I guess it doesn't matter if they do a little smooching as long as they don't do sex.

Sixth grade's okay, especially now that I've got a training bra, 28AAA. Della and I went shopping for it at Nachman's. She sat on the little bench in the dressing room while I tried on the bras and she didn't even say, like Mom would have, "You don't need a bra, there's nothing there." Instead, she picked out one with a little lace on it and said I looked va-va-voom.

Molly's mom got back from the writers'-colony place, and now she's working on a book, all the time writing, writing. She reads me parts while Molly and I sit at their kitchen table eating the apple strudel Mr. Finkelstein likes to bake. I don't understand what she's written, but I like to listen to her words, how they go up and down and around like butterflies in your head.

Mr. Finkelstein tells stories and jokes, and talks to me about all kinds of stuff. He says there are things in the world we may never understand, that there is mystery and magic in the universe. He says it's good to wonder about things because wondering is the first step to discovery. And he's helped me understand that Mom and Dad's problems really weren't my fault, and whatever happens now will be okay because I can make it be okay.

He asks me what I think about all kinds of things, but he never asks about the test pattern anymore.

I haven't watched it since that time I saw the scary news on the test pattern about Mom and Dad and the gun. But tonight's one of those nights when I can't sleep. I'm staring at the ceiling wondering about stuff, not just about Mom, but things like If I could get a pet, would I get a chicken or a monkey, or If your toenails really grow after you die, do they put bigger shoes on you for your funeral?

And then I start to wonder what I'd see if I turned on the test pattern just one more time.

It's a creepy thought, but it's keeping me up. So, like I used to do, I tiptoe down the stairs and turn on the TV. There it is: giant's eye, bull's-eye, round and square at the same time. I hear its hum and wait for the tingling feeling to start pricking at my toes and fingers.

I wait and wait. But nothing happens. No tingling, no spinning, no melting into a picture. Nothing is there but the test pattern.

I feel suddenly free, like something dark and furry just left my head. I turn off the test pattern and open the front door. Out on the porch, the wind washes me clean and fresh and pure as Ivory Snow. Across the bay I see Norfolk, a zipper of light between the water and the sky.

And I make a wish upon it as if it were a star.